KISS FROM A ROSE

ANN BENNETT

Andaman Press

Created with Vellum

For Dot

The Rose Park Chronicles

Book 1

Kiss from a Rose

PROLOGUE

RACHEL HEYWOOD LAY on her back in the corner of the garden at Rose Park, staring up at the flickering sunlight between the branches of the spreading oak tree, its leaves waving gently in the summer breeze. Lethargy, and the heat of the still afternoon made her bones feel heavy and her muscles weak. Even if she wanted to move, she didn't think she would be able to.

It had been a long, hot summer and now it was drawing to a close. Over the past few days, Rachel had felt a subtle shift in the temperature, a chill undercurrent of air that mingled with the warmth of the late summer breeze. The trees had lost their bright sheen and were looking overblown and dry, preparing themselves for autumn. There was an unmistakeable change in the air.

The whole place was waiting, holding its breath. Inside the great house, across the manicured lawn from where she lay, Rachel's grandfather, Hadan Rose, was dying. He was ninety years old. He had survived two world wars and outlived all his contemporaries and several of the younger members of his family.

She thought about him now, lying there in his stuffy, darkened room – the room in which he'd been born – gasping for breath. Hadan had always been a tyrant and a bully, and he had been stubborn to the end. He had refused to be moved to a hospital or a nursing home, instead insisting that Rachel's mother, May, a trained nurse, should drop everything and rush to his side and help him through his final days.

'May! Where are you, girl?' he would boom, at any time of the day or night, his voice echoing through the high rooms and empty corridors of the old house. When May heard him, she would drop whatever she was doing and go running, in her eyes the fear of the little girl she once was.

It felt like the end of an era to Rachel, staring up at the sky through the branches of the old oak tree. This tree had been here for centuries, while the world turned around it, and momentous events ruptured the peace of the estate with its own immutable routines – two world wars, the sweeping away of the old order that had existed when the house was built. Rachel sensed that this ancient tree would outlast even her.

When Hadan drew his last breath, the old house would be sold. It was where Rachel's mother, May, and her three aunts – Blanche, Ivy and Florence – had grown up, and where Rachel herself had spent many long, lazy summers as a child.

Rachel recalled her grandfather now, on the telephone in his office, in a fug of cigar smoke, bawling down the line to his estate manager, his quarry manager, or whoever else in his domain had displeased him that day. Goosebumps still rose on her arms thinking about those days when she was a little girl and her mother used to bring her home to Rose Park for holidays. She would dread her grandfather's footfalls in the corridor. She was still terrified of him even now at the age of nineteen, though he was a weak, old man and his life force was ebbing from him.

She'd come to Rose Park reluctantly at the beginning of the summer, to please her mother rather than herself. They had been constant companions since her father had died when she was ten, and soon Rachel would be going away to university. She'd resigned herself to being bored at Rose Park, but over the course of those two months, she had discovered a lot about what lay beneath the calm façade of this place, the secrets and lies it had been built on, the feuds and passions to which its walls had borne witness over the decades. There was more though, much more that eluded her still. She sometimes wondered if this place would ever give up its dark secrets.

As she lay there, listening to the wood pigeons cooing, the squawk of the squirrels fighting in the branches above, she sensed that her mother must have lain here just like this as a young woman, as had her grandmother, and her great-grandmother before that. Thinking about those generations of women, she closed her eyes and felt the oddest moment of connection with the past. It was almost as if every moment that had ever happened or would ever happen in the future collided in a split second. Rachel sat up, blinking, shocked, her heart pulsing in her throat. It felt as though the world had tilted on its axis. She sat there, her head in her hands, trying to make sense of it all.

Something in the periphery of her vision made her glance across the lawn towards the house. It was her mother, May. She was closing the door of the garden room, coming down the back steps of the house and walking towards Rachel across the sweeping lawn.

Rachel could tell that the old man was dead, just by the movement of May's body, the droop of her shoulders, the length of her stride, and as she drew closer Rachel could see the tears glistening in her eyes.

1

RACHEL

ROSE PARK, SUMMER, 1980

As May's Mini Metro nosed its way along the dark, narrow lane, the headlights lit up the hedgerows on either side. Rachel could see they were full of white dog roses and bramble flowers. She even caught their scent on the warm night air through her open window. At the end of the lane stood the great wrought-iron gates to Rose Park. Her mother drew the car to a halt in front of them.

'You'll have to get out and open them, I'm afraid,' May said, her voice brittle with nerves. 'I'm surprised they're closed.'

May sounded tired. The long drive north from Surrey must have exhausted her. She wasn't used to driving in the dark, and she was worried too, Rachel realised, worried about her father and about what the coming months would bring. Rachel got out of the car and went to open the gates. The balmy evening air enveloped her. It felt good to be back here at Rose Park, despite the circumstances. May drove the car through and stopped to let Rachel back in.

'It's OK, Mum,' Rachel said through the open window. 'I'll walk down to the house. I could do with some fresh air.'

'Alright. See you down there.'

Rachel watched the rear lights of her mother's car bump

down the drive towards the bulky shadow that blocked out the sky at the bottom of the hill. She was surprised at the state of the drive; there were many potholes, and weeds growing down the middle, and she almost tripped a couple of times. It had never been like that in her grandfather's heyday. Everything had been kept shipshape, and staff had to answer to Hadan Rose for anything that was less than perfect.

As she drew closer to the house, she tried to make out how many lights were on. In past years when they'd arrived at the start of the summer holidays late in the evening, the whole place would have been lit up in their honour, but now the house stood shrouded in darkness. Narrow chinks of light leaked from a couple of upstairs windows that Rachel knew to be her grandfather's bedroom.

She walked closer, a feeling of trepidation creeping through her veins. The last time she'd seen her grandfather, about a year before, he'd been in rude health, striding round the estate, giving orders to his estate manager and other staff as he'd done almost every day for sixty-odd years. But now his health was failing fast. He'd suffered a series of strokes.

Rachel had been afraid of him before, with his booming voice and domineering personality, but even in his weakened state, she knew he would still have the power to terrify those around him. She was worried about seeing him like that though, aware that it must be very painful to him to have lost so much of his vigour. She hoped it hadn't enflamed his temper even more. That was probably what her mother was worrying about during the drive too, why she'd been so silent and pensive.

Rachel walked up to the front door and pushed it open. Her mother was already inside the flagstone hall with their bags. Hilda Allen, the housekeeper, was bustling around as she had for the past fifty years.

'He wants to see you as soon as you arrive, Mrs Heywood,'

Mrs Allen said to Rachel's mother. 'Just you, mind. Rachel can see him in the morning.'

Rachel wasn't surprised. It had always been this way and it was to be expected that her grandfather would still want to control everything in his household from his sick bed.

'Of course,' said May. 'I'll speak to his nurse before she leaves.'

Mrs Allen gave a bitter laugh. 'She left this morning. Couldn't stand it a moment longer.'

'Oh dear,' May said and scurried up the stairs.

Mrs Allen turned to Rachel. 'Now, while your mother is upstairs, would you like to come along to the kitchen? I've made some sandwiches for you both and I'll put the kettle on for some tea.'

Rachel followed Mrs Allen's neat form along the flagstone passage to the back kitchen which would once have been filled with staff, but now seemed a little too large for its purpose. Two plates of sandwiches were set on the scrubbed wood table and Rachel gratefully sat down and tucked in, while Mrs Allen put a mug of tea in front of her.

'I'm glad to see you, Rachel. We didn't know you were coming until this morning.'

'I wasn't sure myself. I was meant to go interrailing with some friends, but I decided to come along to help Mum.'

'Oh, what a disappointment for you!'

It was and it wasn't. The day before, when Rachel had walked through the front door of her mother's house at the end of a long shift at the meat factory, May was sitting at the kitchen table clutching a cup of tea, staring into space.

'What's wrong?' Rachel had asked, dumping her backpack and washing her hands at the sink. There was still tea in the pot, so she poured herself a mug. 'You look worried.'

It was unusual to see May sitting still. She was normally always on the go, cleaning, preparing meals, working at the sewing machine, gardening. She had a lot of energy and since she'd retired from her job as an intensive care nurse at the local hospital, had struggled to fill her time.

'It's your grandfather,' May said, biting her nail. 'He's had some sort of seizure and has been told to rest. Mrs Allen phoned this afternoon. He's asked his nurse to leave, apparently. He wants me to go there and look after him. I think... well, I think this is probably the beginning of the end for him, Rachel.'

'Oh, how terrible,' Rachel said, shocked by the news. It was impossible to imagine her grandfather anything other than bullish and full of life.

'It would have been good if you could have come, darling. I could do with some moral support.'

There were only a couple of days to go before Rachel had planned to set off with four other girls on a trip round Europe by train. She hadn't yet bought the interrail ticket, she had been working all summer in a local factory packing sausages and had almost saved up enough to cover the fare and some spending money. But over the past week or two she'd been getting cold feet about the trip. One of the girls who'd been invited, a friend of a friend, had turned out to be overbearing and bossy. She'd been insisting on scheduling their time and their journeys in advance, timetabling everything down to the last half-hour. That wasn't Rachel's idea of an adventure and she'd been starting to dread the trip. Now, looking at her mother's worried face, she felt a pang of sympathy for her. It was a tough time for May. Rachel knew she was already apprehensive about her leaving for university at the end of the summer, despite how much she tried to hide it.

'I'll come with you, Mum,' she said on an impulse.

May brightened instantly. 'Are you sure, darling?... You might even enjoy it there, you know. You used to love it at Rose Park, remember? We would spend whole summers there when you were small. And it might be the last chance you ever get to spend time there. Pa isn't long for this world, I'm sure, and then the old place will be sold.'

So Rachel had broken the news to her friends that she wouldn't be going with them. Only one, her best friend Karen, sounded remotely disappointed. It made it easier for them to book rooms if there were only four instead of five, she realised. Interrailing could wait until next year.

Now they had arrived, seeing how anxious returning to her childhood home was making her mother, Rachel was glad she'd agreed to come along. And looking round at the high-ceilinged Victorian kitchen, so redolent of a bygone era, she remembered how much history there was here at Rose Park. At last, she might have the chance to spend some time looking into her mother's family history.

She'd always been fascinated by history and loved nothing better than uncovering the past – it was the main reason she was going to study archaeology at Cambridge in October. The story of Rose Park and of the Rose family in general was particularly tantalising, but when her grandfather had been up and about, lording it over the household, it would have been impossible to poke around looking for old photographs and letters, unearthing family secrets. If May was going to be busy nursing her father, Rachel would have time on her hands, and she would also have a free run of the place.

May came back into the kitchen, her face ashen, and sat down at the table opposite Rachel.

'Is everything alright?' Mrs Allen came and laid her hand on May's shoulder and May gave a shuddering sob.

'Not really, no. You've seen him, haven't you? It's such a shock. He looks wasted, and he was such a vital man. Now all the stuffing has gone from him. It's painful to see.'

'I know, I know, my dear. It is hard. But he's had a long, long life. You have to remember that.'

May bit into her cheese sandwich absently.

'I'm exhausted from the drive,' she said. 'I think I'll turn in soon. I might feel better able to cope with it all in the morning. Which rooms are best for me and Rachel?'

'I've made up the Rose room for you and the Pink room for Rachel,' Hilda Allen said.

'The Pink room?' May asked, and Rachel thought she detected a note of concern in her voice.

'Yes,' Hilda Allen said steadily, her eyes on May's face. 'It's got a lovely view of the garden. Rachel will be very comfortable there, I'm quite sure.'

Later, after having said goodnight to her mother and Mrs Allen, Rachel carried her backpack up the wide staircase. The Pink room was on the first floor along the corridor, at the very end of the house. There was a big bay window in one corner of the room with a one-hundred-and-eighty-degree view of the garden.

Rachel had a vague idea that it had once been her great-grandmother's room; in fact there was a picture of Emily Rose on the dressing table. Dressed in a Victorian bodice and lace collar, Emily was a frail beauty, pale and thin with fair hair. She was smiling, but her eyes betrayed a deep sadness. Rachel bent down and looked at the photograph, then walked over to the bed and turned back to look at it again. Like the Mona Lisa, Emily's eyes seemed to follow her. A chill went right through her. She dredged her memory for information about her great grandmother, but nothing much came back. With a sigh she got her pyjamas out of her bag and found her washbag. Then she remembered.

'She was rumoured to have died of a broken heart, long before the First World War. Before that she was bedridden for a long time, and although he had nursemaids, Dad was very much left to his own devices,' May had once told her.

Rachel looked back again at her great-grandmother's pleading, soulful eyes. She could well believe that she had died of a broken heart. But why? Grabbing her washbag, she left the room and headed down the corridor to the antiquated bathroom to wash and clean her teeth. Despite his wealth, Hadan had never seen fit to install modern bathrooms. There was a huge bath on clawed feed with copper taps, and an old-fashioned lavatory with a chain pull, where the water thundered down from a high metal tank. In the stained mirror, Rachel washed her face and combed her short, dark hair.

Back in the bedroom, she got into bed and read for a while. Then she put the light out and tried to sleep. But sleep eluded her. Through the open window she could hear the barn owls hooting in the nearby spinney, but apart from that all was still and quiet.

To help her get to sleep, she tried to remember some of the things her mother had told her about the family...

She recalled that her great-grandfather, Gabriel Rose, already a landowner, had built this house beside the limestone quarry on the edge of the village of Perry Cross a few years before Hadan was born. He owned almost all the land around and was rich – living off the rent from the farms and from the spoils from the lucrative quarry, where he was said to exploit his workers. At that time, most people in the village worked for Gabriel and the estate one way or another. Some of the women made lace in their homes to sell in Nottingham – the only source of income that didn't belong to Hadan's father.

She thought too about her grandfather, Hadan – domineering and controlling – and her grandmother, Wilhemena, a pale shadow of a woman who used to live her life in fear of Hadan, but always tried to do her best for her four daughters. There was something else too, that her mother had told her about the past... she struggled to recall, and then she remembered. There had been some talk of bad blood between Hadan and one of the families in the village, but that was all she knew. May hadn't told her who the family was or what the reason was either. Something else she would try to get to the bottom of during the summer, if she had the chance.

With thoughts of the past and of long dead ancestors going round in her mind, Rachel finally drifted off to sleep. But she soon woke with a jolt... and sat bolt upright. To her astonishment, the room seemed to be suffused with a dim light. It felt as if she wasn't alone, as if some unseen presence was bearing down on her, pushing her backwards onto the pillows. With her heart racing and her skin prickling, she opened her mouth to scream, but no sound would come.

2

RACHEL

IN THE MORNING, Rachel woke with her skin prickling all over again, a vivid memory of... was it a dream? She shuddered, glad to see the sunlight streaming in through the thin floral curtains. She got out of bed, went over to the windows and pushed the curtains aside. Down in the garden, old Tom Hallam was already at work, digging the rose bed across the lawn. It was a comforting, familiar sight. Tom had worked in the gardens at Rose Park for as long as Rachel could remember. When she was little, he used to let her help him sometimes, he would give her a trowel to dig weeds, take her around in the wheelbarrow, and even let her sit on the lawnmower.

Beyond the rose garden, a spinney separated Rose Park from the quarry, and even today, Rachel could hear the low rumble of the diggers and caterpillars at work. In Gabriel Rose's day, the quarry would have been worked by hand, with multitudes of workers with their pickaxes and hammers, and all that would have been heard from the big house would have been tapping and banging. If he'd foreseen the mechanised age, Gabriel might have built the house further away, Rachel reflected. Hadan had sold the quarry and its mineral rights about twenty years ago to a big company for a considerable sum, but he'd kept the house and the farms. Rachel couldn't imagine him living anywhere different.

A knock on the door made Rachel start. She turned to see Hilda step into the room.

'Are you alright, Rachel? I've kept breakfast for you. Your grandfather wanted you to pop in to see him at ten o'clock.'

Rachel smiled. How typical of Grandad to be making appointments for his guests from his sick bed.

'Thank you. I'll be down in a few minutes,' she said, trying not to sound as unnerved as she felt. She decided to keep the strange night-time experience to herself. She knew it would only worry her mother, and that Mrs Allen was prone to gossiping in the village.

After a quick wash in the bathroom, Rachel pulled on jeans and a T-shirt and went down to the kitchen. Mrs Allen had set out cereals, toast and hard-boiled eggs for her. She didn't feel hungry, so she contented herself with a piece of toast and a cup of tea.

Her mother appeared while she was eating. She still looked drawn.

'How's Grandad?' Rachel asked.

'Demanding,' May said, sitting down heavily at the table. 'Just as he's always been. Only this time he feels helpless and vulnerable, which is making him worse.'

'Poor you!' Rachel said, sipping her tea.

May drew herself up. 'Of course not. I shouldn't moan. He *is* my father after all. It's the least I can do for him.'

'What about the others?'

'Others?'

'Your sisters?'

May frowned. 'Oh, I wouldn't expect them to come. I'm the nurse in the family after all. Blanche is really busy and she couldn't possibly come all the way from the Philippines. And Florence... well, Florence isn't exactly practical, is she?'

Rachel laughed. 'No, I suppose not.' Her Aunt Florence was a mathematics professor at Oxford. Her house was a delightfully chaotic jumble of books, antiques and dogs. Of course she couldn't be expected to nurse her father. And Auntie Ivy. Well, poor Auntie Ivy had disappeared during the war and Rachel had never met her.

Rachel glanced at the big clock on the kitchen wall. Five to ten.

'I suppose I ought to go up,' she said. 'Apparently he wants to see me at ten.'

'Oh really. He is the limit,' tutted May. 'Well, if you're going up there for a while, I think I'll take the opportunity to have a coffee.'

Rachel left the kitchen, and, feeling a little apprehensive, walked along the flagstone passage to the great hall, then up the stairs and along the corridor to her grandfather's room. As she knocked on the carved oak door, she realised that she'd never actually been in his bedroom before. She'd visited his office on the ground floor plenty of times, with its smell of leather and cigar smoke, its walls lined with bookshelves and his tooled oak desk piled with papers and files.

'Come in!' Despite his illness, her grandfather had retained his commanding voice.

Rachel turned the handle and stepped inside. The room was in semi-darkness and she stood for a second letting her eyes adjust to the gloom. It was a large, rectangular room with four sash windows above the front door of the house. There was a four-poster bed on one side and the rest of the furniture, including a giant wardrobe and an elaborate dressing table, was heavy and old-fashioned. The room was more or less just as she had imagined.

'Ah, Rachel!'

The voice came from beside the window where the curtains had been drawn back a little, giving a view of the garden and the front drive. Hadan wore a navy-blue silk dressing gown. He was reclining on a couch. Various bottles and instruments were set out on a table beside him.

'Come over here so I can see you properly,' he said, and Rachel obediently walked closer, and stood in front of him. 'You've grown taller. I haven't seen you for at least a year,' it sounded like an admonition.

'I'm sorry,' she said. 'I've been busy.'

She was shocked to see how thin he'd grown. His face was sallow and hollow and deeply wrinkled; folds of skin lay around his cheeks and under his chin. One side of his face looked as though it had dropped slightly, making him look lop-sided. From the way his dressing gown hung from his shoulders she could see that he had lost a lot of weight. Rachel knew instantly what her mother had meant. Hadan looked like a hollowed-out version of his former self.

'Yes, I know you've been busy,' he replied. 'You did well to get a place at Cambridge.'

'Thank you, Grandad.'

'Take my advice. Don't waste it,' he said, leaning forward and wagging a bony finger at her. 'Don't spend your time partying and drinking. Make the most of your opportunities.'

'Of course, I will.'

'It's an honour to be accepted there.'

'Yes, I know,' she said, trying not to sound irritated, but wishing he wouldn't lecture her.

'Sit down, Rachel,' Hadan said, waving for her to pull up a chair. 'It's good to see you.'

She placed one of his bedroom chairs opposite him and sat down.

'I'm glad you've come along with your mother,' he said. 'Because there's something I want to say to you.'

'Oh?'

'Hmm. Your mother is a fragile creature, and your aunt Florence is... well, to be quite frank, she's away with the fairies.'

'Oh, Grandad,' Rachel said. This was hardly the way to describe a professor of mathematics, but he waved her protest away.

'And as for Blanche. Living out there in the tropics. Doesn't come home from one decade to the next. I don't even know her anymore.'

Rachel detected a note of sadness in his voice and felt a prickle of surprise. She hadn't thought her grandfather was the least bit sentimental about his daughters.

'No, there's just you and your cousin, Lawrence, though I don't set much store by his common sense, I can tell you.'

'Grandad!' she said again, but she knew what he meant. Lawrence was rather ineffectual. An antiques dealer in a small town near Oxford, he struggled to make a living and had frequently fallen prey to unscrupulous business partners and poor business decisions.

'I put it down to his woolly upbringing by Florence. The airy-fairy atmosphere in that house can't have done the boy any good.'

Rachel was silent. She wanted to protest again, but knew that nothing she could say would change Hadan's old-fashioned views. After Florence's amicable divorce from Lawrence's father, she'd moved in with her long-term companion, Rebecca. It had been a bold move in the 1950s and Hadan had never accepted it fully.

'Well,' Hadan said, then paused to cough. He took a sip of water and banged his glass down on the table.

'I just wanted to say this to you...' He paused again and dabbed his mouth with a handkerchief. 'My father and I worked hard to build this place up. We worked hellish long hours, we took great risks with our investments. Now... there are some people who might want to take advantage after I'm gone,' he said, then he leaned forward and looked Rachel straight in the eye, his face deadly serious. 'For God's sake don't let them!' and he banged his fist on the table so the glass rattled.

'Now, that's all I have to say to you. Off you go and enjoy your day. Send your mother up to me when you go down.'

'But Grandad…' Rachel said, standing up, but he waved her aside and was instantly taken up with another coughing fit.

She left, and stood outside his room for a moment, listening to his hacking cough, wondering what on earth he'd meant. Perhaps he was finally losing his grip on reality. He'd always been paranoid about people taking advantage of him, it was one of the things that made him so controlling. Perhaps his illness had just made it worse. Shrugging, she walked along the corridor towards the stairs. It was just another mystery to add to all the others surrounding Hadan and this house.

She paused at the top of the stairs. There was a sideboard under a window with a few old family photographs set out on it. There was a picture of the four daughters in their teens, all wearing pinafore dresses. It must have been in the late 1930s. Blanche was the tallest and the most beautiful, with her high cheekbones, wistful eyes and blonde hair tumbling around her shoulders. Rachel remembered something her mother had confided about her eldest sister; *'She always struggled a bit at home. Florence and Ivy were so brilliant. Florence at maths and Ivy at languages. Blanche wasn't blessed with that sort of brilliance, but she had intelligence of another kind. She was imaginative and intuitive, she understood people. But that didn't wash with my father. Quite honestly, when the chance to move to the United States came along, she snapped it up and never looked back.'*

There was Florence, with her tomboy looks, her hair in a fashionable bob, looking straight at the camera with a wry smile; Ivy, as deliciously pretty as Blanche was beautiful, curly dark hair framing her heart-shaped face; and finally little May a thin intense-looking child, standing at the front, looking nervous, her eyes wide with surprise. Her grandfather was right, Rachel thought. She was fragile.

Next to that was a photograph of Hadan and Wilhemena at

their wedding in 1919. Hadan looked dashingly handsome in his officer's uniform and Wilhemena, in a fashionably narrow dress and lace veil, looked young and very pretty. She also looked terrified. May had once told her that the marriage was not a love match, that Wilhemena came from another landowning family, the Devereux, and that Gabriel and old Henry Devereux had cooked the match up on a pheasant shoot, knowing their estates would be stronger if they combined their land.

'Poor Grandma,' Rachel whispered, remembering her only as a sick, pale wisp of a lady, who had died when Rachel was very small.

Next to that was a photograph of Hadan with his regiment, the Northamptonshires. He had joined up in 1914 at the same time as many men in the village, Hadan as an officer, commanding men who had once worked in his quarry or on his land. He stood on the back row, an authoritative presence. Scanning the faces, Rachel recognised several of them. Not the men themselves, most of whom were long gone, but from their descendants who still lived in the village. Rachel knew that many of the men and boys in that photograph had never returned. She was astonished at how young many of them looked.

She remembered that someone, one of the old servants, she thought, had once told her that Hadan had changed irrevocably when he'd returned from the Great War early in 1917. The loss of so many of his contemporaries had changed him, as well as the mustard gas he had breathed in. After that, he was more temperamental and volatile than before. The old carefree Hadan of his youth had gone for ever.

Rachel stood back and looked at all the photos on the sideboard. She knew there would be more if she looked, hidden away in albums, shoved into drawers, forgotten in the back of cupboards. The whole family history and all its dark secrets was surely hidden away in this house somewhere, just waiting to be uncovered.

3

RACHEL

On the fourth evening since they'd arrived at Rose Park, May suggested they should take a walk down to the village pub.

'It would make a change,' she said.

Rachel didn't need any persuading. She was already bored with playing Scrabble with her mother before watching the ten o'clock news and turning in to bed.

'I used to go down there sometimes when I was young,' May confided. 'When I wasn't in London, that was. It was run by a lovely couple. A Mr and Mrs Jackson. I think their daughter runs it now.'

'Really, Mum, I didn't have you down for a pub person,' Rachel said.

'Oh, you'd be surprised,' May said, laughing. 'Come on. Let's get ready. I'll ask Mrs Allen to keep an ear out for Pa.'

Rachel felt her spirits lift as they went out of the kitchen door, through the kitchen garden and then a side gate in the high stone wall and out onto the village street. It was good to leave Rose Park and its oppressive atmosphere behind, at least for a couple of hours.

She tucked her arm into May's, and they walked along the

quiet street, between the chocolate-box thatched cottages, to the picture-book pub – the Quarryman's Arms. Although it was still early evening, it was already busy inside, and the atmosphere was hot and steamy. They shouldered their way between the drinkers towards the bar. A couple of locals recognised May and nodded to her, and the lady behind the bar, a dark-haired woman with an ample frame, greeted her like a long-lost friend.

'May! How wonderful to see you. It's been a while. Is this Rachel? My how you've grown! What are you doing back in the village?'

'Hello, Jenny. Yes, this is Rachel. Nineteen now, would you believe? My father's not well, so I'm back for a while to look after him.'

'Oh dear. I'm so sorry to hear that. I hope he gets better soon. What can I get you?'

May ordered them each a gin and tonic.

'If you'd like to sit down at that table in the corner, I'll bring them over to you in a minute. I'm afraid it's a busy night and we're a bit short staffed.'

Rachel and May sat down at the corner table.

'It's good to get out of the house,' said May with a sigh. 'It's tougher than I thought it would be. Father is not an easy patient.'

'I know. No wonder all the other nurses left!'

May laughed. 'Exactly. Only I can't very well do that, and he knows it.'

'Don't let him take advantage, Mum,' Rachel said.

'Well, that's easier said than done,' May replied.

The drinks came and they both took their first sip. Rachel was glad to see her mother visibly unwinding. Nursing Hadan was hard on May, she knew, especially as she'd only recently given up her job in intensive care for a less stressful life. She was a brilliant nurse and it had been her vocation, but she gave so much of herself to the job that it ended up taking a huge toll on her own wellbeing.

'It's so nice having you here, Rachel,' May said. 'I just hope you're not too bored.'

'Of course not,' she said. It was only a little white lie. 'I've been looking at old family photographs.'

'Oh really? Have you found anything interesting?'

'Not much. A few old albums. Nothing very interesting so far.'

For the past two days, Rachel had been sifting through the shelves and drawers in the library and the drawing room. She'd found a couple of albums and some odd packs of loose photos. The albums were full of stiff family groups – Hadan and his parents and possibly even his grandparents, then later Hadan, Wilhemena and their four daughters. There were some pictures of the workers in the quarry – old sepia photographs of men in cloth caps, breeches and kerchiefs, holding pickaxes and shovels; there were also some of the summer bale-carting – carthorses drawing trailers full of hay bales while workers ran behind lifting more onto the trailer. She'd found some studies of the stable block, complete with grooms and stable boys, some pictures of the big house, with all the servants lined up in the hall, some smiling, others looking nervous, taken at the turn of the century. The photos of the outside of the house must have been taken in the summer because the rambling roses that covered the front walls were in full bloom, just as they were now.

'What are you looking for, exactly?' May asked.

Rachel gave her a mischievous look in return. 'Family secrets!' she said in a stage whisper.

'Such as? I always think we're quite a boring family under the surface...' May ventured.

'You're joking, aren't you? There's so much I don't know about. For example, why my great-grandmother died of a broken heart, and why...'

She was about to say why Hadan had told her not to let anyone "take advantage", but something stopped her. Partly because she didn't want to worry her mum, and partly because she wanted to find answers to some of these questions herself.

'Why, what?' May was watching her, curiosity in her eyes.

'Why... well I was also wondering about this feud that people talk about. The bad blood between Grandad and a family in the village.'

'Hmm, I'm not sure about that. I think a lot of it is speculation. Idle gossip, probably.'

'And I don't know much about *your* past either, Mum,' Rachel said. 'About what you did in the war for example.'

'Oh that! Do you really want to know?' May said. 'I'm sure you'd find it as dull as ditchwater.'

'I don't think so. Look, I've been thinking, why don't you tell me while we're here? I want to find out as much about the family as I can before it's too late. To piece it all together. This summer seems like the perfect opportunity. I might even write it up in a journal, a sort of family history.'

'If you really want to hear about it. I suppose being in London during the Blitz was quite memorable now I come to think about it...' suddenly May broke off. She had a faraway look in her eyes.

'What are you thinking about?' Rachel asked.

'I was just remembering what it was like... it was a very long time ago,' she said, but Rachel noticed that her cheeks were flushed with the memory. It made her want to hear her mother's story more than ever.

'I'll tell you what,' May said. 'I'm usually free in the afternoons while Pa is having his nap. Why don't we go out into the garden, sit under the old oak tree and I will tell you what I can about that time.'

'That would be great, Mum,' Rachel said. 'Can we start tomorrow?'

May laughed. 'Of course. Why not?'

Just then, Jenny, the landlady bustled over to take their glasses.

'Would you like another one? Sorry it's so chaotic tonight, but as I mentioned, we are very short staffed at the moment.' She picked up the two glasses and paused beside the table. 'I don't suppose you would like a bar job for a few weeks, would you?' she said, addressing Rachel. 'Just in the evenings, mind. We're quiet at lunchtimes and I can normally cope with that.'

Rachel stared at her, processing the information for a moment, but it didn't take her long. It would be good to get out of the house in the evenings and earn a bit more money for her first term at college. And it would give her the chance to get to know more people in the village. Some of them might even have once worked for Hadan and be able to tell her nuggets of gossip about Rose Park.

'Why don't you take it, Rachel,' her mother said. 'You might even get to meet some people your own age.'

Rachel looked round at the assembled company, mostly men in their fifties and sixties laughing raucously while supping pints, so that seemed rather unlikely. But it didn't matter.

'Alright,' she said, smiling at Jenny. 'I worked in a pub at home last summer, so I do have some experience.'

'That's brilliant. Even better than I'd hoped. When can you start?'

Rachel shrugged. 'Tomorrow?'

'Great. If you turn up at around five, we can get things ready for the evening shift. Oh, and let me get you both a drink on the house to celebrate!' Jenny bustled away beaming from ear to ear.

'Well done, darling,' May said. 'I'm sure you won't regret it.'

'I might,' Rachel said, then shrugged. 'But whatever happens, it's only for a few weeks.'

~

AFTER LUNCH THE NEXT DAY, May was true to her word.

'Well, now's the time, Rachel. Pa is sound asleep. Let's make a jug of lemonade and take some deck chairs out to the oak tree. And don't forget your notebook.'

Mrs Allen stared at them. Rachel could tell she was brimming with questions, but she turned back to the sink and got on with the washing up.

They found some old deck chairs belonging to Hadan in the cupboard under the stairs and set them up under the shade of the great tree. May found a folding table too and brought the jug of lemonade, two glasses and a plate of biscuits. Rachel brought the lined hardback notebook she'd bought especially to write her travel journal in. It would be ideal for noting down nuggets of family history.

They settled down under the tree and May poured them each a glass of lemonade.

'So.' She rested her grey-blue eyes on Rachel's face. 'Where would you like me to start?'

'At the beginning, of course. Your childhood. What you were doing when war broke out; I want to know all about it.'

May laughed. 'My childhood! Well, that *is* a long time ago... but if you really want to know, I'll try my best.

'You know, all I can remember about the early years is how all of us girls had to tiptoe around Father. He was always domineering and had an explosive temper. Poor Mummy was a nervous wreck trying to please him, to head off outbursts. She crept around him as if she were on eggshells.

'She hadn't had much of an education herself. After all, she was married off to Father when she was just eighteen, shortly after he came back from the Great War. I told you, didn't I, it was all cooked up between Gabriel and her father? But, she was an intelligent woman, and very well-read. She made it her business to make sure that us girls got an education. She saw its value.

'She engaged a French governess to teach my older sisters. I was only about five at the time and too young to join in, but I remember the governess well. She was very glamourous – black curly hair and lots of lipstick. Madeleine, her name was. Unfortunately, she didn't last long. She left that same summer under a cloud.'

'Under a cloud?' Rachel looked up from her notebook. 'You can't leave it at that, Mum, you'll have to tell me what happened.'

May frowned and looked down at her lap, deep in thought, dredging through her memories.

'Well, I don't exactly know what happened. Of course none of us knew at the time, but when we were older, we began to speculate. Blanche thought that Father had taken a fancy to Madeleine and that Mummy had put a stop to it by sending her away. But that's all speculation, of course... He did have a bit of a reputation though,' she added as an afterthought. 'A roving eye, some people called it.'

'Oh really?'

May laughed. 'I have absolutely no evidence for any of this. It was all just gossip.'

'So, what happened after Madeleine was sent packing?'

'After that, we were all sent to an old-fashioned private school for girls. It was run by two very strait-laced old sisters and there was a very strict dress code. Collars and ties, pleated skirts and thick tights. Indoor and outdoor shoes, white gloves in summer and woollen ones in winter, straw hats in summer and felt ones in winter. I really don't remember much about what we were taught – apart from Bible studies, of course, but I do remember the deportment lessons, when we had to walk around with a book on our head.'

Rachel laughed.

'Life at home was strict, though,' May said on a more serious note. 'Although we were outwardly wealthy and privileged, none of us girls were very happy. Father was so strict, we could never let our hair down when he was around. The good thing was, he was a workaholic, always in his office or out and about at the quarry or the farms.

'In the late 1930s, I was in my teens then, the quarry started to fail – result of the world depression – and Father started trying to get investors interested. He was up and down to London on the train all the time at that point.

'One American, Thomas Baines, came over to look at the quarry and brought his son, Conor. Blanche fell for him straight away. I remember the first time she saw him, she was dumbstruck, it was as if there were stars in her eyes. It was certainly love at first sight. Thomas and Conor were only here a couple of weeks and off she went with them to America. At least Pa got his investment. He'd gained some capital, but lost a daughter, Mother always used to say.

'Even though I was only a teenager, I remember clearly the buildup to the war, the news reports about Nazi aggression, the invasion of Czechoslovakia and the Munich agreement in 1938, then the invasion of Poland. We were all sitting in the living room that fateful Sunday in September 1939 to listen to the address by Neville Chamberlain. When he said those terrible words, that Germany had not agreed to withdraw its troops from Poland, "so consequently, this country is at war with Germany," a hush fell over the room as we all contemplated what it might mean for us. I remember noticing my father's face, it was completely ashen, like a mask, full of horror and I realised that he was remembering his experiences in the trenches. He rushed over to the radio and turned it off. Then he left the room. I think we realised then that our lives would never be the same again.

'A few months after that, early in spring 1940, Florence, who had just finished her mathematics degree at Cambridge, was recruited to work at Bletchley Park, the newly established Government Communications HQ. She was only just twenty, very advanced for her years. Father took her there in the car. We all stood on the drive and waved her goodbye, while she blew kisses out of the window.

'A few weeks later, Ivy went off to work in London for the

government. Her exact role was shrouded in mystery, but she said she'd be able to use her languages. She always was brilliant at languages. I missed them all desperately.

'So, I was left on my own here at Rose Park and very lonely. It felt so unfair, as if I'd been abandoned. I was just eighteen, and I really didn't want to stay at home. That's when I started yearning to get away from this place. I could hardly bear to stay, in fact.'

4

MAY

ROSE PARK, 1940

At least when Florence left home in April 1940, May still had Ivy as a companion. But little did she know that Ivy was busy making her own plans and would be off soon too.

When Ivy called her into her bedroom a few weeks after Florence's departure, and said, 'Little sis, I've got something to tell you. Now you're not to be mad,' May felt betrayed.

How could Ivy have done that to her? She must have been working towards her departure for months. She'd been for interviews and even sat examinations without telling May. Mother and Father must have known about it too. May dissolved into tears at the news that she was off to London, and let Ivy gather her up in her arms and hug her. She could still remember the feel of her sister's arms around her all these years later. It was all she had to remember her by.

A few days later, May went with Mother and Ivy to the station at Wolverton to see Ivy off. How pretty Ivy looked in her red cotton dress with little white flowers, her glossy, dark curls tucked up into a French-style beret. Her eyes were shining with excitement. It was infectious, and although they were saying goodbye and didn't know when they might see each other again, May didn't feel sad anymore. Instead, she felt thrilled for Ivy, that she was off to London to work in a recently formed part of the War Office. She might even be posted abroad and would certainly be using her languages. It was her dream job and she'd been brimming with excitement since she'd first broken the news of her departure to May.

All these years later, May had kept that image of Ivy in her mind, getting onto the London-bound train with her two leather suitcases. Mother, in her typically generous style, had treated her to a first-class ticket.

'You may as well enjoy the journey, my darling. After all, who knows what hardships you'll have to face in the coming months...'

Hearing this, May frowned, puzzled, guessing there were things about Ivy's new job that her sister hadn't told her. A bowler-hatted man stood aside gallantly and raised his hat with an approving look, letting Ivy onto the train first. After she'd installed her luggage, she came back to the door, pulled down the window and leaned out. She looked dazzling, with her English rose complexion, and her deep red lipstick setting off her dark hair.

'Goodbye, darling,' Mother said, and May had noticed with surprise that tears stood in her eyes.

'Bye-bye. I'll miss you!' Ivy said.

The whistle blew and the engine started puffing and panting, then the train began to move slowly along the platform.

Ivy smiled and waved until the train was out of sight and May and her mother did the same. And May had held onto that last memory of her sister for four decades and had cherished it like a precious jewel.

Walking back to the car, she quizzed her mother.

'Why are you crying?' she asked.

'Oh, darling, we might not see dear Ivy for a while, that's all.' Her mother sniffed dabbing her nose with a handkerchief.

'You didn't cry like that when Florence left.'

'Well...' Wilhemena appeared to be stumped. 'We're not quite sure when Ivy might be able to get back to see us. It could be a long time,' she said finally. 'Florence hasn't gone very far at all, and she'll be back to visit in a few weeks.'

'And what did you mean by hardships?' May persisted.

'Oh... well, the women's hostel she's going to live in isn't very comfortable, apparently.'

Her mother was a hopeless liar, but May didn't ask any more questions. It was clear that there were things about Ivy's new career that she wasn't meant to know. What troubled her more, was that now she was the only Rose daughter at home. There'd never been a day without at least one of her sisters being around to entertain her. She had no idea how she would cope without them for company. There would be no one to confide in, no one to joke with, no one to take a walk with. She wasn't cut out to be an only child, she was sure of that.

Wilhemena drove the lumbering Austin 12 home to Rose Park even more erratically than usual. She ground the gears, stalled the engine several times and almost hit another car when she pulled out of a turning without looking.

'Are you alright, Mother?' May asked.

'Quite alright, darling. I just want to get home, that's all.'

'I was wondering, Mother. I'd like to do something for the war effort myself,' May began. She'd planned to wait a few days until the dust had settled on Ivy's departure before trying, but now she had her mother alone, she thought it was a good time to broach the subject.

'Well, that's admirable, May, but after all, you are only just eighteen.'

May ignored the comment and went on. 'You know my friend, Ruby, from school?'

'Uh-huh,' Wilhemena said absently, focusing on a slow tractor up ahead.

'Well, her parents have a flat in London. She's going to move there and get a job in a hospital. Casualties are coming back from France all the time and hospitals are already overstretched. I was wondering if I might...'

'No,' said Wilhemena sharply, her attention finally fully focused on her daughter. 'Your father would never allow it.' Then, she pulled out onto the opposite carriageway and accelerated past the tractor.

'But what about you? What do you think?'

'What does it matter what I think?' her mother replied with a trace of bitterness. 'But in any case, I don't think it's a good idea. You are far too young.'

'Too young? Father has people working on the farms and in the quarry who are a lot younger than I am.'

'That's beside the point,' her mother said.

'But what can I do here? Sit around on my own and get bored?'

'Well actually, your father was saying they are short of men on the farms now so many have signed up for the army. If you want to be useful, you could help out on one of the farms. How about that?'

Wilhemena turned to her, beaming in triumph, May's spirits plummeted. Her mother had wrong-footed her. She could hardly refuse to do this when she'd been agitating about helping the war effort.

'And perhaps next year, after your birthday, we can think again...'

So, the following Monday, May got up before dawn, put on a pair of sturdy work trousers and a plain cotton blouse, tied her pale hair back in a ribbon and settled a cloth cap she'd found in the tack room on top of it, pulled on a pair of Wellington boots and set out on foot to Park Farm. It was just the other side of the village of Perry Cross. Her father had told the farm manager, Percy Payne, that she would be glad to help out.

'She's as strong as some of those boys you employ,' May had overheard Hadan telling Percy when he'd come to the house to be introduced and to discuss the work. She'd already met Percy. She had been dismissed and was walking along the passage away from her father's office when she heard him say that. She stopped, curious as to what else he would say.

'She's good with horses, but she'll do anything you give her. Don't shrink from giving her jobs to do just because she's my daughter. I wouldn't want her treated any differently from the others.'

Walking through the waking village towards the farm, she realised how beautiful this time of day was, with the morning sun burning the mist off the fields and the birds twittering their dawn chorus in the hedgerows that were filled with summer flowers.

At the farm she was introduced to the labourers: Ken, Joe, Ernie and Michael. Ken, Ernie and Michael were all middle-aged, but Joe was younger, probably in his early twenties.

'We're lucky these four lads are still with us,' Percy said. 'We did have a workforce of seven, but three have already signed up. I hope you boys aren't thinking of doing the same,' he said with a chuckle, and they all grunted their denials and looked down at their hobnailed boots.

'I was thinking of asking for a couple of Land Girls to help out for haymaking and the harvest this summer. But as you've volunteered, Miss Rose, I'm not going to do that for a while. We can see how things pan out. Alright, today is shearing day. Fifty head of sheep to get through. Is everyone ready?'

May had wanted to tell him not to call her Miss Rose, but hadn't had time.

They all trooped into the fields behind the farmhouse where a flock of fifty or so sheep were grazing. Percy fetched his Collie sheepdog from one of the barns and set it to work rounding up the sheep and driving them into the stable yard. May was mesmerised, watching the skill of the dog as, guided by Percy's whistles and shouts, it ran round the back of the flock, harrying the sheep into ever tighter circles, all the time moving them forward towards the farmyard. She was so fascinated watching the dog, that she forgot that she was meant to be blocking the open entrance to another field. Three wayward sheep on the edge of the flock broke away and made a run for it, dashing past May, their eyes wide with fear.

'Miss Rose!' Percy yelled. 'Watch what you're doing, please!'

'Oh, I'm sorry!' she said, colouring. She rushed into the other field to try to chase the three sheep back, but try as she might, she couldn't catch up with them, and every time she approached them, they scattered in all directions. May felt such a fool. She'd failed at her first task. She'd seen the looks Ken and Mike had given her when Percy had yelled at her. They must already resent her and were probably looking for her to trip up at the first opportunity.

She struggled alone for a few minutes, but then Joe appeared through the gap between the fields.

'Need some help?' he yelled. 'You go that way and I'll stand here and stop them running into this part of the field.'

After a few false starts, together they managed to drive the three runaway sheep back into the other field.

'Thank you!' she said, smiling in relief at Joe.

'It's no problem,' he said. 'I made all sorts of mistakes when I started out. I know how it feels.'

'I don't think the others were too impressed,' she said.

'Oh, take no notice of them,' he said. 'I'll look out for you.'

'Thank you,' she repeated, flashing him another smile. She noticed that his eyes were hazel, that his hair was dark, almost black, and that his cheeks were flushed from fresh air and exertion. His body was lean and fit and she could see the hard muscles under his shirt. She was glad that at least someone was prepared to show her kindness. She had expected to be treated as an unwelcome outsider by everyone on the farm.

The rest of the morning was spent herding the sheep into pens in the yard, so they were in groups of ten. Then, when their time came to be sheared, taking them out one at a time and funnelling them down a narrow run between two sets of hurdles. Either Mike or Ernie was at the other end to catch them and to wrestle them to the ground and shear them of their thick wool coats with a pair of sharp shears. It was a hot day and by lunchtime May was running with sweat and ready for a rest.

'Come on into the farmhouse,' Percy said at noon. 'There's bread and cheese and a pint of beer waiting for you.'

May followed the others into the house. Hadan had told her she would be given lunch at the farm, but he hadn't told her about the beer.

They all sat down at a big, square table in the dairy, behind the farmhouse kitchen, and Percy's wife, Ethel, slapped a plate of doorstep cheese and pickle sandwiches down in front of each of them. Then she brought tankards and a jug and proceeded to fill them with beer.

May put her hand over her tankard. 'I don't think I'd better have beer,' she said. 'I'm not used to it, and I wouldn't be able to work this afternoon if I had it.'

There was a general guffawing amongst the others and Percy's wife said, 'We ain't got nothing else though. Only water.'

'Water will be fine,' May said and Ethel brought her a fresh tankard filled with water.

Everyone tucked into their sandwiches and for a while the talk was of the farm and of the morning's work, but soon it turned to what was on everyone's minds; the war and the battle of Dunkirk that was raging across the channel.

'I heard on the radio that our boys are trapped on the coast. Outflanked by the Jerry on every side,' said Mike. 'Dreadful business. It's a bloodbath out there.'

'Johnny and Roddy are out there. I hope to God they are safe. They've started evacuating the troops on a fleet of small boats this morning, though, I heard,' said Percy. 'They're bringing 'em all home. Sounds like a proper defeat if you ask me.'

'Well, they couldn't leave 'em there to be slaughtered, could they?' said Ernie. 'There's already been one massacre. Did you hear about all those French and British POWs, gunned down in cold blood? Nearly a hundred of 'em shot in one go. Jerry's an evil enemy alright.'

'I blame Churchill,' Ken chimed in. 'Did you hear his speech the other day? He called Dunkirk a "military disaster". What sort of talk is that for a leader? No wonder the men are dispirited. I fear for the future.'

May listened with interest. She'd heard the radio reports about Dunkirk herself, but unlike these men, she didn't know anyone out there. It had all sounded rather remote to her, but now she knew that two of the men who had worked on this farm were in the thick of it, it somehow seemed more real and immediate. Like the others, she began to think about them and to hope they were coming home safely.

In the afternoon, the shearing resumed. It was May's job to guide the sheep back into the field once they were sheared. Sometimes the animals were skittish and wouldn't go through the gate. Instead, they started running around the yard. They were quick on their feet and it was difficult to catch them. Each time this happened, Ken and Ernie leaned on the fence, grinning at her attempts to catch the errant animals, but Joe would stop trimming the sheared fleeces, and come and help her. With two on the job, it was much easier to herd the animals back to the field.

By five o'clock, May was exhausted and ready to go home. Joe walked a little way along the high street towards Rose Park with her.

'Where do you live?' she asked.

'With my mum and grandparents,' he said. 'In a tied cottage in the village.'

'Tied cottage?' she asked.

He laughed. 'You don't know what that is? The cottages are owned by the estate – in other words, by your father. They are for workers, and retired workers. My grandad used to work in the quarry. That's why we've got one.'

'Oh, I see,' she said, blushing, ashamed that she'd asked a question which could potentially have embarrassed him. He'd been so kind to her that day, and she was grateful to him for that.

He laughed. 'It's fine. I'm just surprised you didn't know, that's all.'

'My father doesn't let us have anything to do with the business,' she said. 'After all, we're just girls, he always says.'

Again Joe laughed. 'I'm not surprised at that.'

They walked on and soon came to the top of Quarry Lane.

'Well, this is me,' he said. 'I live down there. I'll see you tomorrow, same time.'

'What do you think we'll be doing tomorrow?' she asked, and he shrugged.

'Not sure. Possibly hedge-laying or fence repair. We'll be starting haymaking soon, but maybe not tomorrow. Percy will keep us busy, to be sure.'

They said goodbye and May walked the rest of the way back to Rose Park alone, musing over the day's events and thinking about Joe. She didn't know his surname but would ask him the next day. How strange that she'd lived her life here on the edge of Perry Cross, but she'd never met Joe or any of the other men before. Perhaps they'd passed in the street once or twice and nodded to each other, but their paths had never crossed properly. How unfair the class system was, she reflected. If Joe had been born into a family like hers, he would have been running a business or working in a profession by now, having spent three years at university, not slaving away as a farm labourer as he was.

She let herself into the house through the kitchen door, went straight upstairs and lay down on her bed and fell asleep, exhausted by the day's work.

After that, the days on the farm followed more or less the same pattern. For the rest of that week, the workers were sent out to the fields in groups mending fences and laying hedges. May was assigned to help Joe and he taught her how to cut and lay a hedge, how to weave the top branches into each other to make it strong and thick. He was very patient, and May learned quickly. The first time she managed to lay a section without help, she stood back to admire it.

'That's pretty good,' Joe said, smiling.

'Well, you're a pretty good teacher,' she said, swelling with pride at his words.

The following week the haymaking started in earnest and May discovered what hard work really was. They were out in the fields at daybreak. Three of the men would cut the tall grass in a section of the field with long scythes, then the others would rake up the cut grass with huge wooden rakes and fork it onto the back of a horse-drawn trailer. May's job was to rake and load the hay alongside Joe and Ken. After less than an hour of this work, her back was aching, and all her muscles were screaming out for her to stop. But she kept at it. She wasn't going to let the others think she was soft and weak. She wanted to show them that a mere slip of a girl like her, and a Rose at that, could work just as hard as they could.

At lunchtime, if they were in a far field, Percy would bring them lunch on a pony cart, so they didn't have to waste time traipsing back to the house. They would all sit down on the grass wherever they were and eat the sandwiches and sup the beer that he gave them. May would look around her at the undulating hills, bisected by green hedgerows and dotted with spinneys, basking in the sunshine. How beautiful it was here and how lucky she was to be working on the land.

As with every other day on the farm, the conversation quickly turned to the war. These men were deeply interested in its progress, so much so that the news reports May heard on the

BBC Home Service as she ate breakfast in the mornings started to come alive to her as never before.

Each of the ten days of "Operation Dynamo", the codename for the evacuation of Dunkirk, had been followed closely and discussed in detail by the men, with the numbers of troops reaching Britain each day, being reported and mulled over. Now, in the first week of June, they talked about Winston Churchill's latest speech, in which he'd said, 'We shall fight on the beaches, we shall fight on the landing grounds, we shall fight in the fields and in the streets...' and May noticed that Churchill was now gaining grudging approval amongst the farm workers. They mourned the loss of *HMS Glorious* that week and debated hotly the declaration of war on Britain by Italy, then a few days later expressed outrage at the fall of Paris to the Germans.

In July the harvest began. Once again, the crop was cut with scythes, then May, Joe and Ken went through and gathered up the sheaves and tied them in bundles and Percy went through with a machine pulled by a new-fangled tractor to harvest the seeds and grains from the crop. She was used to hard work now, to the relentless sun beating down on her back when she bent down, to the cuts in her hands from sharp ends of corn, the stings from insects, to the constant back ache. She realised that being on the farm made her happy and contented and she was forced to admit to herself that that was largely to do with Joe.

It was about a week into the harvest that Hadan took a sudden interest in May's work.

'Who's working for Percy nowadays?' he asked over supper one evening, peering at her over his evening paper.

May reeled off the names of the men. When she mentioned Joe, Hadan looked at her sharply.

'Joe? Joe who?'

'Joe Harding, I think he said,' she replied.

Hadan stared at her, his face suddenly ashen.

'Joe Harding? Did I hear you properly?' he said, putting down his newspaper and glaring at her.

'I think so. I'm sure that was the name he said. Why?' May said, putting her fork down, worried now.

'I thought he worked in the quarry. Now look here. I don't want you to have anything to do with that lad, do you hear me?' Hadan boomed.

May swallowed. 'Why? He's nice. He's the only one who helps me. The others just laugh when I can't do things.'

Hadan banged on the table, making the cutlery rattle. 'You are not to have anything to do with him. His family are no good. They're rotten to the core. D'you hear me?'

May considered his words. She was vaguely aware that her father had a longstanding feud with one of the families in the village.

'I don't see how I can avoid him if I'm working on that farm. There aren't that many of us.'

'Well then, this is what you'll do. You'll have to leave the farm. You'll not go back there. I forbid you to have anything to do with Joe Harding. And that is my final word on the subject.'

'That's so unfair,' she said, swallowing hard. She knew she had no bargaining power against her father, but she now realised that it would be a huge wrench to give up seeing Joe. They'd become firm friends. In fact, he was the first male friend she'd ever had.

'Unfair it may be, but it's what's going to happen. I will go and see Percy myself this evening. You needn't go back there at all.'

'Mother, tell him it's not fair,' she said to Wilhemena who had sat silently so far.

'I'm sorry, darling, but it's your father's decision,' she said weakly.

May left the table, ran up to her room and flung herself on her bed, sobbing her heart out. She couldn't understand her father's attitude, but it was typical. He could give or take away on a whim, he was mercurial and capricious. It made her feel powerless and small again. And very, very angry.

Finally her sobs subsided, and as she calmed down, she saw that her mother had left a letter on her dressing table that must have arrived that morning. She went over and picked it up, examining the envelope. She recognised the handwriting immediately and saw the London postmark. She ripped it open. It was from Ruby.

Darling May,

I'm having such a fabulous time here in London. Working really hard but partying just as hard on my evenings off. I'm working at St Thomas's hospital. They were expecting bombings and a lot of casualties, but so far there haven't been too many at all, so the work I'm doing as an auxiliary nurse is light at the moment. Some of the wards have been evacuated from London, so we've been busy organising that for the last couple of weeks.

They are still looking for people though, so there would be an opening for you if you'd like to come. I would love it if you were here. We would have so much fun together!

Do write and let me know your news. And if you can get down to London even for just a visit, I'd love to see you!

Your ever loving,

Ruby

May put the letter down and thought for a long time. If her father wasn't going to let her work on the farm – something he and Mother had originally suggested and insisted on her doing – then she would go to London. It was as simple as that. And if they wouldn't let her do that, she would have to run away from home.

5

RACHEL

ROSE PARK, 1980

AT FOUR-THIRTY THAT AFTERNOON, Rachel set off from Rose Park to walk through the village to start her shift at the Quarryman's Arms. It was a beautiful afternoon, the gentle breeze filled with the sound of birdsong. The cloudless sky was azure blue, and the afternoon sunlight bathed the honeysuckle-coloured cottages in an ochre glow.

As she walked, she thought about her mother's story. She was glad she'd asked May to tell her about what happened to her during the war. Rachel had never known that May had worked on one of the village farms that first summer of the war. She was looking forward to hearing about how May eventually managed to escape to London and whether she'd discovered why Hadan had such antipathy towards the Harding family.

When she arrived at the pub, Jenny was already busy behind the bar, cleaning the taps and making sure there were enough clean glasses set out for the evening rush. She greeted Rachel warmly.

'I'm so pleased you agreed to help out. I've been really struggling lately. I just haven't been able to get the staff over the summer.'

'It's no problem. I'm happy to get out of the house, actually. What can I do to help?'

'Oh, could you just wipe down all the tables and the bar. Then set out the ashtrays. They're on that shelf over there.'

Rachel found a cloth in the sink and got on with the task.

'How is your grandfather today?' Jenny asked as she polished the taps.

'As well as can be expected. I don't think he's the easiest patient in the world though. Poor old Mum.'

'Your mother is a saint,' Jenny said. 'I don't suppose old Mr Rose *is* an easy patient, though. He's been used to getting his own way his whole life. It can't be easy for him, either.'

'Do you know my grandfather?' Rachel asked, surprised. She wouldn't have thought that Hadan would be a regular at the village pub.

'Who doesn't know him in this village?' Jenny said smiling, 'but, actually, my grandmother used to work in the big house in the early days, so I know a little bit about it from her.'

'Oh, how interesting,' Rachel said, making a mental note that Jenny's grandmother might be a good source of information about the old days at some point.

She was kept busy until opening time. Jenny showed her the ropes; where everything was kept, how the till worked, the idiosyncrasies of the beer taps. It was all familiar stuff to Rachel, from her pub job in Surrey the previous summer. Then, when the first customers came in, the two of them took it in turns to serve them.

It was a Friday evening, and most of the customers were labourers, fresh from their week's work at the quarry or on the farms, intent on drinking away a large portion of their weekly pay packet. Most of them hadn't even gone home to get changed before dropping in for a pint. Soon the pub was packed and noisy. It was hard to hear the customers' orders above the hubbub of conversation. Rachel liked it like that, though. It made the time pass more quickly, but looking around she did notice that there were virtually no people of her own age in the bar and only a few women. It didn't matter, she decided, she had a job to do, and she was earning money and not wasting her evening watching soap operas on the crackly TV at Rose Park.

At around nine o' clock when the crowd was thinning out a little, a young man, a few years older than herself, shouldered his way to the bar and ordered a pint.

Rachel watched him from the corner of her eye as she pulled the pint of Phipps for him. He had tousled, shoulder-length dark hair, intense eyes and a stubbly chin. She couldn't tell whether the stubble was a deliberate fashion statement, or inadvertent. He looked a little dishevelled and wore a black leather jacket over a crumpled cheesecloth shirt.

She handed him the pint.

'You're new here, aren't you?' he asked, taking his first sip, leaving a line of foam on his upper lip.

'Yes. It's my very first evening.'

'New to the village too, I take it?'

'Not exactly. I'm just staying for a few weeks. My grandfather isn't well.'

'Oh. I'm sorry to hear that,' he said. 'Anyone I know? Only it's a small place and I know most people...'

'My grandfather is Hadan Rose,' she said and waited for his reaction. Sure enough, his eyes widened and he raised his eyebrows.

Rachel couldn't help laughing.

'So, I take it that you know him?' she asked.

'Of course. Who doesn't, here? Well, I'm sorry to hear he's ill, but he's a very old man, isn't he?'

Rachel nodded. 'He's ninety years old. But I suppose no one ever wants to go, no matter how old they are.'

'You're right about that,' he said, raising his glass.

They chatted for a few more minutes, until Rachel had to serve another customer. In that short time she discovered that his name was Daniel Walters, that he'd lived in the village his whole life, that he was a journalist on the local paper and that he played in a band that toured the local pubs at weekends. She also told him a little about herself, although it sounded very tame in comparison. He seemed quite interested in her family.

'Which of the Rose sisters is your mother?' he asked. 'My money is on the youngest one... May, isn't it?'

'Yes!' she said, surprised. 'You seem to know a lot about my family.'

'Well, people in villages do tend to know a bit about local gentry, don't they? It stands to reason. For centuries your family have been the masters around here.'

'It's not really like that anymore,' she said. 'And when Grandad dies, the house will be sold. It will be the end of an era.'

Daniel raised an eyebrow, clearly interested to hear more, but Rachel stopped herself. She'd already said too much. What business was it of anyone's that the house was going to be sold? It was her nerves that had prompted her to divulge family secrets she told herself. She needed to be careful. After all, Daniel had already told her he was a journalist. He might be sniffing around for a story.

Talking to Daniel had made her feel very young and inexperienced, but she was flattered that he had bothered to spend time chatting with her. After a while though, she got busy again and he moved away from the bar to talk to a group of men who were standing in the middle of the room.

Towards the end of the evening, Daniel came to put his empty glass on the bar and to say goodbye.

'I expect I'll see you again soon. I'm often in here,' he said with a smile and a wave and setting off towards the door.

Rachel turned to see that Jenny was watching her, with a wry smile.

'You want to watch that one,' she said, nodding in the direction of the door.

'Oh? Why?' Rachel asked.

'He's a right charmer. A ladykiller some say. He's left a trail of broken hearts behind him, so watch yourself.'

Rachel felt her cheeks growing hot at the implications of Jenny's words. Was it so obvious that she'd found Daniel interesting and rather attractive? She had no experience with boys at all, and she told herself she needed to be far less obvious in future.

When she got back to Rose Park, Rachel felt fully awake, stimulated by the evening's work. There was no way she would be able to sleep, at least not for an hour or two. Her mother and Mrs Allen were already in bed, so she had the downstairs of the house to herself.

She decided to take another look in the library. She'd only given the room a cursory look for photographs before, and she had to admit to herself, she'd been rather disappointed with what she'd found so far. Perhaps, if she were to delve a little deeper, she might find some more interesting ones. She walked along the flagstone passage and pushed open the creaking door to the library. Despite the heat of the summer evening, the room was cold – it had the chill of an empty church in winter. Rachel switched on the lights. One of them buzzed and flickered, giving the place an eerie feel. She shivered. It reminded her of the strange, soft light she'd occasionally seen in her bedroom. That hadn't happened for a few nights, and she'd put the apparition out of her mind. Now she recalled with a chill the strange force that had pushed down on her chest, stopping her from sitting up in bed.

There was a small, decorative walnut-wood bureau in one corner of the room. Rachel remembered that May had told her that it had originally belonged to her great-grandmother, Emily, but that no one had used it for years. Wilhemena had wanted to get rid of it when they refurbished the library after the war, but Hadan had refused to let her. He was sentimental about his mother, probably because she'd died so young.

To Rachel's surprise, the lid opened easily, and she pulled it down to make a desk. She sat down on the leather stool, just as her great-grandmother would have done a century before, and started to open the small drawers inside the bureau. There was nothing interesting in there, only the usual assortment of paper-clips, treasury tags and a bottle of dried-up ink.

There were two larger drawers underneath the desk. There were several old hardback notebooks stacked in the top one and opening them up, one by one, and scanning through them, she realised that they must have been Emily's household accounts. They listed amounts paid for meat, vegetables, firewood, furniture wax, and then the wages paid to the household servants each week. Only a few shillings each; pitifully small sums, Rachel thought, her eye running down the columns. She was amazed at how many servants there had actually been in 1890 though; a housekeeper, a butler, four housemaids, four kitchen maids, a scullery maid, four gardeners, three stable boys and a coachman. All were paid out of Emily's housekeeping money that Gabriel gave her at the beginning of each month.

The notebooks were all the same. There were about thirty of them, the last one was dated 1895. When Rachel opened that one, she saw that the notebook was only half full, then she realised that halfway through that year, Emily had become sick, struck down by an illness no doctor could diagnose or explain. She had taken to her bed and had wasted away there, dying a few years later.

It was chilling to look at Emily's last entry. A seemingly mundane shopping list of flour, yeast, butter and cheese. The writing was a little faint, but there was nothing to suggest that the woman who'd written it was sickening for an illness that would eventually carry her away. She must have still been a relatively young woman, only in her early forties. How strange, Rachel mused, wondering if there was something that had happened that day, the 15th June 1895, to cause Emily's sudden decline.

She put the books back in the drawers with great reverence. At the very least, they were a piece of social history, a relic from a bygone era that local historians would probably find fascinating.

Rachel opened the bottom drawer of the desk and drew in a sharp breath. There was nothing in that drawer except a large, leather-bound book. She held her breath. Was this the photograph album she'd been searching for? She opened it up and exhaled gratefully.

On the first page were several faded, sepia pictures of a small, chubby baby, whom Rachel immediately assumed must be Hadan. He was dressed in a lace-cap and white, frilly clothes like a baby girl. He was constantly staring at the camera and smiling a wide, gummy smile.

Rachel turned the page and there were more pictures of the same child. This time he was slightly older, sitting up in a pram, standing on the lawn at Rose Park in a sailor suit, sitting on Emily's lap in a studio. In those pictures, Emily didn't look pale or sad, she looked happy and bursting with life. The pictures of that baby went on for a few pages, then, on a subsequent page, they started again, with photos of a small baby. Rachel flicked back to the first page of the album frowning. Was this the same child? She carried on, turning the pages. Once again there were similar shots of a baby getting bigger and taller, then becoming a toddler. On the third or fourth page, she stopped and stared. There was a picture of Emily, holding this baby. But it looked different from the first one. Emily's hair was styled differently and the baby was not as round and chubby as in the first photographs. Whatever did this mean?

She turned to the next page and this time, did a double-take. This photograph was of the two babies together. The chubby one was a toddler and sat beside the younger one, again clearly taken in a studio with a background of a sky with fluffy clouds. She looked at this photograph for a long time wondering what it meant. Had Emily and Gabriel had another son? Were these children not actually theirs? She'd always known Hadan to be an only child, but had he once had a brother? If so, what had happened to him?

She closed the book and slipped it back into the drawer. She would show the pictures to her mother tomorrow and see if she might have an explanation for the seemingly inexplicable. Lost in thought she went up to her bedroom, undressed and lay down on the bed. She was tired and as soon as she'd closed her eyes, her thoughts became jumbled. She was walking across the lawn at Rose Park towards the big oak tree hand in hand with a little boy on each side of her. Under the oak tree, Daniel was waiting for her, smiling sardonically, smoking a cigarette. A bird squawked in the branches, and she awoke with a jerk and sat up. There was that soft, fuzzy light again, but in front of her a shapeless form, blocking out the light. Panic rising in her throat, she tried to get out of bed, but some invisible force was stopping her. Then she realised that the shapeless form was standing in front of her, pushing her backwards, just as it had before, only this time it felt more threatening, more malevolent somehow. And again, she opened her mouth to cry out but no sound would come.

6

MAY

LONDON, 1940

PERSUASION DIDN'T WORK on May's father. She realised after a few days that he didn't think that because he'd stopped her from working on the farm, he owed her the right to go and work in London with his blessing. For a week she tried to persuade him. She tried every version of every argument she could think of, but they all fell on deaf ears. She realised then that her father was a ruthless, self-centred man. It didn't enter his mind that he might owe her anything because of the way he'd treated her. In May's mind, he had no compassion whatsoever.

Each morning when she woke up, she thought about the farm, about all the other workers who had accepted her grudgingly because she was a hard worker, and of Joe who had shown her nothing but friendship and kindness. And each morning, her anger and frustration at what her father had done came back to her afresh. She was determined to do something about it, and after a few days she knew what it would be.

On the fifth day, she went to the post office in the village and withdrew thirty pounds. Then, back in her bedroom, she packed a small knapsack, that she'd found in the servants' boot room, with essentials, and hid it in her wardrobe. She could only take a few things with her. It was a good job it was summertime and the days were warm. She didn't have room to pack a coat or any warm jumpers.

A week after she'd worked her last day at the farm, she was ready to act. She waited until the evening meal was over, then went to her room and sat quietly until she heard her parents going up to bed at around eleven o'clock. She waited a little longer – until half past and she was sure that all was quiet before making her move.

Firstly she scribbled a brief note to her parents.

DEAR MOTHER AND FATHER,

I'm sorry if you're worried about me, but I've decided that I can't sit at home doing nothing when everyone else is working for the war effort. I was enjoying working on the farm, and I don't understand why you stopped me. I would have been quite happy to stay there the whole summer.

Since you won't allow me to do that, I've decided to leave home and to go to London to join Ruby. Please don't try to stop me, it is what I want to do and because I can't work here, I really need to do it.

I will be in touch when I've arrived.

With love,

May

SHE STARED at the note hardly believing that she, May Emily Rose, model pupil and daughter had actually written it. Unlike her sisters, she'd never given her parents a moment's worry in her whole life. Naturally sweet natured and compliant, she'd never felt the need to rebel before. But she felt it now. It burned inside her with a fierce flame, the strength and ferocity of which frightened her.

May didn't write Ruby's address on the note, although she

realised it would be easy for her parents to get it from Ruby's parents. She hadn't been in touch with Ruby to let her know she was coming either, partly because she wasn't sure how long it would take her to get to London and partly because she didn't want Ruby waiting around for her to arrive. There was also a chance that she wouldn't make it, of course.

She folded the letter and put it on her writing table under a paperweight. She tried not to imagine her mother's face crumpling when she read it. She had no desire to cause her mother, or her father for that matter, any pain, but she was angry with both of them; with her father for his unreasonable behaviour in forbidding her to return to the farm, and with her mother for being too weak to take her side against him. Wilhelmina had simply gone along with his wishes, as she always did.

May had already decided it was too risky to go out onto the landing and down the main stairs with her knapsack; her father sometimes prowled about the house if he couldn't sleep, so, she would have to find an alternative way out of the house. She opened her window and peered out. The light in her room cast a pale square on the lawn outside, but as far as she could see, it was the only light left on in the house. She fetched the knapsack, eased it onto the windowsill and out of the window. Then, holding her breath she gave it a final push. There was a cracking of twigs and branches below, and leaning out, she saw that it had landed on a bush in the flowerbed beneath the window. She breathed easily again. It hadn't made much of a noise and it hadn't burst open either.

Then it was her turn. She threw her shoes out onto the lawn, then wriggled herself onto the windowsill so her legs were dangling outside. Now she was sitting there, it seemed a very long way to jump without spraining an ankle, and she looked for alternative ways of getting down. The ivy which clambered all over that side of the house was thick and strong. It was almost as old as the house itself, with big, sinuous branches and strong creepers that clung tenaciously to the brickwork. May turned over on her belly and, feeling around with her foot, found a foothold in the ivy beneath the window, then little by little, she eased herself down. It wasn't difficult – May and her sisters had grown up climbing trees all over the estate – and the ivy was so dense and strong, the branches so close together, that she was on the ground in a matter of minutes. She dusted herself off, found her shoes and slipped them on, eased the knapsack onto her shoulders and set off at a brisk pace.

She'd brought a small torch, some water in a metal canteen and a few biscuits from the kitchen. It was eight miles to Wolverton station where the fast trains that ran between London and Birmingham stopped. She'd calculated that it would take her around three hours to walk there. Then she would only have an hour or two to wait before the first train of the day departed for London Euston. She decided not to walk along the main road, she didn't want to be spotted by motorists, so she had worked out a route on back roads through villages. It was longer but less conspicuous.

She left Rose Park by a side gate, skirted around the edge of the quarry and clambered over a fence onto a country lane. She knew these roads near the estate very well, and wasn't at all fazed by walking in the dark. It was a clear, cool night and there was a full moon which lit up the road ahead. At first, she felt elated and buoyed by the fact that she'd managed to get out of Rose Park without mishap and without being discovered, but as she carried on, and as the miles took their toll on her muscles and joints, she began to feel a little less sure of herself. On one occasion, a badger ran out of the undergrowth making her jump and cry out, and on another, she was spooked by some horses in a field beside the road who started whinnying at her approach. Often, she would hear animals and birds rustling around in the undergrowth which she also found disconcerting, but she told herself that it would be dawn soon and that she didn't have to walk alone in the dark for too much longer.

Sure enough, she entered the suburbs of Wolverton just as dawn was breaking. She put her torch away as she passed the terraces of railway workers' houses where the lights were on; people were just getting ready for their day's work. Nearing the station, she noticed that other people were joining her on the pavement and walking towards it too. Some looked like workmen, in dungarees and hobnailed boots, heading for the railway works, but others were clearly commuters, bound for the city in their three-piece suits and bowler hats.

Wolverton station was more crowded than she'd expected. She hadn't realised that so many people got the early train to London. She looked around nervously for any sign of her father or one of his employees. It was just possible that he'd already discovered her departure and was out looking for her. But none of the anonymous faces queuing at the ticket office or waiting for the London-bound train down on the platform, took any notice of her at all. They hid themselves behind newspapers or sipped from thermos flasks. She glanced at the headlines: "Air raids on Midlands, Liverpool and South Wales. Luftwaffe steps up the tempo..."

May wondered where in the Midlands had been hit. Could it have been Birmingham, where this train was coming from? She shivered. It all felt very close to home now, but she knew it was ironic that she felt like that, when she was deliberately travelling to the city which was the most likely to be bombed in the whole of the United Kingdom. Soon with a blast of the horn, the express train was puffing into the station, steam and smoke billowing onto the platform. When it ground to a halt, the place became a sea of movement as people thronged around the doors to get on the train.

May deliberately chose an inconspicuous corner seat and spent the journey staring out of the window at the undulating countryside, golden after the harvest in the morning sunlight, and the small, red-brick communities in Buckinghamshire and Hertfordshire that the train rumbled through.

More than once she wondered if she was crazy to take this step. It was the boldest thing she had ever done in her life. She knew she could have just sat the summer out in the safety of Rose Park, minding her own business. But she felt that what she was doing marked a rite of passage for her, a statement that she was no longer prepared to be trampled underfoot, to be treated like a child.

In less than an hour, the train was rattling through the suburbs of North London, the back-to-back terraces, with their narrow gardens running down to the railway track, the apartment blocks, the rows of shops. The streets got denser and the buildings taller as they drew closer to the city centre. Then came the warehouses, factories and office blocks north of Euston and finally they rolled into the station itself, just before six a.m. May wondered at all these people pouring off the train bound for their offices in the city. Did they do this every day? What kind of a life would that be? Then she stopped herself. Those were the questions only someone with her privilege might ask. It was easy to forget that for ordinary people, without the advantages her background had given her, daily life was a constant struggle.

She got off the train and walked with the crowd towards the underground. She had rarely been on an underground train before. Normally, her visits to London had taken the form of a shopping trip with her mother and sisters, when they would be driven by Barlow, her father's driver, to Selfridges or Harrods and home again. They also had an annual family trip to the theatre. For some reason that May could never understand, her mother loved opera. Again, the car would take them to the doors of the Royal Opera House or the Coliseum and be there waiting when they emerged, ready to whisk them home to Northamptonshire again. Her mother had once taken them on a tube train, more to show them what it was like than anything else. Now, May was glad that she'd done that because she vaguely remembered how the tube map worked, how to get a ticket from the machine and what signs to follow when she headed along the tiled passageways towards the platforms deep in the bowels of the earth.

She spent a long time looking at the tube map. It seemed a more complex journey to Pimlico, where Ruby's flat was, than she'd previously thought, with a change at Edgeware Road and a fairly long walk at the other end. She was alarmed by the crowds of workers heading for their offices, and how busy the platforms and escalators were. When she squeezed on to a smoky carriage on the tube train, her eyes immediately watered and she tried to hold her breath between stops.

She got off at Westminster and once she'd surfaced, she headed past the Houses of Parliament, then along the river Thames towards Pimlico. She was glad to get out in the open air again and it was a glorious late-summer's day. She was developing a blister on her left heel though and she was glad it wasn't far to Dolphin Square where Ruby's apartment was. Ruby's father was the local Member of Parliament and he'd purchased the apartment to be near the Palace of Westminster, but Ruby had told her that he hardly ever stayed there, that he preferred to motor back home in the evenings even if the House sat late. May found herself hoping that he wasn't there that day. She had never met him and wasn't sure how he might react to a strange runaway teenager turning up unannounced.

When she reached the front entrance to Dolphin Square she stood staring at it, stunned. It wasn't just a single building, but over a dozen monolithic art-deco apartment blocks, each of them ten stories high. She walked through the imposing arched entrance and into an immaculate formal garden bounded on every side by apartment blocks. Gradually, following the neat signs, she guided herself to Flat number 45, Raleigh Block. It was on the fourth floor and letting herself in through the glass doors to the block and climbing the concrete stairs, May couldn't help feeling a little apprehensive. What if Ruby wasn't in? What if her father was there instead? What if Ruby had someone else living there now and wasn't keen on May staying? All these things raced through her mind as she approached the door and knocked on it firmly.

To her relief, she heard a familiar voice say, 'I won't be a minute...' then seconds later, Ruby opened the door in her dressing gown.

'May?' she said, her face registering shock, but she instantly smiled broadly, put her arms around May and hugged her tight. 'I'm so glad you came! But why didn't you let me know you were coming? I would have tidied up a bit. The place is in a bit of a state as you'll see!'

Ruby beckoned her along a passage and into a small living room. As Ruby had said, it was indeed in a bit of a state. There were dirty cups and dishes everywhere. Magazines were strewn about, and empty beer and wine bottles jostled on a coffee table with overflowing ashtrays for space. May looked at her friend and Ruby had the grace to go a little pink. The air was stale with cigarette smoke and alcohol. Ruby went to the window and threw it open.

'I'm sorry, May. As I said, if I'd known you were coming...'

'What's been going on here?' May asked, realising after she's spoken just how judgmental and prudish she must sound.

'Oh, I often have people back here after work or a night out,' Ruby said.

'Have you started smoking?' May asked.

'Yes! And what of it?' Ruby said defensively. 'All women smoke nowadays. I expect you'll soon start if you stay here. Look, let me show you the spare bedroom,' Ruby said, quickly leading her away from the untidy living room. She showed her into a narrow room with a single bed and a small window looking out over the gardens. There was a tiny utility chest of drawers and a mirror and a chair in the other corner and that was it. To May's relief at least the room was tidy and the bed was made.

'It's lovely, Ruby,' she said, sitting down on the bed. 'And I'm sorry I was offish. I've had a hell of a night.'

'Don't worry, May. I understand. Let's go and get a cup of tea and you can tell me all about it.'

In the tiny kitchen, May sat down at the small table and Ruby put the kettle onto a gas hob.

'I've got very lazy living on my own,' she said. 'There's a lady who comes in to clean, but she only comes on Tuesdays and Fridays. I tend to get a bit lazy in between times, especially at weekends. But there's no excuse and now you're here, I will turn over a new leaf. Now, come on. Tell me all about your journey.'

So May took a deep breath and told her everything. Ruby's mouth fell open when she heard that May had run away from home.

'You're joking! May Rose. I would never have guessed. It's so unlike you!'

'Well I've changed now,' May said drawing herself up. 'Something inside me snapped when Pa stopped me going back to the farm.'

'And what are you going to say when your father comes to take you home?'

'I'm not sure yet. But I've probably got a day or two to think about it.'

'Well, I hope he lets you stay. I need the company and the hospital needs every pair of hands it can get. Oh, and by the way, they are going to open up a hospital in the basement here in Dolphin Square. They've asked me to help set it up – make up the beds etc. I can put in a word for you too if you like?'

'That sounds marvellous,' May said.

'Oh, and most of the residents of Dolphin Square have moved out in case it is bombed. I've managed to sweet-talk the caretaker. But if we ever hear an air-raid siren we have to go straight to the basement. He made me promise. But there's been nothing so far. I listen out every night.'

'I saw in the paper that Birmingham was bombed last night, so perhaps London will be next,' May said.

When they'd finished their tea and Ruby had got dressed, they set to and cleared up the living room. May stood at the kitchen sink washing up while Ruby brought through the dirty dishes, and swept and tidied. By the end of the morning, the place was looking vaguely respectable.

'Time for a coffee, don't you think?' Ruby said, with a satisfied smile.

At that moment the doorbell rang and, with a quick glance at May, Ruby went to open it. May stood in the living room and listened to the conversation.

'Good morning, Ruby,' said a familiar voice which set May's heart beating ten to the dozen. 'You know who I am, don't you? I'm Hadan Rose. I understand my daughter, May, is with you. Could I come in and have a word with her please?'

7

RACHEL

ROSE PARK, 1980

THE NEXT DAY was Saturday and the Quarryman's Arms was just as busy as the previous evening. Rachel was just getting into her stride, getting to know some of the faces and becoming familiar with the routines of the place. After a couple of hours she realised she was even quite enjoying herself.

'You're doing well.' Jenny smiled at her halfway through the evening. 'The customers seem to like you and that's saying something around here.'

'Oh?'

'They can be a miserable bunch, stuck in their ways. They don't take to everyone, but they probably recognise that you're a native.'

'Well, hardly...'

Rachel hadn't been born at Rose Park, but rather in Surrey where her father had hailed from. She and May still lived in the same small town, almost ten years after his death. But Surrey was her father's county and she'd always sensed that May never felt completely at home there. But Rachel counted Rose Park as her second home and was glad that she was being accepted by the villagers.

She hadn't expected to see Daniel that night. But he came in towards closing time and made straight for the bar.

'Rachel!' he said, smiling broadly when he saw her. 'I'm glad to see your first night here didn't put you off altogether!'

He asked for a pint of Phipps' and when she handed it to him, he said, 'I was wondering if you'd like to come out with me after your shift? There's a lock-in at a pub in Grey's Norton. It's usually quite lively.'

'Lock-in?' she looked at him blankly and he laughed.

'Don't tell me you don't have those down in Surrey? Well, basically, the landlord locks the pub door and carries on serving until the small hours. The local coppers normally turn a blind eye.'

Rachel felt her cheeks heat up in embarrassment. She'd let herself down again, betraying her lack of experience and sophistication in front of someone she was quite keen on impressing. How humiliating!

'Well, anyway, if you'd like to come along when you've finished here, I can take you in the van.'

She hesitated, thinking about her mother. She didn't want May to worry – she had enough on her plate with Grandad already.

'You could always give your mum a call,' Daniel said, watching her face. 'I'm sure Jenny would let you use the phone.'

'Alright,' she said on an impulse. 'I'll come along.'

Jenny looked sceptical when Rachel asked to use the phone at the end of the evening. She'd noticed Daniel waiting for her on a stool by the door.

'You're not going out with him, are you?'

'I'm afraid so,' Rachel said.

Jenny raised her eyebrows. 'Well, all I can say is, be careful.'

After Rachel had called her mother, she joined Daniel, and they went outside. His small Ford Escort van was parked opposite the pub. Rachel got into the passenger seat.

'This doesn't seem a typical journalist's vehicle,' she said looking around her at the cab. The van was old, and the inside was scruffy, the plastic peeling from the seats.

When Daniel started the engine, it roared noisily and everything rattled. Once they got going it was even more noisy, and the tinny radio blared out jazz music as well.

'It's useful for carting stuff about for gigs,' he said. 'I know it's a bit of an old banger, but we're not all local gentry now, are we?' he said with a twinkle in his eye.

'Well, I haven't actually got a car and my mum drives a Mini Metro for your information,' she said, in an equally teasing tone.

'I'm only kidding,' he replied, then focused on the road. They were out of the village now and heading down a narrow country lane where the headlights lit up the leafy verges. Moths and insects fluttered in their beams. Rachel thought about her mother, walking alone down lanes just like this on her way to Wolverton station, forty years before.

'How's your grandfather?' Daniel asked.

'He's just the same. Mum says that each day he gets a little worse. The doctor came this morning and said he hasn't got long, sadly.'

Then she stopped herself again. Why was she telling Daniel this? These were private matters that should be kept within the family.

'Do you have grandparents?' she asked, trying to shift the subject away from her family.

'Actually, my grandfather died in the First World War,' he said. 'He would have been about the same age as your grandfather.'

'I wonder if they knew each other?' Rachel asked. 'Perry Cross is a small place.'

'Probably. They served in the same regiment. I know that. The Northamptonshires. Your grandfather was an officer, but mine was just a foot soldier.'

Rachel glanced at him out of the corner of her eye, was Daniel bitter about that? But if he was, his face wasn't betraying it.

They were silent then until they reached the next village. There was a pub on the village green, the Barley Mow, and although the curtains were drawn, chinks of light spilled out around them. Daniel parked the van on the edge of the green and they walked across the grass to the pub.

When he pushed open the door a blast of hot air hit Rachel. The bar was thronging with people, and she was relieved to see that the crowd was a lot younger than the locals at the Quarryman's Arms. The atmosphere was lively and the music loud. Daniel went to the bar and bought them both a drink, then led her through the press of drinkers to a back room where a few young men were playing pool. They all looked up and greeted him warmly and he introduced Rachel to his friends – Andy, Ian and Tim. She felt a little awkward, being the only girl amongst them, but they all seemed friendly enough.

Conversation was limited – the juke box was playing "Love Will Tear Us Apart" by Joy Division at top volume – but Rachel soon gleaned that these three were the other members of the band Daniel played in.

'We're having a well-earned night off,' Andy told her between shots of pool. 'Do you know how to play?'

She shook her head apologetically, once again feeling very naïve and very young. She'd never played before. So Daniel showed her how to line up the balls, position the cue and to take a shot. The first time she tried she missed the ball, but after a couple of attempts, she managed to pot her first ball. The boys all cheered and clapped her on the back, and she began to lose her initial shyness and to enjoy the evening.

They played for an hour or so, then the landlord put his head round the door.

'Lock-in's over, lads. It's half past twelve.'

They finished their drinks and spilled out onto the village green and said their goodbyes. The others all drifted off in different directions.

When Rachel got into the van, she realised that she was feeling a little light-headed. She'd had at least three gin and tonics, and she wasn't used to drinking.

On the way back to Perry Cross, Daniel asked her more about her family.

'You've got three aunts, haven't you?' he asked.

'No. Only two. One of them went missing during the war.'

'Oh yes. I heard about that. That was Ivy, wasn't it?'

'Yes, so I have two. Aunt Florence and Aunt Blanche.'

'Do you think they'll come home to Rose Park when your grandfather dies?'

'I really don't know,' she said and then went quiet, thinking what a strange question that was.

She looked at Daniel frowning, but he was concentrating on the road. She wondered suddenly why he was interested in her. Was he digging around for a story? She felt let down. As well as being attracted to Daniel, she'd started to like him too. He'd seemed interesting, different from most of the boys she knew at home, and she'd been flattered that he'd taken an interest in her. But now she was doubting his motives.

He turned to her smiling.

'Don't worry. It's an old journalist's habit. Being nosey. But I am interested in your family. Our two families go back a long way.'

'Really?'

'Yeah, as we were saying earlier, our grandfathers served in the First World War together, only mine died and yours survived.'

She had no reply to that comment. She still had the feeling that he was fishing for information, but by that time they were outside the gates of Rose Park.

'Do you want me to take you down to the house?'

'It's OK,' she said. 'It's no distance, and the engine might wake everyone up.'

'Oh, sorry. Yes, I need to get that silencer fixed.' He smiled, leaning towards her, looking deep into her eyes.

He took her face in his hands and kissed her full on the lips. She hadn't expected that. It took her completely by surprise, but after a moment's hesitation, she kissed him back, enjoying the feel of his lips on hers, the musky smell of his cologne.

'I'll see you very soon,' he said after they'd broken apart.

She got out of the van and let herself in through the tall, metal gates. She stood on the other side watching his taillights as he drove away down the lane. Then, she turned and walked towards the house, her emotions in turmoil. She put aside his odd questions, putting them down to awkwardness, or the fact that he was a journalist, and thought again of the feel of his lips on hers. She realised she had completely fallen under his spell and that there was no going back.

THE NEXT AFTERNOON, when Rachel and May were sitting under the oak tree, May gave her a mischievous look and said, 'Did you enjoy your evening? You didn't tell me who you were going out with.'

'Yes. I had a lovely time, thanks,' she said. 'We went to Greys Norton, to the pub there. They had a lock-in.'

'A lock-in!' May raised her eyebrows. 'And who did you go with, may I ask?'

'Someone called Daniel. Daniel Walters, I think his name is.'

'Walters? Walters... it doesn't ring a bell. Has he lived here for long?'

'Yes. All his life. In fact, he told me that his grandfather had died in the Great War. That he and Grandad served together in the Northamptonshires.'

'Oh... oh really?' May looked a little unsettled by those words, but quickly recovered.

'You don't mind, do you? Me going out after work? I tried to be quiet when I came in.'

'Of course not, darling,' May put her hand out and squeezed Rachel's arm. 'I'm glad. You know you've spent far too long locked up in your room studying and staying at home to keep me company. It's good that you're making friends and getting out at last. Is he nice, this Daniel Walters?'

'He's OK,' Rachel said, she didn't want May asking difficult questions about Daniel. In the cold light of day, she was feeling a little confused about him herself. Despite the thrill of the kiss, she kept wondering about all those questions he'd asked about her family; it didn't feel quite right.

'Why don't you tell me some more about your time in London during the war, Mum,' she said, changing the subject. 'What happened when Grandad came to Ruby's flat? What did you say to him?'

May sat back in her chair and looked wistful.

'Poor Grandad. I'm sure he thought he was doing the right thing coming to fetch me. He came inside and Ruby made him a cup of tea. At first he was angry at me for having run away, but after a while he saw how determined I was. I think he relented. I can't remember exactly how we talked him round, but after about an hour he got up to go. I'd managed to convince him that if I couldn't work on the farm any more, I really needed to make myself useful somewhere else. Then Ruby chimed in to say that they were opening a hospital up in the building and that they needed all the help they could get. That seemed to swing it for him. He said he would call Ruby's father and make sure he was happy with the arrangement. And before he left, he gave me a stern lecture about not staying out late and about calling home every day to set my mother's fears at rest, but then he fished in his pocket and got out ten pounds and handed it to me.

'I think he finally felt guilty about the way he'd treated me and was trying to make it up to me. To me it was a breakthrough. It felt like a victory over my father. Thinking about it, Rachel, it was the first one I'd ever had and probably the last one I'll ever have too.'

8

MAY

LONDON, SEPTEMBER 1940

THE DAY after she arrived at Dolphin Square, Ruby took May to the hospital that was being set up on the ground floor of one of the apartment blocks. It was in a huge, high-ceilinged room with high windows that ran the length of each wall. The place was a hive of activity. Beds were being moved into position by workmen, who were also bringing cabinets, chairs and medical equipment.

'Until last week, this was the residents' gymnasium,' Ruby told her. 'Look, there are the ladders and ropes on the walls still. All the rest of the equipment has been taken out.'

'It's amazing,' May said, looking around.

A man with a clipboard bustled up.

'Good morning, Miss Ruby. The linen has arrived now, so if you'd like to help out today, the beds need making up.'

'Alright. This is my friend, May Rose. She'd like to help too.'

The man smiled. 'That's good to know. The more the merrier. You can work together. You know how to do hospital corners, I take it?'

'Of course. The nurse showed me yesterday.'

They set to work at the far end of the gymnasium hall,

making up the beds. Ruby showed May how to tuck and fold the sheets neatly at the corners.

'They must be expecting a lot of casualties,' May said, wondering at all this activity. 'What if it doesn't happen?'

Ruby stared at her. 'I can tell you've been holed up in the country for too long, May Rose! It *will* happen. People are sure of it. That's why they're making all these preparations. As I told you, all the patients in the main London hospitals have already been evacuated and the medical facilities moved down to the basements.'

May had her answer the next afternoon. It was a Saturday, but despite that, she and Ruby went to help out in the hospital in the morning, sweeping and cleaning the floors. They were sitting in the gardens resting, soaking up the afternoon sun, when the shrill, wailing sound of a siren blared out from one of the buildings. The hairs on the back of May's neck stood on end.

'This is it!' Ruby said. 'We need to go to the basement straight away. It's over here.'

She took May's hand and they ran across the garden towards one of the apartment blocks. Before they'd reached the door, the droning sound of engines that had been a distant hum they'd barely noticed at first, suddenly became deafening. A group of aircraft burst into view overhead. There must have been ten of them, flying in precise formation. The girls stopped and looked up in amazement. The sky darkened as the aircraft passed over the square, blotting out the sun. The planes were flying very low. It seemed to May as if they were just brushing the tops of the buildings. She shuddered to see the black cross on the underside of their wings that she knew from the newspapers was called the Balkenkreuz. There was no doubt about it. These were Luftwaffe planes, coming to bomb London, to cause death and destruction.

A man rushed up to them red-faced, in a panic. He was wearing a black uniform and a helmet with the letters ARP on the front. 'You need to get inside, right away,' he said. 'With your gas masks.'

'Come on!' Ruby was pulling her arm and she realised she'd been mesmerised by the sight of the sinister aircraft. She came back to earth and followed her friend in through the door of the building, then down some concrete stairs and into a long basement corridor. Neither of them had their gas masks with them, they'd left them up in the flat by mistake. May promised herself she would be more vigilant about hers in future.

There were several people rushing about in the basement. They must be the remaining residents, together with building staff, gardeners and hospital staff. There were three or four rooms set up for air raids, with chairs and tables, and at the end was a tea urn, manned by one of the cleaners.

All the talk was of the attack and where the bombers were headed.

'It'll be the docks for sure,' someone said. 'That's where they'll go first. They'll be after the ships and the warehouses.'

'God help the East End,' someone else put in. 'Right next to the docks it is. Those poor people. I wouldn't fancy me chances there, I can tell you.'

Ruby brought May a cup of tea and she was grateful to sip the hot liquid. Despite the warmth of the day, the shock of seeing the planes had chilled her through to her bones. She thought of her mother and father. They would hear about the raid on the evening news and worry about her. She bit her nail, hoping her father wouldn't go back on his word because of this. She would try to call them when the raid was over and let them know she was safe.

Ruby, outgoing and confident in a way that May knew she could never be, had opened a conversation with a man at the next table. He was in uniform with the Red Cross on his arm. Ruby turned to May.

'This gentleman tells me they are setting up an ambulance

station in the building too. They are looking for volunteers to drive and operate ambulances.'

'Count me in!' said May immediately.

'Can you drive, young lady?' asked the man.

'Of course. I learned to drive on tractors at home.'

It was true, it was one of the things Joe had taught her that summer, although she had to admit she didn't have a lot of experience.

'But do you have a driving licence?'

'Er... not exactly, I'm afraid.'

'In that case, you won't be able to drive, my dear, but you could possibly be a stretcher-bearer.'

'Of course,' she said, 'I'd love to help.'

'Me too,' said Ruby.

'In which case, you can both start tomorrow morning. Report to the ambulance station in Dolphin Square at nine o'clock. It's in the garage, if you know where that is. Wear sensible clothes and bring your gas masks – we can sort out uniforms later on – and be prepared for some hard work.'

May was elated that she'd managed to find something worthwhile to do, but she was already getting fed up with sitting there in the basement. It was hot and fuggy down there and the one toilet was already blocked and smelly.

To her relief the "All Clear" siren sounded soon after that and everyone trooped out into the gardens and dispersed to their apartments. As they walked towards their block, May noticed the sky in the east was lit up with an orange glow.

'Look at that.' She pointed to Ruby.

'My God. That's the docks on fire from the bombings. That man was right. That's where the planes were heading.' They stared at the burning sky for a moment, thinking about those poor souls who were trapped there, burning to death.

Back in their apartment a couple of hours later, the air raid siren sounded again. They picked up their gas masks along with a few books May suggested they take to help pass the time and went down to the garden, heading for the basement once more. Running across the grass towards the basement door, they saw that the sky was still red with fire. It was a terrifying sight.

Having the books to read had been a great idea, but still this raid went on for four long hours.

'They would have known where to head for alright,' one man said. 'The fires will have lit up the whole area for them. The earlier raid was so they could find their way to this one.'

Someone had brought a wireless and everyone sat round rapt, listening to the regular news reports about buildings that had been hit and casualties sustained. By the end of the evening, it was reported that at least 300 German bombers had descended on the Port of London and the East End Docks that day, escorted by fighter planes. In the docks, ships being loaded with cargo had been damaged, many of the docks themselves, including Surrey Docks, the Royal Albert Dock, the Queen Victoria Dock and the King George V Dock were burning, as were all the industrial areas in the dockland including many factories. But tragically too, many, many residential streets had been reduced to rubble by the bombings, including streets in Barking, East and West Ham and Bethnal Green. The number of casualties was not yet known but was expected to be high.

May and Ruby stared at each other, tears in their eyes, thinking of all those innocent people who must have been killed in their homes, in terraced houses or tenements in those crowded, narrow streets in the East End, crushed to death, or perishing in the fires. What had started out as an adventure for them both had quickly become deadly serious. But this was it, May thought, she was needed here and despite the dangers, she was glad she'd come.

The next day, the BBC reported that over 850 people had died in the bombings, most of them in the East End. But the bombs had not been confined completely to that area. They had fallen in Chelsea and Battersea, and Victoria Station, less than a mile from Dolphin Square, had been bombed four times; one had landed on a train, killing a train driver. May and Ruby listened to the reports over breakfast. They looked at each other, wide-eyed with shock. It was worse than they had expected.

May telephoned Rose Park and spoke to her father. He sounded relieved to hear her voice.

'I would like you to come home, May, but I know it is useless to ask you. I am pleading with you though; take care and keep safe. Oh, and go and see your sister Ivy as soon as you can.'

After breakfast, May and Ruby reported to the ambulance depot in the Dolphin Square garage. May was feeling nervous. She was dressed in a pair of Ruby's trousers, sensible, flat shoes and an old shirt. What would the day bring? Would there be more air raids? Would she be up to the task?

There was a small crowd of people in the garage, including the man they had met in the basement the day before. They were divided into groups, or crews of four, then given some rudimentary first-aid training by a doctor dressed in a white coat with a Red Cross armband.

'Your aim is to get casualties to hospital as quickly as you can, but you are likely to need to minister to them first. So, for those of you who haven't done this before, we are going to teach you the basics of first aid this morning. It will act as a refresher for those who are already familiar.'

For the next hour they were taught mouth-to-mouth resuscitation, how to dress wounds, strap up sprains and broken limbs and how to deal with concussion. May was glad she was learning these vital skills, although she had already been paired with Jane, an experienced nurse whom she hoped would be the one actually performing first aid out in the streets. After the first-aid lesson, they were taught how to load patients onto stretchers and carry them without jolting them, even over rough ground.

Then, armed with this basic knowledge, the crews set off for the East End where casualties were still being dug out of wrecked buildings. May's crew was sent to East Ham High Street. All four of them squeezed into the cab of the ambulance which was a converted Ford van.

The crew consisted of May, Jane, Tommy, an experienced ambulance worker who was the unofficial leader of the crew and John, who drove the ambulance. On the way over to East Ham, Tommy explained that a huge bomb had wreaked havoc when it destroyed a railway bridge which had collapsed onto a Woolworth's Store, trapping people inside the shop and the basement. Rescue workers were still digging people from the wrecked building.

'Some have been taken to hospital already, some haven't survived, sadly, but we need to be there in case they manage to get any more people out alive.'

They passed through the streets of the City of London itself, past the proud dome of St Paul's, down Cheapside and past the monolithic white building, the Bank of England; that area looked relatively unscathed. Then they continued into the East End which had clearly suffered heavy bombing.

May stared out of the ambulance window at the devastation that had been caused by just one night of bombing. Whole streets had been flattened, row upon row of houses reduced to rubble. People sat around, dazed, on piles of bricks beside whatever belongings they'd managed to salvage. Others were walking the streets, looking for somewhere to stay. Whole families walked together, pushing their belongings in prams, looking overwhelmed and desperate, small children and babies amongst them. It was a pitiful sight.

And beyond those streets, over towards the River Thames, fires were still raging, twelve hours after the bombings. Red and yellow flames and black smoke billowed above the houses to the south, darkening the sky, blotting out the sun.

Progress was slow through the bombed-out streets. Many were impassable, and they frequently had to reverse up and find alternative routes. When they finally arrived in East Ham High Street, it was impossible to get near the site of the bombing. John skilfully manoeuvred the ambulance as close as possible and reversed it as far as he could without ripping the tyres. The crew got out and went to report to the rescue workers who were still sifting through the rubble of the Woolworth's building. A man wearing an ARP helmet came to speak to them.

'There are women and children still trapped underground in there. We've been passing them food and drink down a shaft, but they are exhausted and terrified. Some of them are badly hurt too. We've almost got two of the children out, just need to take out a few more bricks, so bring your stretchers as close as you can.'

With Jane in the lead, May helped to carry the empty stretcher over the enormous pile of rubble and into the wrecked shop which was full of collapsed shelves. Stock was scattered all over the floor and May nearly slipped over on some stray boiled sweets. Once her eyes had adjusted to the gloom inside, she could see what the rescuers were up against. The ceiling had collapsed onto the ground floor, so you had to crawl to the place where they were trying to get survivors up from the basement. They were pulling them up through a lift shaft that had been partially blocked by masonry. As they approached, May could see that a small child, a little girl, was being brought slowly and carefully to the surface. She was clearly hurt and was screaming and crying inconsolably. Jane leaped forward once she was clear of the wall. They laid the girl on the stretcher and Jane got to work examining her.

'What's your name, darling?' she asked the little girl, who was probably only four or five.

'Betty,' she replied, still sobbing. Her face was stained with tears and there was blood on her cardigan.

Jane felt her body all over and the little girl cried out when she touched her arms.

'I think this one is broken, I will splint it up. She's also very bruised. There might be some internal bleeding too.'

As Jane was working on the little girl, another child, a boy, was brought to the surface and then a young woman, whose head was bleeding profusely. Tommy helped her to walk to the ambulance, then came back with John and the other stretcher to take the boy, who had also suffered head injuries.

May was shocked by what she was seeing and by the fact that there were clearly many more people trapped underground, but she tried to keep calm. She knew it wouldn't help anyone if she began to panic or if she passed out. She had to keep a grip on herself as the sight of some of the wounds was making her feel nauseous.

When Jane had finished splinting Betty's arm, they picked up the stretcher and carried it as carefully as they could towards the ambulance. It was difficult climbing over the pile of rubble with the stretcher, even though the little girl wasn't heavy, and more than once, the bricks beneath her feet gave way and May slipped and stumbled, almost dropping her precious cargo. Coming down the other side was even harder, but soon they were at the ambulance and loading Betty's stretcher onto the trolley inside. The little boy was already stowed safely on one side of the vehicle.

'I'll ride in the back with them,' Jane said, climbing in. Tommy slammed the door shut and May got into the front beside the injured woman who had been patched up with a bandage. Tommy got in beside her and shut the door.

'We'll take them to Mile End Hospital,' John said, and they set off, back through the devastated streets, the siren blaring. The injured woman didn't speak at all on the journey, she was clearly finding it hard to stay conscious, and kept passing out on May's shoulder. May put her arm around her so she didn't slip off the seat.

She couldn't stop thinking about all those innocent people trapped beneath the buildings they were driving past and how twenty-four hours before, they would have been completely unaware of what was about to happen and how their lives would soon be blown apart. How precarious life was, she thought as the ambulance swung into the entrance of a huge Victorian, red-brick hospital. It was time to get out and carry the stretchers inside.

When they'd delivered their patients, they headed back to East Ham High Street. By the time they'd returned four more people had been brought up from the basement. Two were uninjured and were treated for shock at the scene, but two more – two women – were very badly injured. One had splinters of glass all up her arm and some serious looking head injuries, the other had been crushed under a falling beam and couldn't move her legs. The sight of these injured people shocked May to the core, but as they were loading the second woman onto the stretcher, the rescuers brought up another woman who hadn't made it. Her face was bruised black and blue. They laid her out on the floor of the shop and covered her with a sheet.

May found her eyes filled with tears at the injustice of it all. This was probably someone's mother, sister, daughter and wife, cut down in the prime of life.

'I know, it's hard. But you'll get used to it,' Jane said, placing a sympathetic hand on her arm. 'But we mustn't let it distract us from our work. We need to get this lady to the ambulance straight away if we've any chance of saving her.'

Once again, they set off back to the hospital to deliver their patients, then returned once again to the bombed-out shop. That carried on for the rest of the day and by the time they set off back to Dolphin Square, they had taken fifteen people to hospital and the rescuers had recovered twenty-five bodies. May was reeling from the shocking events of the day. She couldn't believe the devastation she'd witnessed, the injuries people had sustained and the fact that people had lost their lives. All the same, amongst the rescue workers and those who had been rescued, the volunteers she'd met serving tea and coffee from a trestle table near the bombed Woolworth's, people seemed determined to carry on and not to let these dreadful events beat them.

When they arrived back at the ambulance station in the Dolphin Square garage, the whole crew looked white-faced and exhausted.

'Well done, crew,' Tommy said. 'We did well today. Now, try to get a few hours' rest. We have another shift at nine o'clock this evening, so be sure to be back in time.'

May stumbled out into the sunshine and wandered like a sleepwalker back to the apartment. When she went in, Ruby was sitting at the kitchen table, sobbing. When May got closer, she saw that her friend was trembling all over.

'What's the matter, Ruby?'

'It's all so awful, isn't it? We were sent to a house where a bomb had landed on an Anderson shelter and killed everyone inside. We had to pull them out to see if any of them were alive, but they were all dead. Just the sight of them. I can't get it out of my head. Babies and children too. It was so... so shocking, May.'

'I know,' May said putting her arms around her friend and squeezing her tight. 'I'll make you a cup of tea.'

After they'd finished their drinks, May ran Ruby a hot bath and helped her into it. Ruby gave her a thin smile and lay back in the warm water.

'Thanks, May. You're a true friend.'

'When you've finished, why don't you go and lie down. I'll use your water,' May said, realising from looking in the mirror that her clothes were filthy, but also her skin and hair were covered in smuts, plaster dust and dried blood.

'Alright,' Ruby said. 'Are you going to rest too?'

May shook her head. 'I need to go and see my sister.'

LATER, after she'd bathed and changed into her own clothes, May said goodbye to Ruby and set off towards Vauxhall and the address of the hostel where her father had said Ivy was staying. She walked along beside the Thames towards Vauxhall Bridge. It was hard to imagine the devastation of the East End looking at the tranquil scene around her. The sun was sparkling on the water, there was no breeze to rustle the leaves in the plane trees that lined the riverbank. May knew it was deceptive, that the bombers could return after dark to wreak their havoc again.

She crossed Vauxhall Bridge, walked along the river a little way on the other side and found the entrance to a large building, that looked a little like a warehouse, tucked into one of the streets set back from the river.

She let herself in and saw that there was a door marked "Office" on the right-hand side of a long corridor. She knocked and a woman's voice said, 'Come in.'

Inside the office, a middle-aged woman with immaculate hair and a lot of red lipstick sat at a typewriter. She looked up enquiringly at May.

'I'd like to see my sister, Ivy Rose,' she said.

'Ah, Ivy Rose. She left two days ago,' the woman said.

'Left?' May asked, confused.

'Yes. You might want to speak to her roommate. I'm not sure exactly where she's gone. Go and knock on the door. Room 238 on the second floor. She should be in on a Sunday.'

Thanking the woman, May made her way up the bare concrete stairs to the second floor and along the sparse corridor. She knocked on the door of Room 238. The door opened after a few seconds. It was a girl a little older than May. She had a look of sophistication about her, despite the fact she was dressed in striped pyjamas.

'I'm looking for Ivy Rose,' May said. 'I'm her sister.'

The girl pulled open the door and let May into the room. It was small and square with a bed on each side.

'I'm Ethel Sharp, her roommate. I'm afraid she left a couple of days ago.'

'Left? But I don't understand,' May said, still puzzled. 'Where has she gone?'

'Oh dear. Well, I suppose I can tell you as long as you don't tell anyone else. She's been posted to France. It was all rather last-minute, I'm afraid.'

'France?' May was aghast. All she knew about France was that it was overrun with Nazis. How could Ivy have been posted there? She'd come to London to take up a job with the government, surely.

'You don't know, do you?' said Ethel. 'Ivy works for Military Intelligence. She's been posted to France as part of her work. That's all I can tell you. It was all very last-minute and hush-hush, which is why she couldn't say goodbye.'

'Oh! Well, thank you,' May said, leaving the room and walking away.

She walked slowly down the stairs to the ground floor, thinking carefully. Everything was falling into place now; her mother's tears at Wolverton Station, the odd words she'd said to Ivy when they were saying goodbye. Her mother knew. Both her parents did, although they probably didn't know that Ivy had already departed for France. May felt slighted that none of them had trusted her enough to tell her the true nature of Ivy's new job. They must have thought she was a child still, who had to be protected from the truth.

May squared her shoulders and went out into the street. She wasn't going to let that get to her. What did her feelings matter in the face of the risks her sister was taking? She pictured Ivy sitting in a battered RAF transport plane being flown into France, possibly under German fire. Where was she going? How would she land? What dangers would the coming months bring for Ivy? With a heavy heart, she turned and walked back along the river towards Pimlico.

9

RACHEL

ROSE PARK, 1980

THE MORNING after her trip to the lock-in at the Barley Mow with Daniel, Rachel couldn't stop thinking about him. Her mind went over and over the evening, especially those moments when they'd said goodbye, and he'd surprised her by kissing her. She'd never been kissed before, not properly like that at least. There had been the odd innocent but chaste kiss at school discos with pupils from the boys' school, but nothing as direct and passionate, from someone she admired and found attractive. She wondered if he would ask her out again, or if the kiss was just an impulse that would never be repeated. She sincerely hoped not. She couldn't wait for her next shift at the Quarryman's Arms on the off chance that he would come into the pub again.

To distract herself from thinking about Daniel, she went back to her great-grandmother's bureau in the library and took the album of baby photos out of the bottom drawer. They were easier to see in the light of day. The similarities between her great-grandmother, Emily, and Hadan, were striking, even when he was a tiny child. They both also looked a lot like the other baby. Carefully, she took various photographs out of their clips and scanned the back of them for any clues, but there was no writing on any of them, so she slipped them back into the album again, disappointed.

Her mother seemed to be busy caring for Hadan that morning; the doctor had arrived to examine him again. Rachel waited until they had finished and the doctor had departed, then she caught up with May in the kitchen. She had not wanted to bother her mother with this, but as there were no further clues on closer examination of the album, she was becoming desperate for answers.

'Mum, I've found something incredible in these old albums,' she said. 'I'm wondering if you might be able to explain it.'

May looked mystified. 'I can try,' she said.

Rachel laid the album down on the kitchen table and opened it up. She turned the pages quickly, skimming through the photographs of Emily and Gabriel together, the ones of their wedding, the portraits of Emily as a young woman. Then she turned the next page and showed her mother the photograph of Emily with the first baby.

May smiled. 'Wasn't Pa a cute baby?' she said. 'It's hard to imagine that that tiny scrap is actually him.'

'Well, perhaps that's because it isn't him,' Rachel replied.

May frowned. 'What?'

'Look.'

Rachel carried on turning the pages and eventually came to the photographs of Emily cuddling a second baby. May looked down at them and Rachel could tell that she was thinking that this was the same baby as in the earlier photos, just as she herself had thought at first. Then finally, she turned the page to the photograph of the two boys sitting together looking out at the camera. They were clearly around two years apart in age.

'That is Grandad, and that is another, older boy,' Rachel said, pointing to them one by one.

May stared down at the photograph of the two little boys, the colour draining from her face.

'What on earth...?' she said, frowning and looking incredulously at Rachel, 'I can't believe it.'

'Neither could I,' Rachel said. 'I thought you might know something about it.'

May sat down heavily on the chair. Just then, Mrs Allen bustled through from the laundry room.

'Is everything alright, Miss May?' she asked.

'Quite alright thank you,' May replied, closing the photograph album quickly, as if by instinct.

Mrs Allen pottered around at the sink for a few minutes, but when she had finally left the room, May said, 'I just can't understand it. I'm wondering how we could find out more about it.'

'Perhaps we could ask Grandad?' Rachel ventured.

'I don't think so, Rachel. He's very ill. It might make him worse.'

'Maybe I'll just have to keep on digging then,' Rachel said with a sigh.

'Well, perhaps there might be another way,' said May, deep in thought. 'Maybe you could pay a visit to the records office in Northampton. It's in the old Guildhall. At least I think local records are still kept there. I had to go to get a duplicate birth certificate once. You could look and see if there are any records of babies born to Emily and Gabriel before Pa was born. It might yield nothing, but it could be worth a shot. What do you think?'

'Alright,' said Rachel. 'I could go tomorrow maybe... Could I borrow the car?'

'Of course. And, depending on what you find, there is a very old lady who lives in the village who was once a housemaid here at Rose Park. She's about the same age as Pa, so she wouldn't have been around when he was a baby, but she might know something.'

'Oh, what's her name?' Rachel asked, thinking of Jenny's grandmother.

'Mrs Sutton, I think. She might not remember, and she might

not have known anything, but the chances are, if there had been any type of scandal, the servants would have talked about it for decades afterwards.'

'Jenny told me that her grandmother worked here once too,' Rachel remembered.

May frowned, thinking deeply. 'Ah yes,' she said. 'But that was quite a bit later. And if I remember correctly, she was "let go" as they say nowadays.'

'Oh? Why was that?'

'Because she was a gossip, apparently. My mother found out that she'd been spreading rumours about the family. And Mother was very strict about that sort of thing. Jenny's grandmother wasn't the only one. A few of them had to go at the same time, or so I heard. That was when my parents first got married.'

Rachel wondered what the servants had been gossiping about. It must have been serious to warrant dismissal. She would love to know, but for the time being she was keen on solving the mystery of the two boys.

'Where does this Mrs Sutton live?' she said.

'I'm not quite sure. I'll ask Mrs Allen, discreetly of course, without giving anything else away. But why don't you plan your trip to the records office first? See what you find? Those photographs are truly amazing though. I had absolutely no idea. And to think that the album has just been sitting there, in that desk under our noses, for all these years!'

Just then, one of the bells on the bell rack high up on the kitchen wall sounded. They were the old service bells, that Hadan had kept so he could summon Mrs Allen from wherever he happened to be in the house.

'Oh, that's Pa,' May said, looking anxious again. 'I'd better go and see what he wants.'

When May had gone, with a sigh, Rachel took the albums upstairs to the Pink room and sat on the bed flicking through the pages again. She stared at the photograph of the two boys and then turned to one of Emily towards the end of the book. She was looking anxious in this one, far less self-assured and happy than the beaming young mother in earlier photos. What had made this woman so sad that she took to her bed and went into a decline that led to her death at an early age?

Rachel looked around at the room. She knew that the Pink room had been the one Emily had occupied. It was probably the one she'd died in. She shivered, and wondered if it was Emily's presence she sometimes felt at night. The same unnerving experience had happened several times now. Rachel was determined not to give in to fear, but she was keen on finding out as much as she could about her great- grandmother, and what had made her so sad.

At four o'clock that afternoon, Rachel put away all thoughts of family history, pulled on her jeans and a white cotton shirt and looked at her face in the mirror. She hardly ever wore makeup, but she did have some which she'd bought for various parties and discos she'd been to after her A Levels. She knew it made her look older and more attractive. Feeling a little guilty, she sat down at the dressing table, applied foundation, blusher, eyeliner, mascara and lipstick. Looking back at herself, she was rather pleased with the result. The eyeliner emphasised the blue of her eyes and the lipstick made her lips look fuller. She pulled a brush through her bouncy dark-blonde hair and stood up.

'Goodness.' Glancing at her watch she realised that if she didn't hurry, she would be late for her shift and this was only her third day. She didn't want to let Jenny down or to appear as if the job didn't mean anything to her. She pulled her sandals on and hurried downstairs.

'Goodbye,' May called from the kitchen. 'Will you be gadding about again tonight?'

'I very much doubt it,' Rachel replied, hurrying out of the house.

When she arrived at the pub, Jenny looked her up and down.

'Well! You've made an effort tonight,' she said. 'You look gorgeous, my dear. Is that for lover boy?'

Rachel felt her cheeks colouring at Jenny's words. Was it so obvious? 'Of course not,' she lied. 'I thought a bit of makeup might be appropriate for a barmaid. It's sort of expected.'

Jenny laughed out loud. 'Pull the other one, it's got bells on,' she said.

To Rachel's disappointment, Daniel didn't turn up at all that evening. The pub was very quiet, only a few regulars were in, sitting at the tables or propping up the bar.

'Sundays are always a bit like this,' Jenny said. 'People tend to go out on Fridays and Saturdays. Sunday is a family day.'

Rachel wondered if Daniel was at home with his family. He hadn't told her anything about them at all, in contrast to everything she'd told him about hers. She wondered if he had brothers and sisters, whether he lived alone or with his parents. She realised then that she knew next to nothing about him. She tried to disguise her disappointment that he hadn't turned up by busying herself behind the bar. She polished all the glasses, cleaned all the surfaces down and even mopped the floor.

At closing time, Jenny said, 'You've worked hard this evening, Rachel. Thank you. Don't be too disappointed that you-know-who didn't come in, though. He often spends time with his mum on Sundays. Her being on her own and all.'

'On her own?' Rachel asked, curious.

'Yes. She was the original single mum. She brought that boy up all on her own. People in the village disapproved but she didn't care. She's got a lot of guts has Gill Walters. And he's turned out very well, considering. He's got a good job on the newspaper, he plays in a band. He keeps it all together.'

'And what about his father?' Rachel couldn't resist asking.

'No one knows, my love. Apart from her, of course. She's kept that a secret all these years.'

'Does Daniel know?'

Jenny smiled and squeezed her arm. 'You'll have to ask him, but I suspect he has a shrewd idea.'

Later, as she prepared to leave, Jenny said, 'Why don't you take tomorrow off? It's going to be really quiet, it being a Monday, so I can manage on my own.'

'Alright. That will fit in quite well. I need to go to Northampton during the day, so I needn't hurry back.'

'Doing a spot of shopping?'

Rachel shook her head. 'No, I'm going to the records office. Family history.'

'Sounds fascinating,' Jenny said. 'Can you tell me what it's about?'

'Not at the moment, I'm afraid,' Rachel said, cursing her indiscretion yet again. She really must learn to be more circumspect in future.

The next morning, she set off early in May's car and drove the twelve miles or so into the centre of Northampton. It was a beautiful morning, the late-summer meadows golden in the sunshine, and she was enjoying getting away from Rose Park and striking out on her own. She'd forgotten how pretty Northamptonshire was, with its rolling countryside and ancient villages with thatched, stone cottages. The centre of the town was a different matter. She drove past the modern, high-tech brewery, all glass and chrome and steel chimneys, remembering fondly the old Victorian red-brick brewery warehouses that used to crowd the waterfront, but had recently been demolished. She recalled that Hadan had been incensed at the demolition of those old, heritage buildings. He'd campaigned fiercely and tried to do everything he could to save them, but had failed. The failure had hit him hard; it was only a few years before that the last of the old buildings had been razed to the ground, and Rachel realised now that it was probably that which had marked the beginning of her grandfather's descent into ill-health. It was maybe the first time he'd ever admitted failure to himself.

After parking up on a cleared former bombsite that now served as a car park, she walked to the Guildhall. As she turned to go up the steps towards the entrance, she noticed two people deep in conversation on the steps of a building. A man and a woman. There would be nothing unusual about them, except the man was Daniel Walters. Rachel's heart thumped. The way their heads were tilted together, it looked as if they were very close, intimate even.

She turned away and went quickly up the front steps to the Guildhall, feeling stung and foolish, recalling the way he'd kissed her only two nights before. What an idiot she'd been. He clearly had a girlfriend here in Northampton. Someone older and more experienced than her. Then she remembered Jenny's warnings about Daniel leaving a trail of broken hearts wherever he went. She should have listened to her, instead of rushing headlong into something that was bound to leave her hurt.

She didn't look back, and pushed open the swing door to the entrance hall and went inside. The receptionist guided her to the records office on the first floor, and she walked through the corridors noting the coloured floor tiles, decorative friezes around the tops of the walls and stained-glass windows. At least this Victorian building had survived the drive to modernisation.

Inside the office, a middle-aged woman in large spectacles looked interested in her query.

'We don't get many people looking so far back. They mostly want replacement birth certificates because they've lost their own,' she said. 'Are you doing some research?'

'Yes. Family history,' Rachel said, but didn't elaborate.

The woman promised to help her to find details of births in Perry Cross parish from the 1880s and 90s. Rachel knew that Hadan had been born in 1890, so the older boy would have been born a couple of years before that.

After waiting a few minutes, while the woman went to the archives, she returned and handed Rachel three large ledgers, which contained records of births in Perry Cross as well as those in surrounding parishes. Rachel took them to a table in the middle of the room and opened the first ledger with a thrill of anticipation.

The entries were all made in the same flowing handwriting in black ink that was fading with age. She started with 1890 and quickly found Hadan's entry; "Hadan Gabriel Rose", it read. "Born 13th September 1890, Rose Park, Perry Cross. Father, Gabriel Henry Rose, Landowner, Mother, Emily Jane Rose, lady of the parish".

It gave Rachel a little thrill to look at this evidence of her ancestry, to imagine the old Victorian scribe, the keeper of the county records, perhaps even in this very room, dipping his pen in an inkwell and writing these words in the ledger. But this entry only confirmed what she already knew. There was nothing new to learn here at all.

She set the 1890 ledger aside and thumbed through the one from 1889. There were no entries mentioning Rose Park at all in that one, but there were several from Perry Cross, one of which caught her eye: Thomas James Harding, was born in December 1889, to William and Dorothea Harding. William was described as "Quarryman and Union Representative", and Dorothea was described as "Lacemaker". Was this the Harding who'd been the thorn in her great-grandfather's side? Thomas was about Hadan's age. Had they known each other? Grown up together perhaps? The relationships in the village were fascinating to Rachel, but impossible to discern from just looking at the records. If only she could speak to her grandfather. He would surely be able to shed light on everything, but her mother was right. The old man was far too ill to talk about the past.

She turned to the 1888 register and went through it slowly, running her finger down each column. She went through several months with no sign of what she was looking for, but then in June 1888 something caught her eye. There it was! A baby boy, Henry

Joseph Rose, born to Gabriel, landowner and Emily Jane, lady of the parish of Perry Cross.

She stared at the entry for a long time. So here it was in black and white, evidence that her grandfather had had an older brother. But what had happened to Henry Joseph Rose? Did Hadan know about him? Had he died in childhood? All these questions ran through Rachel's mind as she looked at that entry in the ledger. They would have to be answered, now this had come to light, but quite how that would happen, she had no idea.

She picked up the ledger and took it to the desk.

'I'd like a copy of this birth certificate please,' she said, pointing to the line in the ledger.

10

MAY

SEPTEMBER, 1940

May arrived back at Dolphin Square from Ivy's hostel in Vauxhall feeling very low. The devastation, deaths and injuries she'd witnessed that morning had come home to roost, and on top of that the news about Ivy's departure for France weighed heavily on her. Her legs felt sluggish, and she had to drag herself up the stairs and let herself back into the flat. She was relieved to see that Ruby was looking a little better now that she was up and dressed again, and sitting in the kitchen drinking tea.

'Where have you been?' Ruby asked, then seeing May's expression, 'And what's the matter?'

'I went to see Ivy in her hostel in Vauxhall. Only she's not there. She's been sent to France.'

'To France?' Ruby looked as aghast as May was feeling. May knew what Ruby was thinking – that France was occupied by the Nazis, the same people who had wreaked death and destruction on London only a few hours beforehand.

Ruby poured May a cup of tea and May sat down at the table and talked about Ivy.

'Ivy and I got so close during those few weeks when it was just us two at home,' she said. 'I really admire her. She's got so much strength, so much get up and go. But I had no idea she was preparing to work for the intelligence services. She was good at keeping a secret, I'll say that for her,' May finished with a wry smile.

'I was listening to the wireless earlier,' Ruby said. 'Apparently the government has issued the codeword "Cromwell" to all military bases. It means that invasion is imminent.'

'Invasion?'

Shock went through May like lightning at those words. She imagined German soldiers goosestepping into London behind tanks, bearing swastika flags. She'd seen the newsreels of similar events in Poland, Czechoslovakia and Austria. Could it really happen here? Suddenly she felt afraid, but was determined not to show it. At the same time, she realised she should get in touch with her parents to tell them what she'd found out about Ivy.

Mr Farrow, the butler, answered the telephone at Rose Park. May asked for her father and when Mr Farrow laid the telephone down on the hall table and went to find Hadan, May could hear the peaceful sounds of Rose Park; the birds twittering on the lawn outside the open front door, the grandfather clock in the hall chiming the hour. She visualised the peaceful scene, sun slanting in through the front door onto the flagstones, the smell of lavender furniture polish. It felt a million miles away from this cramped flat in the heart of a war zone. For the first time since she'd arrived in London, May wished she was back at home in Rose Park, in comfort and safety, not facing another night of danger and horror. But she wasn't about to give in, or even admit to having had qualms. She heard footsteps at the other end of the line and then her father's anxious voice.

'May? Is that you? You must come home immediately. It's not safe for you in London.'

'We've talked about this, Pa,' she replied calmly. 'I'm not coming home. I've started a new job; I'm volunteering with an ambulance crew now, doing valuable work. I can't abandon it now. The crew need me.'

'Dear God, that means you'll be going into the heart of the bombing. Your mother is already beside herself with worry.'

'I phoned to tell you that I went to see Ivy today,' May said, changing the subject. She didn't like to think of her mother worrying. She knew Wilhemena struggled with anxiety and that what she was doing was probably making her worse than ever.

'And how was Ivy? I haven't heard anything from her for a couple of weeks.'

'She wasn't at the hostel,' May replied. 'She's been sent away.'

She hesitated, realising that it might not be safe for her to say where Ivy had been sent to. Were phone lines listened in to? She knew that the apartment shared a party line with at least two other apartments in Dolphin Square. Ruby had once mentioned that spies were thought to live in the complex and that there had been a surveillance operation leading to the arrest of Oswald Moseley, the Fascist leader, and his wife, who had been residents. Could there be enemy agents living here too?

'Sent away?' her father sounded worried.

'Yes. You might be able to guess where.'

'Ah... I see. Well, we can speak about it another time,' he said.

May wanted to tell him how upset she'd been that neither he, Wilhemena or Ivy had wanted to share the true nature of Ivy's job with her, but she held back. What did hurt feelings matter in the face of so much suffering? She told herself that she needed to move on and put those hurt feelings behind her.

'I need to go now, Father,' she said, catching sight of Ruby tapping her watch and making a face. They both needed to get ready for the evening shift. 'We'll talk soon.'

'May, I really wish you would—'

'Bye, Pa,' she said, cutting him off and putting the phone down abruptly. She wasn't about to go home, and she didn't want him trying to persuade her. He was the most persuasive person she knew and given her earlier wobbles that day she didn't want to be tempted.

There wasn't much food in the flat, but Ruby made them some cheese sandwiches that looked like doorsteps. Biting into them, May realised how hungry she was and afterwards she felt a little better. Then, together they went back downstairs to the garage where, in the common room beside the garage itself, uniforms had arrived for the crews. May was dismayed to see that they consisted of a navy-blue gabardine wraparound coat with an insignia on the sleeve. It was the badge of the London Auxiliary Ambulance Service. There was also a navy-blue cap and a tin helmet to be worn on dangerous assignments. Ruby gave her a look.

'I can see what you're thinking,' Ruby said. 'The uniforms look a bit hot for summer. But, actually, it is starting to get cold at night now, so we might be glad of them.'

'Ruby, I wish I could always be as positive as you!' May laughed, but she slipped her coat and cap on and looked around at all the others doing the same and she realised that there was some sense in it. Putting on the uniform instantly made her feel part of a professional team, rather than one of a random bunch of assorted volunteers just trying to do their best.

She went over to the table where Jane, John and Tommy were sitting, already in their uniforms. They greeted her with warm smiles.

'More raids are expected this evening, but we need to sit here and wait. The telephone operators will tell us where to go when calls start coming in,' Tommy said, nodding in the direction of the corner of the common room. There, in a makeshift office, two women were already at work on a switchboard, which must have been brought in and set up during the day.

'They don't expect Jerry will come until after dark,' Tommy went on. 'Probably at blackout time.'

May knew that blackout time was eight o'clock. It was now only six.

'I know what you're thinking. We're in for a boring evening. Well, I've brought Monopoly!' he said, producing a set from his bag. 'Anyone fancy a game?'

May wasn't keen, but realised it was at least a way of passing the time, so agreed to join in. Once the game had got going, it did indeed make the hours pass more quickly.

She was just puzzling over whether to buy Old Kent Road, when the building began to shiver and she looked up to hear the tell-tale drone of aircraft engines overhead. Then, a moment later, something they hadn't heard the day before, the ack-ack of anti-aircraft guns, followed by the whine of the air-raid siren. They all stared at each other, waiting for the inevitable. It came within a minute, the crash and boom of explosions, probably miles away downriver at the docks, but still audible from where they sat in Dolphin Square.

It was impossible to carry on playing after that. All the crews, who had been entertaining themselves with cards or board games, sat and waited for the phones to ring. It started happening within a minute and they all watched and waited tensely while the leader of the station, a man called Ernie Baker conferred with the telephonists. Then he came out of the office and dispatched the first crew to St Katharine's dock.

'They've gone for the docks again,' Ernie said. 'More factories on fire. More collapsed buildings.'

Calls came in thick and fast after that and ambulances were dispatched in different directions. Then it was May and her crew's turn.

'Peabody Estate in John Fisher Street, Stepney,' Ernie said. 'Sounds like a bomb fell through into an underground shelter. Lots of casualties.'

May gave Jane an anxious look, and Jane reached out and

squeezed her arm. 'You did well on the last shift. Don't worry. We're doing this together,' she said.

May felt a little reassured as she got up into the front seat of the ambulance after they'd stowed blankets, bandages and dressings in the back and made sure that the four stretchers were securely loaded, two on either side of the vehicle.

The drive across town to Stepney was terrifying. Because of the blackout, the headlights had to be dimmed and the ambulance could only proceed very slowly. The fires from the blazes lit up the sky, but as well as that, the beam of searchlights shone on the buildings in front of them. Then there was the never-ending ack-ack of the anti-aircraft fire, the drone of bombers and the occasional boom from an explosion which shook everything around. The explosions seemed to be coming from every different direction this evening. Perhaps the docks weren't their only target.

As they turned into the end of John Fisher Street, John had to slow the ambulance down and skirt around fallen masonry and timbers from buildings either side that had been hit and were still collapsing onto the road, showering bricks and dust all around. Up ahead was the building they were making for – a big, square tenement block. It was silhouetted against a bright orange sky that was lit by the fires from the docks and sprays of golden light like fireworks. The roof to the apartment block looked jagged against the sky. There was a huge, gaping hole where a large bomb had entered less than an hour before.

Two air-raid wardens approached the ambulance carrying torches. As they spoke to John through the open window, May noticed the look of shock and bewilderment in their eyes.

'We'll guide you down to the building, so you don't get punctures. This is bad, really bad. Prepare yourselves.'

The two wardens walked in front of the ambulance, guiding John round debris and broken glass, until they had drawn up in front of the stricken building. They all got out.

'This building took a direct hit,' the ARP warden said. 'Somehow the bomb ripped straight down through the whole building and ended up in the basement. That's where the residents were sheltering. It's a shocking sight. Many dead. We're trying to find survivors.'

They followed him along the front wall of the building to a gaping hole in the ground, it must have been fifty feet in diameter, filled with broken beams and collapsed walls. Dust was billowing all around, the explosion had been so recent. There was a terrible smell in the air, a mixture of smoke, fireworks and burning flesh. Small fires burned all around them, on the street and down in the wrecked basement.

Rescue workers were already inside, their torches lighting up terrible sights. May gasped in horror. Bodies and body parts were strewn about the floor, in a sea of blood. People had landed on top of each other, some in heaps several bodies thick. She could see from the clothing that many of the dead were women and children. She wiped away a tear. How grotesquely unfair. They had obeyed orders and gone down to the safest place in the building, but still the German bomb had sought them out.

'Here's someone alive, bring a stretcher!' one of the rescuers yelled from down below. May jumped out of her reverie and ran back to the ambulance to fetch one of the collapsible stretchers. By the time she got back to the edge of the crater, the survivor had been pulled up out of the wreckage. She assembled the stretcher while Jane bent over the young woman, feeling her limbs, checking her pulse.

'Could you bring the dressing box?' she asked and again May ran back to the ambulance and collected a box of bandages and wound dressings. She also collected some blankets.

Jane bandaged the woman's arm which had been crushed by a falling beam. She was covered in cuts too, and Jane bathed them gently with a damp sponge from the dressing box. May tucked a blanket around her. Then Jane nodded to May and the two of them lifted the woman gently onto the stretcher. At that moment her eyes flickered open and she looked around wildly.

'Where am I?'

'You've been in a bombing raid,' Jane said. 'You've been hurt, but we're going to take you to hospital.'

'Where's Dotty?' she asked, trying to lift her head to look around.

'Dotty?'

'My little girl, where is she?'

'The rescue workers are bringing people out of the basement. We'll find her later.'

'I don't want to go without her,' she said, but collapsed back on the stretcher weakly and closed her eyes. She can't have had the strength to protest.

With a nod from Jane, May lifted one end of the stretcher and they carried it carefully the hundred yards or so to the ambulance. It was difficult not to trip with so much debris and broken glass in the road, and they had to proceed slowly, but they reached it safely and slotted the stretcher into the ambulance, then, they took another one and returned to the top of the crater. By that time, John and Tommy had loaded another patient onto their stretcher. This was an old man with blood in his grey hair. He was shaking all over and moaning in pain.

'It's alright, mate,' Tommy kept saying. 'You're safe now. You'll be in hospital soon.'

Another young woman had been brought to the surface. This one had cuts and bruises all over her face and was clutching her ribs and crying softly. Jane knelt down and examined her and looked up.

'She's got a couple of broken ribs,' she said. 'Could you hand me a bandage?'

May watched Jane bandage the woman's chest quickly and deftly, then they manoeuvred her onto the stretcher and carried her to the ambulance, by which time Tommy and John were also bringing the final stretcher on which lay an old woman, who was writhing in pain.

'Can you take any more?' one of the ARP wardens asked.

'Only if they can sit on the floor. We've no more stretchers.'

'This woman has a broken arm, and this one has head injuries,' the rescuer said.

Tommy nodded and guided the two walking wounded to the ambulance, where May helped them inside and sat them down in between the banks of stretchers.

They all climbed back into the cab and Tommy turned the ambulance round. By now there was a queue of ambulances behind theirs in the street, waiting to take survivors to hospital. They set off, their bell ringing, proceeding at the standard sixteen miles per hour. Still the bombs were raining down on the docks and surrounding streets; searchlights raked the orange sky and the sound of aircraft and ack-ack anti-aircraft fire filled the air. But May couldn't stop thinking of the terrible scene she'd witnessed in the basement of that building, the mangled bodies of women and children, the severed arms and legs floating in a sea of blood.

The nearest hospital was the London on Whitechapel Road. There were so many ambulances in the forecourt that they had to wait several minutes to be able to offload their patients, but it was a relief to take them inside the hospital and deliver them to the care of the nurses and doctors there.

They returned to Dolphin Square, drank hot sugary tea to help get over the shock of what they'd just witnessed and waited for another call out. It didn't seem appropriate to play games. They just sat at the table silently, each deep in their own thoughts.

The next call came quite soon after they'd arrived. This time, it was to St Thomas' Hospital across the river, where a bomb had fallen on a nurses' home killing six people. When they arrived on the scene, rescue workers were pulling survivors from the wreckage and May and her crew took three loads of injured nurses the short distance to the main hospital.

By the time her shift ended at midnight, May felt shattered. She was reeling from the horror of what she'd seen that night. Mechanically, she washed the blood off her hands and face in the bathroom beside the common room, then wandered out into Dolphin Square.

She didn't want to go back to the flat just yet. She wanted to be alone for a while, to walk and to reflect, to come to terms with what she'd seen that night.

She wandered along beside the river towards Vauxhall, walking away from the East End and the burning sky. Even so, the sky above the river glowed with reflected light from the fires and she could hear the anti-aircraft guns miles away at the docks.

Halfway along, opposite the Tate Gallery, there was a Salvation Army bus parked up. It had been converted into a tea stall with a serving hatch on one side. There were a few people standing round, drinking tea and chatting. Normally Londoners didn't speak to strangers, but the bombings seemed to have brought them closer. Everyone had a common experience and wanted to share it.

May approached the bus and ordered a tea. A kindly woman with a Salvation Army bonnet handed it to her and asked her for a few pence. She stood sipping it beside the counter and was glad of the warm liquid coursing through her body, warming her through. Although the air wasn't cold, she'd been shivering since she'd first peered into that hellish basement full of bodies. It must be delayed shock.

'Are you alright, my darling?' the woman behind the counter asked. 'You look rather pale.'

'I'm fine,' she said. 'I've been on duty with the Ambulance Service this evening. It's been a bit tough.'

The woman's face was a picture of concern. 'Oh, I'm so sorry to hear that. What terrible times we're living through.'

A young man who had been standing at the other end of the counter approached.

'Could I buy you a cake or muffin?' he asked. 'You people are doing such brave work.'

She shook her head. 'I'm not hungry. But thank you.' She turned to look at him, surprised at his kindness.

He smiled and held out his hand. 'I'm Gerald. Gerald Clifford,' he said. 'I think we are neighbours. I've seen you about in Dolphin Square.'

'Oh!' She shook his hand surprised, but looking at him now she realised he was vaguely familiar and that he might well have been one of the people in the basement shelter at Dolphin Square during the first raid. He looked a few years older than her. Late twenties or early thirties perhaps. He had wavy, sandy-coloured hair and gentle blue eyes. His face was earnest and his eyes kind.

'Have you had a dreadful time this evening? Why don't you sit down?' he asked, beckoning her towards some folding chairs that were stacked beside the van. He pulled a couple out and put them up opposite each other.

May sat down on one of them.

'It's been pretty bad,' she said, 'but we've been told not to talk about it.'

'That's tough,' Gerald said, sitting down opposite her. 'But do you mind me asking why you are staying in Dolphin Square? You're new there, aren't you?'

'Yes,' she said. 'My schoolfriend, Ruby Winter, lives there. It's her father's flat. We both wanted to help out with the war effort.'

'And where do you come from?' he asked, a look of genuine interest in his eyes.

'Northamptonshire,' she said. 'A little village called Perry Cross. There's nothing much happening there and all my sisters have left home.'

With a warm smile, Gerald asked her to tell him about her

family and before she knew it, she was talking about her sisters, giving him a potted history about each one. She was telling him about her parents too and her work on the farm. He nodded and smiled and asked encouraging questions and soon she'd forgotten all about the horrors of the evening. He bought her another tea and she began to feel quite human again.

Later, when they'd finished their drinks and the Salvation Army had started to pack up the stall, he offered to walk her home. They wandered back in companionable silence along the river, the glow of the fires from the Port of London and surrounding streets still lighting up the sky ahead.

When they reached Dolphin Square, they entered the complex under the portico together and he walked her across the courtyard to her block.

'It's been wonderful talking to you,' Gerald said. 'Perhaps we could go out for tea another time. During daylight hours, of course. I'll put a note in your postbox when I've looked at my work schedule.'

'I'd love that,' May said.

'Excellent! I look forward to it. For now, I bid you goodnight.' Gerald tipped his hat and walked away.

May went on up to the flat, feeling an unexpected surge of pleasure in her heart at having made a new friend.

11

RACHEL

ROSE PARK, 1980

When Rachel got back to Rose Park from the records office in Northampton that afternoon, she went into the kitchen, made sure that Mrs Allen wasn't around, then laid the birth certificate of Henry Joseph Rose out on the table for May to look at.

May put her reading glasses on and peered down at the document. She looked at it for a long time, her eyebrows raised. Gradually, the blood drained from her face.

'I'm stunned,' she said. 'Just as I was when you showed me those photographs. But this is concrete proof. I have no explanation for any of this.'

'Shall we pay a visit to this Mrs Sutton you mentioned?' Rachel asked.

May sighed. 'She's very old. It's doubtful that she would remember... but I suppose we could try.'

'Shall we go down there now, then?' Rachel asked, desperate for immediate answers.

Her mother hesitated. 'I don't think we should just go and knock on her door out of the blue. I think her daughter might live with her. I'll see if I can give her a ring and ask if it's OK for us to pay the old lady a visit.'

'OK. That would be good.'

'But it will probably have to wait until tomorrow, Rachel. It's late afternoon now. They'll probably be having their meal and settling down for the evening.'

'If you say so,' Rachel said, trying to suppress her impatience.

'Are you not working this evening?' May asked.

'No, I've got the evening off,' Rachel replied.

'Oh, that's good. How about a game of Scrabble after supper? I think Mrs Allen said she was going out this evening.'

Rachel tried not to look as bored by the suggestion as she felt. She knew her mother valued her company and that soon she would be away at university and May would be alone every evening again.

'Alright, that would be nice,' she said, smiling.

May went off to telephone Mrs Sutton's daughter. Later, over their supper of shepherd's pie, she told Rachel that Mrs Sutton was happy for them to pay her a visit the following morning.

'Her daughter didn't sound that thrilled though,' May said, looking anxious.

Rachel shrugged. 'If she doesn't know anything, at least we will have tried.'

When they'd finished supper and had washed up together at the huge, Butler's sink, May produced the Scrabble board and they sat down at opposite sides of the kitchen table.

'I've always liked board games,' May said, collecting her first set of pieces from the bag. 'I suppose it's a hang on from the war and all those evenings in the ambulance garage in Dolphin Square.'

'From what you've said, Mum, I wouldn't have thought you would want to remember those times very much.'

'No, on the contrary, they were the most memorable days of my life...' May said, her eyes misty. But then she backtracked, seeing Rachel's crestfallen face. 'Apart from when I met your father after the war of course, and when I had you...'

Rachel laughed. 'You don't need to spare my feelings, Mum,' she said. 'I understand what you mean.'

They played for a couple of hours, then, yawning, May said, 'I suppose I had better check in with Pa, then I'm ready for bed.'

Rachel went upstairs and laid down on the bed in the Pink room, putting the birth certificate beside her on the nightstand. She was tired, and closed her eyes before even getting undressed and ready for bed, but she was soon jolted awake by a great gust of air that swept through the room, blowing the birth certificate onto the floor. Realising she'd left the window open, she swung her legs from the bed and bent down to reach for the birth certificate but froze – there was that change in the air again, as if somehow what light there was became diffused. She swiped up the birth certificate, but by the time she sat up on the bed again, the strange light was no more.

She sat for a few moments, fully awake now, wondering if it would return, but when nothing happened, she got up and went to the window, pulling it closed and fastening the latch.

She realised then that there was no wind. The trees were still.

A feeling of unease settled over her and she shivered, hugging herself before running to the bathroom.

Mrs Sutton lived in a picture-perfect, thatched cottage with whitewashed walls smothered with roses. It was tucked away down a narrow lane, along with other similarly pretty dwellings. Rachel and May walked there together the next morning after a leisurely breakfast. Rachel had never been down that lane before and looked around her, admiring the flower-filled gardens, the hedgerows laden with blossom.

'I think this is it,' May said nervously when they reached number 10 Blossom Lane. 'Have you got the birth certificate?'

Rachel nodded, her mother's nerves making her own

stomach jangle in sympathy. How could she be afraid of an old lady, she asked herself, then she realised that what she was feeling wasn't fear, it was anticipation of discovering some long-buried secrets.

Mrs Sutton's daughter opened the door when May knocked tentatively. She nodded when she saw them standing there, but didn't smile. She was a neat, dark-haired woman, with a severe face.

'Good morning, Mrs Heywood, Miss Heywood,' she said, holding the door open for them. 'I'm Alice Johnson, Mrs Sutton's daughter. Come on through. Mother is in the conservatory. She likes to look out at the garden in the mornings.'

They followed Mrs Johnson through rooms with their low beams and inglenook fireplaces and into a sunny conservatory at the back of the house. The glass doors stood open and the scent from the rose-filled borders and freshly mowed grass wafted in from the garden.

A very old lady sat in a recliner close to the open doors. She was thin and bent, her hair was snow-white and permed into tight curls, and her skin was parchment thin and deeply wrinkled. She was dozing when they entered, but looked up when her daughter spoke.

'Mother. Here are the ladies from Rose Park to see you,' she said.

'What?' Mrs Sutton looked bewildered as she jolted out of her doze. 'Who is it, did you say?'

'Miss May and Miss Rachel, from Rose Park. Remember? You agreed to see them this morning.'

'Oh!'

Alice Johnson turned to May and Rachel. 'I'm sorry. She gets very confused nowadays. Please sit down. She'll remember soon enough. Would you like a coffee or tea?'

'Coffee would be nice,' May said, taking a seat opposite Mrs Sutton. 'We both have milk, no sugar please.'

As soon as Mrs Johnson had left the room, May leaned forward and spoke gently to Mrs Sutton.

'Do you remember working at Rose Park? For Gabriel and Emily?' she asked.

Slowly, the old lady nodded. 'Of course. It was a long time ago,' she said. 'A very long time ago. I was fifteen when I first went there. Mr Hadan was only ten in those days. Seems hard to credit now. He's old now. Just like me.'

'Well.' May cleared her throat. 'Did you know that Miss Emily and Mr Gabriel had another son? A boy a little older than Hadan?'

The old lady started visibly at those words. 'What? Another child?' Then she shook her head vehemently. 'Mr Hadan was an only child. You can be sure of that. They doted on him because he was their only one. He could do no wrong. Not that Miss Emily was much of a mother. She spent much of her time up in bed. In the Pink room. And those nursemaids they had looking after him were no good. That boy was allowed to run riot. He got into all sorts of trouble.'

'Well, it was a surprise to us too, but we found photographs of Emily with another child. And then we discovered this birth certificate.'

Rachel took the birth certificate out of her bag and handed it to her mother who then passed it to Mrs Sutton.

'I need my glasses to see this. Alice! Alice! Could you bring my glasses?'

Mrs Johnson came bustling through with a tray of coffee. She also had a glasses case on the tray. When she'd handed the coffees round, she took a pair of thick glasses out of the case and put them on her mother's nose. Mrs Sutton took the certificate and held it in trembling hands, then she looked down at it, frowning deeply. She studied it for a long time, tracing the words with a bony finger, before handing it back to Rachel.

'I don't know anything about it. There was no other child at

Rose Park. Perhaps this boy died when he was a baby. Have you thought of that?'

'Yes. Perhaps. We will look into that possibility. But we wanted to ask you first.'

The old woman drew herself up in the chair.

'You know my mother always said to me, "No good will come of gossiping about that family. You need to keep your mouth shut. Be more subtle, Edna," she would say. I never did know what she meant by that.'

'Your mother?' Rachel asked.

'Yes. My mother worked up at the big house. She was housekeeper there. I remember, she was worried, when Miss Emily died so young, that Mr Gabriel wouldn't keep us on. She told me she was taking steps to protect us. But they did keep us on, so she needn't have worried.'

'Steps?' May said. 'What do you mean?'

The old lady shrugged. 'Search me. That's what she said though. I never did know what she meant. Perhaps she meant looking for another job. She was always on the lookout. Yes, that must be it come to think of it.'

Rachel sipped the bitter coffee and looked at Mrs Sutton from behind her cup. Did she know more than she was letting on? It was hard to imagine her as a young woman, working for Emily and Gabriel, even before the turn of the century, and later on for Hadan and Wilhemena. She'd finally retired in 1945. She must have picked up a lot of information about the family over all those decades.

May drained her cup. 'Thank you for talking to us, Mrs Sutton. It's very kind of you to see us.'

'I'm just sorry I couldn't help more,' she said. Then she reached out and took May's hand. 'I remember you, my dear. From before the war. Such a pretty girl you were. You and your sisters. You all used to run your mother a merry dance...'

Alice Johnson stood in the doorway, watching with a cold expression. 'Shall I see you out?' she asked.

'Yes please, and thank you for the coffee,' May said.

On their way out, Rachel noticed an old, framed photograph hanging on the wall in the narrow hallway. It was sepia-coloured, it was so old. She stopped and took a quick look, although she was conscious that Mrs Johnson was ushering them towards the front door, clearly keen to get them out of the house. The photo was of the assembled staff of Rose Park all standing on the front drive, with Emily and Gabriel sitting in the centre with Hadan beside them, a young fresh-faced boy, a couple of dogs at their feet, the big house looming in the background. There were twenty or so staff, the women in pinafores and white caps, the men dressed formally in jackets and ties. All of them looked serious, there were few smiles and Rachel had the instant impression that Gabriel ran a tight ship. At the bottom was printed the words: *Joseph Lily photographers, Midchester, Presented to the staff of Rose Park, January 1st 1900.*

Mrs Johnson turned round from where she stood at the front door and saw Rachel looking at the photograph.

'They gave the best years of their lives to Rose Park,' Mrs Johnson said. 'With precious little return. It's good that those days are long gone.'

Rachel stopped looking at the photograph and straightened up. She saw the colour rise in her mother's cheeks. May hated confrontation of any kind and this outburst was completely out of the blue.

'Well, I'm very sorry you feel that way,' May said. 'Thank you again for the coffee and sorry to have troubled you.'

Mrs Johnson didn't reply, so Rachel followed her mother as she walked quickly out of the house, up the garden path and along the lane until they were out of sight of the cottage.

'What was that all about?' May said. 'It was mortifying!'

'A lifetime of resentment by the sounds of things,' Rachel

replied, tucking her arm into her mother's. 'Forget about it, Mum. It's not worth worrying about.'

'I know, but I don't like awkwardness.'

'Let's get home and have another coffee,' Rachel said, 'that one was bloody awful.'

'You're not wrong there,' May said. 'It was as bitter as its maker's face.'

Rachel laughed, squeezed her mother's arm, and kept on walking with a grin on her face. At least she had a decent mother. Others weren't so lucky.

12

MAY

LONDON, 1941

As she walked down the sweeping steps from the upper balcony and into the Café de Paris, arm in arm with Ruby, May looked around her in awe. She'd never been anywhere like this before. Between extravagant potted palms, there were tables spread with linen tablecloths where diners in evening dress were already eating and drinking. At the front of the grand room was a band on the podium, with black musicians playing swing music, and on the dance floor in front of it, couples were circling the room to the music. The glamour was palpable. Everywhere she looked was beauty and elegance. She was sure she spotted more than one famous face in the crowd of revellers.

'Have you been here before?' she asked Ruby, raising her voice to be heard above the music.

'Of course, loads of times. It's the best place in London to forget all about the war. Did you know, they modelled this room on the ballroom of the Titanic?'

'Oh really?' May looked around her dubiously, that didn't sound very auspicious, but she'd just come down four flights of steps from the ground floor. This ballroom was deep underground and was surely very safe.

'Yeah, really,' Ruby said. 'Now, shall I get you a drink?'

'Yes please,' May said, worried that she would appear unsophisticated, knowing nothing about what to order from a bar. She knew precious little about alcohol and had only ever sipped Joe Harding's beer out in the fields occasionally. But she suddenly recalled a conversation she'd overheard between Ivy and Florence a few months before, when they'd been discussing a recent night out and what they'd been drinking.

'I'll have a vermouth please,' she said, and Ruby looked suitably impressed. They made their way to the bar and Ruby leaned forward and shouted her order of two dry vermouths to the barman.

May drank in the atmosphere. The revolving silver chandelier enhanced the glamour of the place, as did the sweeping double staircase, the uniformed waiters, who were serving tables with champagne in ice buckets, the men in dinner jackets, the women in evening dress. It was a far cry from the ambulance station and the terror of the callout.

"The Blitz" as everyone was calling it now, had been raging for several months, and in that time, May had barely had a night off. She knew what she was doing was desperately needed, but seeing death, mass destruction and horrific injuries daily, knowing there was little she could do to alleviate the suffering, was having an effect on her. She was losing weight and hardly sleeping, and when she had slipped on one of Ruby's evening dresses earlier, it had hung loosely on her bony shoulders.

'You're looking a bit wan,' Ruby had said. 'Come and put some rouge on at my dressing table.'

Ruby had helped her put make-up on and put her hair up. Ruby was artistic; she had a gift for knowing what would look good. When May's face and hair were done, Ruby produced a glittering choker and fastened it round May's neck, then finished that off with a pair of matching earrings. May had stared at herself in the mirror, hardly recognising the sophisticated, slightly hollow-cheeked blonde who stared back at her.

'Wow!' Ruby said. 'You'll knock 'em dead tonight!'

It was Ruby who had persuaded her that she needed a night off from the ambulance station. Ruby herself had been working just as hard as May, but unlike May had recognised the strain it was having on both of them.

'I used to go out all the time before we started on the ambulances,' she told May. 'Remember that first morning you arrived? All the glasses and bottles that were piled up in the living room? It used to be like that all the time here.'

'Well thank goodness it's not like that anymore,' May said, laughing.

'I agree, but too much work and no play... as they say,' Ruby said.

'But they need us...'

'They can do without us for one night...'

May had been hesitant. She wasn't sure about going out and the prospect of meeting new people. Her confidence had deserted her recently and all she wanted to do every evening was to put her shapeless uniform on and go out with her familiar crew whom she now counted as her closest friends.

Now, she stood at the bar and sipped the vermouth that Ruby had bought for her and couldn't disguise her expression when she first tasted the bitterness of the drink.

Ruby laughed. 'You're such an innocent, May Rose,' she said. 'Don't worry, it's alright once you get used to it.'

May took a few more sips and realised that Ruby was right. She was already getting used to the taste, and the drink was gradually giving her a pleasant, fuzzy feeling.

A waiter approached them. 'Allow me to show you to a table, ladies,' he said, and they followed him across the busy room to a table with a perfect view of the dance floor.

'There are a lot of very good-looking servicemen here,' Ruby said, her eyes scanning the room, pausing to scrutinise each of the men in uniform. 'Only a lot of them seem to be already taken.'

'Already taken? Is that what you came here for?' May said, mildly shocked.

She knew Ruby was what was described as "fast" with men, but since she'd been staying at the flat, she'd seen no evidence of that. Ruby had been as conscientious a volunteer as May herself had been, but May had been aware that Ruby had been getting restless over the past couple of weeks.

May wasn't the least bit interested in finding a man tonight. The only man she was remotely attracted to was Gerald Clifford, the man she'd met at the tea stall outside the Tate Gallery, several weeks ago now. He had taken her out to tea twice since they'd met. They'd gone to a little place tucked away in a backstreet behind Horseferry Road – a small, old-fashioned café with linen tablecloths and chintzy curtains where elderly ladies served home-made cakes on cake stands. That was during the first fortnight after they'd met, but on the second occasion he had confided that he needed to go away for his work for a few weeks.

May had tried to hide her disappointment, and he assured her he would be in touch as soon as he returned.

On those two short outings, she'd had a glimpse of a man with many surprising traits, and she'd found herself wanting to get to know him better. The first fascinating thing she found out about him was about his work. He worked for the War Office, that much he told her, but he wouldn't be drawn on what he was actually doing.

Whenever she pressed him, he just smiled his sweet smile and said, 'Oh, my work is terribly boring, May. There's nothing interesting about it at all.'

'I'm sure that can't be the case...' she said. 'So, what are you working on now?'

'Ah! I can't talk about that, I'm afraid,' he said dropping his gaze and she knew, from what he'd already said, that he wasn't telling her the whole story. He didn't just work for the War Office, she guessed, he actually worked in Military Intelligence. She was tempted to tell him about Ivy, but held back.

Conversation flowed easily between them, and despite her lack of experience with men, she felt instantly at home with Gerald. He was kind, spontaneous and unaffected. He told her that he'd been born in North London and that he'd lived there his entire life and that he knew the city like the back of his hand.

'I'll show you around if you like,' he said. 'I know some surprising places. Abandoned railways, hidden churches, overgrown cemeteries, that sort of thing.'

'I'd love that,' May said. 'Only so much is being destroyed by bombs at the moment.'

He nodded. 'I know. It's a tragedy. I love this city,' he said. 'It breaks my heart to see what is happening to so many old neighbourhoods. But enough about me. What about you? Tell me some more about where you come from.'

May took a deep breath and told him more stories about Rose Park, about her parents, about her sisters, how she'd been the only one left at home and how she'd had to get away.

'So, you did a moonlight flit?' he asked, his eyes shining with amusement.

'More or less,' May admitted.

'Well, I'm jolly glad you did,' he said, leaning forward and looking earnestly at her. 'Or we would never have met.'

In that moment, looking back into his clear blue eyes, she was jolly glad they had met too, but now, sitting at the table in the Café de Paris, she wondered what had become of Gerald and why he hadn't been in touch since that day. The only fly in the ointment regarding Gerald was Ruby. Ruby had met him once when he came to the flat to collect May and afterwards she'd told May in no uncertain terms that she could do better.

'He's a bit of a bore, and not at all good looking,' she'd told May.

May wasn't surprised that Ruby didn't find him attractive, he had far more subtle charms than the dashing, ambitious types that Ruby tended to go for. May found his face both interesting and beautiful in its own way, with his intense blue eyes that often looked faraway, his delicate complexion and chiselled cheekbones. He had the look of someone intelligent and principled.

If he'd had to go away because of work, was he in danger? Was he one of those agents who risked their lives by sneaking into Nazi Germany? She knew they existed, and the more she thought about it, the more likely she thought it was why he'd had to go away. She bit her nail, suddenly paralysed with anxiety. She was already worried about Ivy, and now she had someone else to worry about too. It felt overwhelming.

At that moment, two young officers approached the table.

'Would you two ladies like to dance?' one of them asked and before May had a chance to consider, Ruby jumped up.

'We'd love to,' she said and was instantly whisked away to the dance floor by one of the men. The other one, who was tall and dark-haired, laughed good-naturedly and offered May his arm. They followed Ruby and her new partner onto the dance floor. The pace of the music had slowed down to a waltz and the young man, who had pleasing dark eyes, took her in his arms. They circled the dance floor and May was relieved to discover that he was a good dancer. She, along with all the girls at her school, had learned to dance at school and she always found it embarrassing and frustrating if her dance partner wasn't similarly accomplished.

When they'd finished, they returned to the table and the young man asked her if she wanted a drink. She asked for another vermouth, and he called the waiter. Then he sat down beside her and offered her a cigarette. She shook her head and he lit himself one, sat back on his chair and crossed his legs.

'My name's Tony,' he said. 'It's nice to dance, but I should tell you at the outset that I'm already engaged to be married. Just to set my cards on the table, so to speak.'

'Oh... I didn't think...' May stumbled, insulted at the insinuation.

'It doesn't mean a boy can't have fun though, know what I mean?' he said, blowing a smoke ring into the air and giving her a lewd wink.

May didn't reply. She just sat there miserably, sipping her vermouth, waiting for Ruby to finish her dance. But Ruby looked as though she wanted the dance to carry on for ever. The music was a schmaltzy jazz number now and she and her officer were dancing very close, Ruby's arms around his neck. She was looking up into his eyes.

May looked away. She didn't want to sit here with this lecherous man, while Ruby was giving every indication that the two of them were in the market for some serious fun.

Tony moved his chair nearer to hers. He put an elbow on the table and leaned in close. She could smell from his breath that he'd been drinking heavily.

'How about another dance?' he asked. 'You're awfully pretty. Did you know that?'

'I think I'll just sit this one out,' she replied and sipped her drink slowly, trying to ignore his looming presence.

How disappointing, she thought, that the evening should turn out like this. She really would have preferred to be on duty at the ambulance garage, if this was how things were going to be. She took another sip of her drink and as she put the glass back on the table, Tony lurched towards her and to her astonishment, slid his hand up inside her skirt.

'What do you think you're doing?' she said at the top of her voice, jumping up out of her chair, but no one noticed, the music was too loud.

Then, she picked up her evening bag and walked across the

dance floor, weaving her way between the dancers, and tapped Ruby on the arm. Ruby and her partner stopped dancing.

'What's the matter?'

'I'm going home. I got landed with a real letch.'

'Oh, don't go, May, please!' Ruby said.

'No, I'm not enjoying myself. I'll get a taxi. I really don't mind if you stay.'

Ruby relented then. 'Well, if you're sure. I want to stay, though. I'm having a lovely time.'

'I'm quite sure, Ruby. Enjoy yourself.'

She walked off the dance floor with as much dignity as she could muster, but as she stepped off the boards onto the carpet, Tony was waiting for her.

'Come on, don't be like this,' he said. 'I'm sorry, I misjudged the situation. How about another dance?'

'No,' she said. 'I'm going home. I don't feel well.'

She walked towards the stairs, but he followed her, grabbing her arm, his fingers gripping so tight he was hurting her. He pulled her to a stop and leaned towards her, his face red with anger and humiliation.

'You're a stuck-up, frigid bitch. I'm glad you're going. Good riddance to you!'

Shaken, she made her way to the stairs and hurried up them, tears stinging her eyes. She collected her wrap from the cloakroom then, brushing past the doormen, she hurried on up the three further flights of steps until she emerged onto the street. There, she took a grateful gulp of air, glad to be away from the chaotic, noisy nightclub and from the clutches of that lecherous oaf.

13

MAY

LONDON, 1941

THERE WAS a line of taxis waiting along Coventry Street. The cabbies were leaning on the bonnets chatting and smoking. May got into the first one in the row.

'Where to, miss?' The elderly driver got into the driving seat and turned round to smile at her. He had a friendly, reassuring face which calmed her down a little.

'Dolphin Square, please,' she said, her voice shaking.

As the vehicle pulled off, she collapsed back onto the seat, sobbing with relief.

All the way home, through the darkened streets, May went over and over the disastrous evening in her mind. Was it her fault that she'd ended up with such an oaf, or was it just bad luck? She shuddered, recalling his hand on her thigh. The cheek of the man.

She looked out at the gloomy streets, the headlights of the taxi were dimmed, so it was difficult to see anything, but she could just about make out the piles of rubble of collapsed buildings from the previous night's raids, the exposed walls of the upper floors with patterned wallpaper on view. They passed lines of people weighed down with blankets and pillows, queuing to go down into the Underground to shelter for the night. Occasionally another vehicle would hove into view, looking ghostly in the misty air. A bus rumbled past, its headlights dipped, its passengers travelling through the night in complete darkness.

At last, they reached the river at the end of Northumberland Avenue, turned right and drove along the Embankment. Within ten minutes the taxi was drawing up outside the porticoed entrance of Dolphin Square. It was when May got out of the taxi and was paying the driver that she heard the whine of the air-raid siren. Glancing at her watch she saw that it was half past nine.

'You'd better go straight to your shelter, miss,' the driver said. 'Jerry's on 'is way again.'

She thanked him and went in through the entrance as the taxi swung out into the road and turned round to return to the West End.

The mist from the river was dank and chilly now, so May pulled her wrap tightly around her shoulders, walked briskly through the courtyard garden and made straight for the basement shelter. Because she'd been on duty with the ambulance service most evenings since she'd arrived in Dolphin Square, she'd barely visited the shelter since that first evening, and she dreaded the thought of going down there now. All she wanted to do was to go up to the flat, brew a cup of tea and lie down on her bed. But she knew she must; bombs had frequently fallen in the vicinity in recent weeks as the Houses of Parliament were so close.

Crossing the garden, she could see other residents making for the shelter, some with blankets and cushions, others carrying books, board games and even bottles of wine. She reached the door and put her hand on the handle at the same time as a man.

'Oh, I'm sorry.' She looked up into his face and a bolt of recognition went through her.

'Gerald!'

'May, you look so beautiful,' he said, his eyes widening in appreciation. 'Have you been dancing?'

'Yes, but not for long.'

He pulled back the door and they hurried down the steps and into the basement. There, they found a bench seat behind a trestle table in the first room along the corridor and sat down side by side.

'When did you get back?' May asked, still reeling from the surprise and pleasure of seeing Gerald again.

'Yesterday,' he said. 'I've already been up to your flat to say hello, but there was no one in.'

'No, we both went to the Café de Paris. It was our night off.'

'So, where's your flatmate?' Gerald asked.

'She's still there. I came home alone. I wasn't enjoying it.'

'Such a shame,' Gerald said. 'But I'm glad you've come. It will make the next few hours a pleasure rather than a terrible bore.'

She smiled. He always said such nice things.

'I've got a bottle of wine in my bag, or would you prefer some tea?'

'Oh, tea please. I was dreaming of a nice cup of tea all the way home in the taxi,' she said.

The drone of aircraft sounded above and Gerald looked up at the ceiling. His smile disappeared and his forehead furrowed into a frown.

'Won't they ever stop?' he muttered, getting up from the seat. 'I'll get some teas from the urn.'

Just then the ack-ack guns started up their familiar chatter. May sighed and sat back on her seat, wondering if she should go along to the ambulance station and offer her services. She wasn't going to get any sleep anyway. But after a little thought, she decided against it. She was entitled to an evening off and she knew the crew had enough cover. Besides, she wanted to catch up with Gerald after all these weeks.

Explosions were rumbling all around them, shaking the walls

of the buildings, even the basement felt the shocks. May wondered how close the bombs were. The Houses of Parliament had already been hit a couple of times, the Commons chamber had been destroyed and sittings had had to move to another building in Westminster. She wondered how long it would be before Dolphin Square itself was hit. It was inevitable, she supposed, big buildings seemed to be targets for the Luftwaffe.

Gerald appeared with two tin mugs of tea. May took hers and sipped it gratefully. It was very strong, but that didn't matter.

'So, where have you been all these weeks?' she asked.

'Ah,' he replied. 'I thought you might ask that. I'm sorry, but I can't say.'

'I thought you might say that. At least you're back safely. I was worried about you.'

'Really?' He looked amazed. 'I'm flattered. But I'm back safely now. If anyone is safe in this city nowadays that is...'

They fell silent for a few moments, sipping their tea and listening to the rumblings of explosions across the city and the constant rattle of the aircraft guns.

'Why don't you tell me about what you've been doing while I've been away? How has it been?'

'Oh, terrible,' she said. 'Just terrible.' And she went on to describe some of the incidents she'd been called out to since he'd left: the sight of bombed houses trapping their residents, so pulverised it was difficult to imagine anyone surviving the blast; crawling under collapsed ceilings to help extract trapped people; the time she'd managed to carry a bruised and unconscious child from the wreckage of a building, only to watch him die on the stretcher when she put him down, the time the mortuary vans had been unable to attend a bombsite, and she and her crew had to collect and bag up body parts from a wrecked Anderson shelter and transport them to the morgue. That had been one of the lowest points of the past few weeks and she couldn't prevent the tears from flowing when she talked about it.

Gerald put his arm around her and pulled her close and she leaned on his shoulder and sobbed.

'You're so brave,' he said. 'Why are you doing this when you could be back at home keeping safe?'

She looked up at him and stopped crying.

'I could ask you why you do what you do. You could have done something safer. It's a sense of duty, isn't it? Knowing that if you can do something to help, you *should* do it.'

'You're right. But not everyone feels that way. They just want to keep themselves and their families away from harm.'

'My father is like that,' she reflected. 'He's desperate for me to go home out of harm's way. But then he served in the Great War. He never talks about it, but I know that dreadful things happened to him in France. He's seen his share of horror.'

Gerald's question set her thinking. It was more than simply a sense of duty that drove her each evening to go down to the ambulance garage. She didn't have to go, after all, she was only paid minimal expenses. She realised that a lot of her drive to do good came from her background. She'd had a privileged, sheltered upbringing. She'd never had to work, and even at home, everything was done for her by servants. Working on the ambulances was a way of transcending all that, of showing that she was no different from anyone else, a way of playing her part.

They carried on talking amiably, slipping back into where they'd left off a few weeks beforehand, while the bombers roared on outside. At last the All-Clear sounded at about two o'clock in the morning. People yawned and got out of their seats and, rubbing sleep from their eyes, slowly made their way out of the shelter and back to their homes.

'I'll see you up to your flat,' Gerald said, and May was glad to take his arm when they got outside into the courtyard, and let him guide her through the gardens to the door to her block.

'Shall I take you up?' he asked.

'I'll be fine from here,' she said. 'I expect Ruby will be home by now.'

'So, I'll say goodnight then,' Gerald said, then, to her surprise he took her face in his hands and kissed her full on the lips. Little thrills of pleasure went right through May at the shock of it, and after her initial surprise, she realised she was enjoying the kiss and was kissing him back.

'I've missed you so much, May,' he said when they broke apart.

'I've missed you too. I was beginning to think I would never see you again.'

They stood looking into one another's eyes a little awkwardly. May was still revelling in the thrill of the kiss.

'Can we go out sometime?' he asked then. 'I'd like to spend more time with you. Make up for lost time so to speak.'

'Of course,' she said. 'But I'm on duty most evenings. The time varies.'

'How about tomorrow afternoon?' he asked. 'We could go for a walk.'

'Why not?' she said.

'I'll come and fetch you around three o'clock then,' he said. 'Goodnight, May.'

Then he turned and walked away. She stood watching him cross the gardens and enter the block opposite, then, with a spring in her step, she went upstairs to the flat.

She was half expecting Ruby to greet her there, her eye makeup smudged, her skin glowing from the night's dancing, but the flat was empty and rather chilly. May lit the gas fire in the living room and made herself some tea and toast. Then she went round tidying. In their excitement getting dressed earlier, they'd thrown aside dresses and shawls, so the floor of every room was strewn with clothing. May smiled as she did it, recalling their excitement as they tried on different clothes and compared results in Ruby's bedroom mirror.

When she finally sat down to eat her toast, weariness overcame her and she fell asleep almost instantly, leaving the toast untouched and the tea to get cold in the cup.

She was woken a few hours later by the shrill buzz of the doorbell. She started, rubbing her eyes. Instinctively she pulled her wrap around her shoulders. She must look a sight, but the person ringing the bell was clearly in no mood to wait.

'I'm coming,' she shouted, running to the door. Perhaps Ruby had forgotten her key?

She pulled the door open and a stranger stood on the landing outside. He wore a tin helmet with ARP written on the front and he looked exhausted and shocked to the core. She recognised that look from all her nights out with the ambulance. He was carrying a woman's bag over his shoulder, but apart from registering that it looked rather odd, for the time being, she didn't register what it was.

'Hello?' she said.

'Is this the home of Ruby Winter?' he asked and she nodded. 'Are you a relative?'

'No... a friend. Oh, and flatmate. Is Ruby in trouble?'

'I'm afraid I have some bad news. You might want to sit down.'

Confused, May went back into the living room and sat down where she'd just been asleep. The man sat down opposite her.

'I'm afraid the Café de Paris took a direct hit from a German bomb this evening. There were several casualties. Ruby Winter was one of them. She was hit by falling masonry and didn't survive. I'm so sorry.'

14

RACHEL

PERRY CROSS, 1980

RACHEL STOOD with her elbows on the bar of the Quarryman's Arms deep in thought. It was a quiet night again and she'd just served a group of customers who had gone to sit in the garden, so there was no one in the pub itself. Jenny was in the cellar, changing the beer barrels.

There were so many things swirling around in her mind that she was having a hard time making sense of everything. It was good, she thought, that she was learning so much about the Rose family, but it was a lot to process too. That afternoon, under the shade of the old oak tree, sipping lemon barley water, May had told her more about her life during the Blitz and how she'd met and become friendly with Gerald Clifford. Rachel had never really thought that her mother might have had boyfriends before she met Rachel's father after the war, and from May's wistful expression when she spoke about Gerald, it was clear that she must have felt very warmly towards him. Rachel wouldn't be surprised if her mother were to tell her at some point that she'd fallen in love with Gerald. That would be a strange thing to come to terms with. Her heart had gone out to May when she'd told her that Ruby had been killed in the bombing of the Café de Paris.

'How terrible!' Rachel had been genuinely shocked at the news, and she'd seen that May had tears in her eyes thinking about it even forty years later.

'I still blame myself for her death,' May had told Rachel, blinking away the tears.

'But why, Mum? How were you to blame?'

'I should have made her come home with me. I could feel it in my bones. Something wasn't right in that place that evening.'

'But, Mum, you said that Ruby was enjoying herself. Why would she have come with you?'

May closed her eyes for a few moments and when she opened them, she shook her head.

'I'm not really sure, but I still blame myself. Whatever the rights and wrongs of it might be.'

It had been time for Rachel to leave to go to the pub then. She'd lost track of time. She rushed into the house to get ready and as she left to go to the pub, through the kitchen window she caught a glimpse of May wandering across the lawn towards the house, lost in thought. Poor May, she took so much upon herself. But from the stories she was telling Rachel about the Blitz, she'd clearly always been that way.

And then there was the mystery surrounding Hadan's brother, Henry. What had happened to him? Mrs Sutton had been no help at all, but Rachel wondered if she did know something and was holding back through a long-held fear of Hadan.

Earlier that day, before settling down under the oak tree to talk about May's youth, Rachel and May had walked to the small family cemetery on the edge of the Rose Park grounds. It was set in the corner of a decaying wood beside the disused estate chapel, and grass and weeds were growing up everywhere, almost smothering the gravestones.

'I'm surprised Pa doesn't get the gardeners to tidy this up,' May mused. 'But then, I suppose Pa never did set much store by religion, or by remembering the dead.'

'Look, here's my mother.' Her voice brightened and she bent down and peered at a moss-covered gravestone. The inscription was just about legible: "Here lies Wilhemena Beatrix Rose, Born 5th May 1901, died 19th January 1965. Beloved wife to Hadan, and mother of Blanche, Florence, Ivy and May. Rest in Peace."

'She went too young,' May said. 'She was only in her mid-sixties. Died of nerves, poor Ma. She never did get used to Pa's temper, not in over forty years of marriage. Do you remember her, Rachel?'

'Of course. I must have been five when she died. She used to sit me on her lap and tell me stories. And take me out to walk in the grounds. She was so kind. I was very upset when she died. I remember coming here, to her funeral. It was the first funeral I'd ever been to, and it seemed so sad.'

'It was sad. We were all devastated.'

The graves of Gabriel and Emily were together in the middle of the cemetery. The headstones were rather elaborate with statues of angels standing sentinel over the graves. There were no graves older than those two in the little graveyard.

'Gabriel built the house, so I suppose Emily would have been the first person to be buried here,' May told Rachel. 'She died young too, didn't she?'

Rachel peered down at Emily's headstone. She'd been born in 1860 and had died in 1900, so she was only forty. A shiver went through Rachel thinking about Emily lying in the Pink room, nursing her depression and finally simply fading away. No wonder there was a strange atmosphere in the room.

Of course, there was no grave for Henry Joseph Rose. They hadn't expected there to be really.

'It was worth checking, wasn't it?' May said as they left the cemetery and she closed the rickety wrought-iron gate. 'I think I'll ask Tom Hallam to come down here and tidy this all up one afternoon,' May said when they were walking back to the house.

'I thought Grandad didn't want to bother, with it?' Rachel

said, surprised. It wasn't like May to take charge and override Hadan's wishes.

'Well, it's not completely up to him, Rachel. Although it's sad to say it, but it won't be long before another grave will need to be dug in that graveyard. And I'm sure he wouldn't want the place to look so unkept for his funeral.'

'Mum!' Rachel was mildly shocked by her mother's practical approach, but she supposed it was best to meet her grandfather's impending demise head-on.

Rachel was still none the wiser about Hadan's brother, and she hadn't yet had time to look for more evidence of his existence in the cupboards and shelves in the house. Hadan's office, she knew, was likely to be a fertile ground for evidence, but so far she hadn't dared enter. It was Hadan's domain, and his presence was still too strong in there to go poking around. Perhaps though, she might be able to, with his consent. Although the thought of actually asking him if she could go rooting around in his papers made shivers go right through her.

But as well as all these different strands of family history competing for her attention, she was also spending a lot of mental energy thinking about Daniel Walters. The memory of him deep in conversation with that woman in front of the building in Northampton the day before kept returning to her. She hadn't got a clear picture of the woman in her mind. She remembered that she was smartly dressed, had dark hair, and looked quite young. It was the way their heads were almost touching, they were so deep in conversation, that Rachel couldn't let go of. She sighed thinking about it, remembering Daniel's kiss the last time they'd parted and how she'd thought they were getting close. Should she challenge him about what she'd seen? She didn't want to seem possessive before there was anything to be possessive about. She decided that she probably wouldn't bring it up, she would just see how things went between them.

She looked up and as if to answer her thoughts, Daniel

himself came through the pub door and walked straight up to the bar. He looked as if he was dressed for a night out, in a leather jacket and tight jeans.

'Well, hello stranger,' he said, beaming. He looked genuinely pleased to see her and she hoped he wouldn't notice that her cheeks had coloured upon seeing him. It was almost as if he knew what she was thinking, as if he'd caught her spying on him. Then he leaned forward and kissed her on the lips.

'Hey!' she said laughing and drawing away. 'Jenny might see.'

'Oh, she wouldn't mind. I'm one of her best customers.'

He asked for a pint of Phipps and Rachel pulled it and put it on the bar.

'I'm sorry I haven't been in the last couple of nights,' he said. 'My mum's not been well, I've been keeping her company.'

'Oh, I'm sorry to hear that,' Rachel replied, remembering what Jenny had told her about Daniel's mother. 'Are you two close?'

'We are, although we argue hammer and tongs sometimes. Mum's a very strong personality. She likes to get her own way.'

'Do you live at home?' Rachel asked and he nodded.

'It's just me and her. She brought me up on her own. Sometimes I'd like to leave – get my own place, but I'd feel a bit guilty abandoning her.'

'I know exactly how you feel,' Rachel said, thinking suddenly of her own mother being left alone when she went off to university in October. They hadn't spoken about it, but it was weighing on both their minds; she knew that May was worried about it.

'I came in to see you actually,' Daniel said. 'Me and the boys have a gig over in Midchester this evening. I was wondering if you'd like to come along? We could have a drink afterwards and I could drop you off home after that.'

'I'd love to,' she said instantly, delighted that he'd asked her out again, 'only I'm working here until ten thirty.'

'Well – you could come for the end of the gig, and we could

have a drink after that. The bar stays open late when they have bands playing.'

'Alright,' she said, still thinking it through. 'I'm not quite sure how I'd get there though. I suppose I might be able to borrow Mum's car...'

'Taxi? One of my mates down our lane is a taxi driver. He often does me favours.'

'OK,' she said. 'That would be great.'

Daniel downed his pint and put the glass on the bar.

'OK then, I'll get Ray to pick you up about ten thirty. I need to get off and get over there now.'

With that he leaned forward, kissed her on the lips and left the pub. Rachel stared after him, reeling from the speed of his visit and the impromptu kiss, but already looking forward to what the evening might bring later on.

RACHEL CALLED May on the pub phone to let her know she would be home late again.

May sounded amused. 'It's nice that you're going out and having fun,' she said. 'But take care, won't you?'

'Of course, Mum,' she said.

After that, the evening dragged, the hands of the big clock above the inglenook fireplace seemed to be on a go-slow, although the pub did get a little busier later on and she was kept on her toes pulling pints and talking to customers.

'Are you all right this evening, Rachel?' Jenny asked. 'You're not thinking about lover boy, are you? I saw him pop in earlier when I was putting the empty barrels in the yard.'

Rachel felt her cheeks heating up.

'I wouldn't exactly call him lover boy,' Rachel said. 'We hardly know each other.'

'I just know, with that one,' she said. 'And as I told you, you want to watch him.'

Rachel wondered exactly what she meant by that, but she didn't want to ask for fear of sounding naïve.

Daniel's friend Ray arrived at the Quarryman's Arms just after ten thirty. He shambled up to the bar. Rachel was surprised to see that Ray was a few years older than Daniel. He was running to fat and had a quiff and fuzzy "Elvis" sideburns. In contrast, he was dressed in a grey cardigan and old jeans.

'Are you Rachel?' he asked. 'Danny Walters asked me to take you into Midchester. I've got me car outside when you're ready.'

'I'll just grab my things.'

Rachel popped to the ladies, grabbed her handbag and cardigan, and hastily touched up her make-up that had started to smudge in the warmth of the summer evening. Then, she went back into the bar.

'Come on then,' Ray said, walking ahead of her and opening the door.

The car was an old Ford Cortina that had been customised, with wide wheels like a racing car and a huge double exhaust pipe. When Ray opened the back door of the car for her, Rachel saw that the interior was covered in synthetic fur. She slid onto the back seat and Ray got into the driver's seat and roared away.

'How do you know our Danny boy then?' he asked above the reggae music that was blaring out from oversized speakers.

'Oh, I just met him in the pub the other night,' she said.

'You're the Rose girl, aren't you?' he asked, watching her face in the mirror.

'My mother was a Rose, yes. I'm staying at Rose Park at the moment.'

'Ah,' Ray replied, as if this answered a question that hadn't yet been asked.

'Why?' she asked him, feeling slightly unsettled by his line of questioning.

'Oh nothing,' he said, then added, as if by way of explanation, 'Everyone in the village knows about the Rose family.'

She didn't answer, wondering if that was a good or a bad thing. Then, Ray added, 'Danny and I go back a long way. I'm a bit older than 'im, but we've always been mates.'

Ray dropped her on the square in Midchester.

'That's the pub,' he said pointing to a building with a metal pub sign hanging above the door, its windows ablaze with light. 'The Brave Old Oak. Just go in and find a seat. It's a very friendly crowd.'

'Thank you, Ray. How much do I owe you?'

'Nothing. It's a favour for a mate.'

She thanked him again, got out of the car, and stood on the pavement watching it roar off down the High Street. Then she walked the few steps across the square to the pub and opened the door. She was greeted by a fug of steam and smoke and a wall of noise from the band. The room was packed with rowdy locals, but Rachel managed to shoulder her way through to the bar and order herself a soft drink. She was thirsty and didn't want to start drinking alcohol too early.

When she'd been served, she turned her attention to the band. There was Daniel and the three young men she'd played pool with the other day, but there under the revolving coloured lights, dancing, and playing their instruments, they looked a lot more glamourous this evening. They were all dressed in leather jackets, jeans and white T-shirts. They were performing "Going Underground" by the Jam and pouring their heart and soul into the music. To her surprise, Daniel was the singer; for some reason she'd imagined him as playing lead guitar, and he had a surprisingly good voice, gravelly but tuneful at the same time.

When the number finished, the bar erupted with applause, cheering and whooping, and whistles, and before the applause had even died down, the band was moving on to another recent hit, "Ashes to Ashes" by David Bowie. They were astonishingly versatile. Rachel closed her eyes and listened to the music. She loved David Bowie and although this wasn't quite the real thing, it came very close.

They carried on for the next half hour, performing rock hits from the past few years, to the appreciation of the audience who clapped and cheered at the end of every number. The final song was "My Sharona" that got everyone clapping and banging on the tables to the beat.

With a final elaborate guitar solo from Andy, the set was over, and the band put their instruments down and made their way over to the bar, through the press of people who all wanted to slap them on the back and congratulate them on a great night's music.

Daniel waved as he pushed his way through and when he joined her, and put his arm around her, she saw that his face was bathed in sweat, his clothes were sticking to his skin and he was breathing quickly.

He ordered a pint of Phipps and a gin and tonic for Rachel.

'There's a back room behind the bar,' he said. 'The landlord lets the band use it. It's quieter in there.'

He went ahead of her through a passage and into a quiet little snug with panelled walls and a flagstone floor. They sat down at a table in the corner.

'Thank you for coming,' he said. 'I hope it went OK with Ray?'

'Yes. It was nice of him to bring me,' she said.

'I hope you liked the car!' he said, and they both laughed. 'It's his pride and joy.'

'I loved it!' she said. 'Especially the furry interior.'

'Did you enjoy the band too?' he asked and she could see from the look in his eyes that her answer would mean a lot to him.

'It was brilliant!' she said and meant it. 'And you've obviously got loads of appreciative fans.'

'We just cover hits,' he said. 'But it seems to go down well round here, and we get plenty of bookings.'

'I'm not surprised.'

The conversation moved on. Rachel asked him how his mother was, and he thanked her and said she was a lot better.

'How is your grandfather doing?' he asked, and she replied that she didn't really see much of him, but relied on her mother telling her about him, and that she didn't think he was doing very well.

'He sleeps every afternoon,' she said. 'That's when Mum and I go out and sit in the garden and she tells me all about what happened to her during the war. I'm trying to find out as much as I can about the family history while I'm here.'

'That sounds interesting,' Daniel said leaning forward and looking into her eyes. 'What did your mother do during the war?'

'She ran away from home and volunteered to drive ambulances during the Blitz. She saw some terrible, shocking things. Her best friend died when the Café de Paris was bombed too.'

'Incredible!' he said. 'How brave of her. And what about your aunts? Didn't one of them work at Bletchley Park?'

'Yes, and one of them was sent off to France, but I don't know much more than that.'

'And what about the other one? Blanche, isn't it?'

'Yes... she went to America.' She looked at him. He was all attention, and the thought flitted across her mind that he was incredibly interested in her family. It occurred to her that it was rather strange. Her family was fascinating to her, but why should it be to him? On the other hand, she told herself, it was nice that he was looking at her with such rapt attention.

'She was actually at Pearl Harbor during the Japanese attack,' she went on.

'Really? Now that *is* interesting.'

'That's all I know I'm afraid. I'm hoping that when she and Aunt Florence come to Rose Park, which they inevitably will when Grandad dies, I will be able to ask them about their wartime experiences. I hardly know Blanche though. She's only been to the UK once or twice during my entire life. The last time was for my dad's funeral when I was ten.'

'That must have been a really sad time for you,' Daniel said. 'I never actually knew my father. My mum brought me up all by herself.'

'Did you never meet him?'

'Well, I probably met him, but neither of us knew about our relationship at the time.'

'But you do now?'

Daniel fell silent. 'It's not something I want to talk about,' he said with an air of finality and she could see that the question had rattled him.

Rachel opened her mouth to protest. After all, he was always pumping her for details about her family, but he wouldn't be drawn on anything to do with his own. Daniel downed his pint in silence. A palpable tension had developed between them and Rachel was regretting having probed him about his parents.

Daniel cleared his throat and got to his feet. 'I'll go and get some more drinks,' he said and disappeared through to the bar with the empty glasses. Rachel was left alone feeling awkward and uneasy, wondering what she'd done to offend him.

He came back in about ten minutes.

'I've given Ray a call and asked him to come and collect you,' he said. Rachel's heart sank. This was proof that she'd offended him and he didn't want to take her home.

'Is it something I said?' she asked, feeling near to tears, her heart pulsing in her throat.

'No, of course not. It's just that Andy can't start his van and I have to take him and all his equipment home to Whittlebury. I'm afraid there's no room for an extra passenger.'

'Oh, poor Andy,' she said, relieved at least that there was a reason Daniel wasn't going to drop her home as planned.

Then, as if there'd been no frostiness between them, he took her hand, then leaned in and kissed her full on the lips. She kissed him back, flooded with relief that everything was alright after all and that she hadn't spoiled things with her clumsy questioning.

There were footsteps in the passage and they pulled apart.

'Hello, lovebirds,' Ray said cheerfully. 'I'll be outside whenever you're ready, Rachel.'

They kissed again, then Daniel said, 'I'm sorry about this evening. I really wanted to take you home. I'll come into the pub tomorrow and let's go out another time?'

'That would be lovely.'

He walked her out to the square and opened the back door to Ray's car and she got in.

'I owe you one, mate,' he said to Ray. 'Drive safely.'

Ray took off down the High Street, heading towards Perry Cross.

'Did you have a nice evening?' he asked.

'It was great, thanks,' she said. 'The band was really good.'

'They are. They've made a bit of a name for themselves around here. It's great. I always said Dan Walters was a good singer when he was a nipper. And I was right.'

'So you've known each other a long time, then?' she asked. She was suddenly wondering if she could ask Ray some questions about Dan that he hadn't answered himself. Perhaps, if they were such close friends, Ray would know something about the woman Rachel had seen Daniel talking to in Northampton. Could she risk the embarrassment of asking him? She bit her nail and stared out of the window at the dark hedgerows whipping past. They reached the end of the lane and turned onto the main road. It was only another five minutes to Perry Cross, she needed to ask quickly if she was going to.

'I was just thinking... I saw Daniel in Northampton the other day,' she said. 'Talking to someone... a woman actually. I was wondering...'

Ray's eyes registered amusement in the mirror and he laughed out loud.

'And you was wondering if he's already got a girlfriend?'

'Well, sort of...'

'Not as far as I know. Not at the moment, but he's a wild card our Danny. Come to think of it, 'e told me he was going into town on Monday to see a solicitor.'

'A solicitor?' gasped Rachel, the wind taken out of her sails by this development.

'Yes. Some lady by the name of Mary Dove. Maybe that's who you saw him with. Her office is opposite the Guildhall.'

'Oh... that might explain it,' she said, a weight gradually lifting from her, but at the same time more questions were crowding her mind.

'But do you know why?' she asked.

Ray took one hand off the furry steering wheel and rubbed his chin.

'Some family matter...' He didn't elaborate. 'That's all I know.'

Rachel fell silent. It didn't matter what Daniel had gone to see a solicitor about; if it was a family matter it must be private. She realised that she had jumped to the wrong conclusion and completely mistaken the nature of the conversation she'd seen. She was relieved at least that he didn't have a girlfriend, but she still felt uneasy for some reason. There were so many things about Daniel that she didn't know or understand. And yet, she did know that in spite of everything, she was falling under his spell.

15

MAY

LONDON, 1941

May sat in the living room of Ruby's flat, paralysed with shock, staring at the man who'd just delivered the devastating blow. All she could think of was Ruby's shining eyes while she danced with the officer. She'd looked so happy. How could this possibly have happened?

'I'm sorry, my dear, but I have to ask; do you have the details of Miss Winter's parents?' the ARP warden asked after a few moments. 'I need to inform them as soon as I can. They will have to come and identify her body.'

'Oh!' May's hand flew to her mouth at the thought of Ruby's poor parents having to go to the morgue to see her battered and bruised body drained of life. No parent should ever have to do that.

'One moment,' she said vaguely, realising it was unavoidable, 'I think they must be in the address book.'

She went to the telephone table and with shaking hands flicked through Ruby's leather address book and found the details of the Winters' address in Northamptonshire and their telephone number. She scribbled them down on a piece of paper, having to pause several times to wipe the tears from her eyes with the back of her hand. She couldn't get that final image of Ruby's face out of her mind, bursting with pleasure at being at the Café de Paris and dancing with a handsome officer. If only... if only...

'Thank you, miss. I will ask the local police to inform Mr and Mrs Winter straight away. Now, do you have anyone you could ask to keep you company? You look very shocked.'

She shook her head. All her friends from the Ambulance Service would be on duty. But then she thought of Gerald. He was only across the courtyard. The thought of talking to him made her feel a little better.

'Actually, there is someone. They live in Dolphin Square, in another block.'

'Could you go over there now do you think? Only I need to get off.'

She nodded and showed the man to the door, then she wandered back into the living room and collapsed into the armchair, her head in her hands. She was sobbing her heart out, still hardly able to believe what had happened. It suddenly occurred to her that, but for her unfortunate experience with the lecherous officer, she herself would have been in the Café de Paris when the bomb hit. Shock washed through her, thinking about it. It was difficult to believe that she owed that odious creep of an officer her life.

She couldn't stop shaking. On the sideboard were some bottles of spirits and liqueurs Ruby's father kept for his infrequent visits. She needed something to calm her down. She poured a generous measure of brandy into a glass and drank it in one gulp. The fiery liquid burned her throat, but within a few seconds she was feeling the effects, the instant relaxing of her limbs, a heavy feeling creeping through her body.

She wanted to collapse on the settee and go to sleep, but she remembered the ARP warden's words. It would be good to have some company. He was right. She pulled on a coat, left the flat, locking the door behind her, went down the stairs and crossed the gardens to Gerald's block. She didn't know which flat he lived in, but a quick look at the postboxes told her he was in Flat 610 on the sixth floor. The door to the block was unlocked, so she pushed it open and went inside and took the lift to the sixth floor.

She knocked at the door to number 610, but there was no answer. She knocked again. On the third attempt, she heard some movement from inside, some footsteps shuffling on a polished floor, then the unlocking of bolts and chains, and the door opened. Gerald was wearing striped, blue pyjamas and was blinking in the harsh light of the hallway.

'May?' he gasped. 'Are you alright? Whatever are you doing here?'

'Ruby is dead,' she said through her tears. 'She was killed in an air raid at the Café de Paris.'

The colour drained from Gerald's face, and he was instantly awake.

'I'm so, so sorry, May. You must be feeling terrible. Come here.'

He took her into his arms and she fell sobbing onto his shoulder. He held her there for what seemed like an age while she sobbed her heart out.

'Come on inside. I'll get you a brandy,' he said, when her sobs had subsided. He led her along the passage to a small, bare living room. 'Please, May, sit down,' he said and she sat on a hard, utility settee while he fixed her a drink.

'I've just had one of these,' she said as he handed it to her.

'Don't worry. You need it.'

He sat beside her and put his arm around her again and drew her close, while she sipped the brandy which did seem to gradually numb her senses.

'How did you find out about it?' he asked in the end.

'An ARP warden came round and told me. I was so shocked, Gerald. If I hadn't left the nightclub when I did, I would have been there when the bomb landed too.'

She heard Gerald's sharp intake of breath as the implications of this hit him.

'Thank God you left when you did,' he said.

'But I should have made Ruby come with me. It's because of me she died,' May sobbed.

Gerald pulled her closer. 'You mustn't think like that, May. It isn't your fault. How could you possibly have known that the place would be bombed?'

'I should have known. I should have known,' she said.

'No. Don't torture yourself. No one could have known.'

They sat there for a long time, May sobbing quietly on his shoulder, Gerald stroking her hair and saying soothing words, but gradually the sobs subsided as the brandy had its effect and finally May slipped into oblivion.

She slept for a long time and when she awoke she could hear pigeons cooing on the windowsill. It was broad daylight and as she came to, she registered that she was still lying on Gerald's settee, but he was not with her and a blanket was spread over her. Checking her watch, she saw that it was past nine o'clock. In that moment the news about Ruby came back to her and her heart sank; the horrific realisation that something terrible had happened the night before – that her life would never be the same again. She closed her eyes and tried to hold back the flood of tears. She wished she'd never woken up.

She got up, needing the bathroom. Her body felt stiff, and her head was pounding from the brandy. She left the living room and found the bathroom beside the front door, in the same location as the bathroom in Ruby's flat. When she'd finished and had splashed her face with cold water, she went out into the hallway again. Wondering where Gerald was, she headed to the kitchen.

She could hear his voice coming from a room halfway along the corridor which in Ruby's flat was the spare bedroom. She paused outside the half-open door and peeped in. She was about to knock, but what she saw made her hesitate. Gerald was sitting with his back to the door, with headphones on, talking into a microphone. May's heart sped up. This was surely proof that he didn't just have some boring administrative role in the War Office.

Suddenly he turned round and saw her standing there. He instantly pulled the headphones off, high colour in his cheeks, got out of his chair and came towards her.

'May! I should have shut the door, I'm sorry. This is to do with my work. Please... come to the kitchen. I will make you some tea.'

When he came out of the room, he shut the door firmly behind him.

'I'm not actually supposed to have visitors here,' he said sounding apologetic.

'It's alright. I will go,' she said.

'No! No, I didn't mean for you to go. Not at all. These are exceptional circumstances. Come into the kitchen.'

The kitchen was as sparsely furnished as the living room and very tidy.

'None of this is mine,' he explained, indicating the shelves stacked with plain cream china, the dresser, the picture on the wall of Big Ben in a snowstorm. He put a whistle kettle on the gas cooker. 'It all belongs to the government. Standard issue.'

'I see,' she said, sitting down at the yellow Formica table. He made them both tea in chipped china mugs and sat down opposite her.

'Would you like some toast?' he asked, and she shook her head. She couldn't face eating, not this morning.

'I'd better go back to the flat,' she said. 'Ruby's parents might come, and I should be there for them.'

'Of course,' he said. 'I'll walk you back.'

'Thank you for... well, for being kind to me last night.'

'It's the least I could have done, May. And you know,' he said, gripping his mug and looking straight into her eyes, 'I would do anything for you.'

May didn't know what to say. No one had ever said anything like that to her before, but her mind was full of thoughts of Ruby. She didn't feel she had room to process what he was saying to her. She just looked back at him and smiled, hoping he would understand.

When she'd finished her tea, Gerald walked her back to her block and up the stairs to the apartment. No one was there and she let herself in with her key.

'Are you going to be alright?' he asked. 'Give me a call if you need anything, or if you just want to talk.'

He scribbled his phone number on a piece of paper beside the telephone, kissed her firmly on the cheek and left.

May wandered round the flat, still in a state of profound shock. In the doorway to Ruby's room she stopped, taking in the devastation that was the result of Ruby trying on virtually her entire wardrobe before being satisfied with what she was wearing. May couldn't go in there. Not yet.

She ran herself a bath and soaked in there for a long time, then dressed in clean clothes and brushed her hair. Just then the doorbell rang.

Mr and Mrs Winter stood on the doorstep, their eyes full of grief, their faces haggard. As soon as she saw May, Mrs Winter burst into tears.

'May, darling.' Mrs Winter stepped forward and flung her arms around May and held her so tight it crushed the breath out of her. 'We weren't sure what had happened to you. I'm so glad you're safe and sound.'

'I'm so sorry about Ruby,' May said. 'I just can't believe it.'

They went into the sitting room and Mr Winter immediately crossed to the drinks tray and poured himself a whisky.

'Do you want anything, Margaret? May?'

They both shook their heads. May couldn't face any alcohol the way she was feeling.

Mrs Winter leaned forward and took May's hand.

'We wanted you to know, that you are welcome to stay here in the flat, my dear,' she said, her voice wobbling. 'For as long as you like. We know you are doing good work with the Ambulance Service and I'm sure Ruby would want you to carry on.'

Mr Winter came and sat on the other side of her. 'The flat is yours for as long as you need it, May. I won't need to stay. I like to travel home after debates. Please accept it, in memory of Ruby. We know she was very fond of you.'

'We can't let Jerry win,' Mrs Winter joined in. 'And you're doing vital war work, my dear.'

May hung her head in shame. 'It's very kind of you, but I can't accept it,' she said. 'It's my fault. It's my fault she died.'

They both frowned. 'How could it possibly be your fault?' Mr Winter asked.

'I left the Café de Paris before she did. I shouldn't have left her there. If I'd insisted she come home with me, she would still be here.'

Mrs Winter wiped her eyes and smiled. She said, 'If I know Ruby, you'd have had a hard time getting her off a dance floor before the last number was over. Please don't blame yourself, May. Nobody holds you responsible one tiny bit.'

THAT EVENING, May steeled herself, pulled on her uniform and went down to the ambulance garage. She had prepared herself to break the news of Ruby's death to her colleagues, but as soon as she stepped inside the common room, and everyone turned to look at her, she knew from their sombre faces that the news must have already reached them.

Jane got up from the table she was sitting at with the rest of May's crew and came and put her arms around May.

'We're all so, so sorry,' she said, tears in her eyes. 'Come and sit down. You shouldn't be at work, you must still be in shock.'

'No,' May said, 'I want to be here. I want to do everything I can to help. If me working means the difference between life and death for someone trapped under a building like Ruby, then I want to work as often as I can.'

'I know what you mean. We all feel that way,' Jane said, 'Only you do need time to grieve.'

May looked at Jane, her eyes pleading. 'Don't send me home. I'd much prefer to be out making a difference to bomb victims than sitting in the flat amongst Ruby's belongings, thinking about her.'

'Alright,' Jane said. 'But make sure you don't overdo it.'

One by one, the members of Ruby's crew came over to speak to May and say how devastated they were at Ruby's loss.

'She was one in a million,' Kenneth, the driver, said. 'She kept us on our toes alright. Always cracking jokes she was, keeping up our spirits. I don't know how we're going to get by without her.'

'Me neither, Ken,' May said, shaking her head, 'me neither.'

May felt heartened by the company that evening. For the first time, she was glad to play rummy and even Monopoly. It made her realise how much these people, from very different walks of life to herself, meant to her. They'd forged a common bond through the experiences they'd shared. And when they heard the drone of bombers overhead and the rumble of the first explosions of the evening in the East End, May felt a tingle of anticipation; a mixture of nerves and adrenaline at what the evening would bring. A few minutes later, Ernie came out of the office with a piece of paper and handed it to Tom.

'East India Dock area. A tenement block nearby has been hit. Many casualties,' Tommy said, looking at the paper. 'Let's get going.'

May ran with the rest of her crew to their ambulance and slid onto the front seat between John and Jane and they roared out of the garage, bell ringing frantically. And as they made their way with dimmed headlights through the streets of the devastated city towards the East End, May said a quiet prayer for the friend who had changed her life, but who she would never see again.

16

MAY

ROSE PARK, 1941

A WEEK LATER, May stood in a pew in Midchester church between her mother and Florence. They all wore black. Her father stood on the other side of her mother. The church was filled with people who'd known Ruby, from schoolfriends to neighbours. There were also several colleagues from the Ambulance Service looking sombre in their uniforms. Looking around at the packed congregation, May realised how popular Ruby had been and how her outgoing, generous personality had touched all those she met.

The organist struck the first few chords of the funeral march, which sent shivers through May. She couldn't remember going to a funeral before, and when she'd entered the church, the sight of Ruby's coffin surrounded by flowers, standing before the altar had shocked her profoundly. Now, she felt Florence's hand take hers and she gripped it hard, biting back tears.

It had been good to see Florence when she'd arrived by bus from Bletchley Park that morning. May hadn't seen her for months. She looked well, and there was something fresh in her eyes, a new confidence about her. May knew that she had something to tell, but was holding back.

Since May had arrived from London two days before, Hadan and Wilhemena had done their best to dissuade her from carrying on with her work, or even from returning to London.

'You should come home, my darling,' Wilhemena had said. 'You've now seen first-hand how dangerous it is there.'

'I saw that the first night of the Blitz,' May said, but all the same she knew what her mother meant.

All those Londoners she'd helped over the past months, all those people she'd dragged from buildings or carried over rubble to the ambulance, had been strangers. However much her heart had gone out to those who had lost loved ones, however much she had been shocked by the things she had seen, Ruby's death had affected her like no other. Losing her friend had left a gaping hole in her life that could never be filled. Since that tragic night at the Café de Paris, the Blitz had become personal.

Hadan hadn't tried too hard to make her come home.

'I can't make you stay here, May, but I wish you would think about the effect all this is having on your mother. You know how she worries.'

'I know, Pa, but I've got to do this. In fact, why don't you speak to Ruby's parents about it? They came to the flat straight from seeing her body and asked me to carry on. How could I refuse? They've even said I can stay in the flat. So I'm doing it for them and for Ruby as much as anything.'

Hadan hadn't tried to persuade her any further and she could tell from his eyes that he had a grudging respect for her tenacity.

The organ music faded away, the congregation sat down on the wooden pews, and the vicar started the service. May found it hard to listen, it all seemed so terribly sad, and it took all her concentration to keep from crying. She thought she'd already done all the crying she could for poor Ruby, but since she'd been home she'd found that wasn't true. She'd been bursting into tears at the slightest thing.

Sitting there, staring at the service leaflet, she thought about

Gerald and what a rock he had been for her since Ruby's death. He'd popped into the flat to see her every day, sometimes staying for a couple of hours, or other times, if he was working, just a short while to check she was alright. He kissed her each time he left, properly, on the lips, but hadn't attempted anything further and they hadn't talked about it. May was glad of that. She already knew that she loved Gerald. It was a slow, steady love that had started as a tiny flame and had grown stronger and stronger each day until it burned constantly in her heart, but she felt too numb and too full of grief to make any commitments at that point.

Gerald had asked if she wanted him to come to the funeral with her, but she'd declined. It was going to be tough enough as it was without the worry of subjecting Gerald to the scrutiny of her parents. She already knew that he wouldn't be good enough for her father. They were so different, and she knew Hadan well enough to realise that he wanted his daughters to marry younger versions of himself. But now, after only two days away from him, she was missing Gerald with a physical ache and was keen to get back to London to see him as soon as she could.

May stood up to sing "All things bright and beautiful", one of Ruby's favourite hymns apparently, although she had such a pain in her throat from her grief that she found it hard to make a sound. After the service, the coffin was carried out into the churchyard and the burial service was conducted at the graveside. May found it hard to watch Ruby's coffin being lowered into the grave, to think that her friend's young body would be underground for the rest of time. After Ruby's parents had thrown flowers onto the coffin, May approached the grave with a red rose. She had to close her eyes, but the tears still oozed out as she threw it down into the grave.

Then, everyone walked the few hundred yards to the Winters' house. It was a large, square, stone-built pile on the edge of town, with huge gardens and a deer park running down to the river. The wake, held in their dining room, felt very awkward, with Mr and Mrs Winter, red-eyed, circulating amongst the subdued mourners, shaking their hands and thanking them for coming.

May stood alone in the corner beside the window sipping tea, while Hadan and Wilhemena talked to the Winters. She was relieved when Florence came to join her.

'This is unbearable,' Florence said, dabbing her nose with her handkerchief. 'I can hardly get my head round it.'

'I know. It's terrible,' May said.

'I'm glad I found you on your own though, May. There's something I want to tell you.'

'I knew it. Go ahead.'

'I'm going to get married.'

May's mouth fell open in surprise. She stared at her sister. 'But you're only twenty-one, Flo. And you've never had a boyfriend in your life to my knowledge.'

'It's a marriage of convenience,' Florence said with an air of mystery.

'But you don't need money, Florence,' May said. 'And you have your own career.'

'It's not for money. It's for a different reason.'

May was all ears. She couldn't get over the surprise of hearing this news. 'What reason?'

Florence cleared her throat, leaned towards May and lowered her voice.

'Well, I'm not sure if I've ever told you this, or if you've picked it up yourself, but I'm not actually... well, I've never been interested in men.'

'So why then?' May began and then the truth of what her sister was trying to tell her began to dawn on her.

Since as long as May could remember, Florence had always been a tomboy. She'd loved dressing in boy's clothes, playing with toy cars, messing about on the estate farms, driving tractors. She'd never been interested in the girlie things like the other sisters. May had put it down to the fact that Florence was so brilliant, she simply didn't have time for that sort of trivial stuff, but now she realised with a shock that it was something different, something deeper.

'You see?' Florence said, watching her face. 'I've met someone at Bletchley Park. Rebecca. She does the same work as me. She's wonderful. Brilliant and beautiful. You should meet her one day... you *will* meet her. But we can't be together. Not properly. It's impossible, it's such a close-knit place, everyone knows everyone else's business. I thought, if I were to get married, it would provide cover for us, and no one would ever guess.'

'Apart from your husband,' May said grimly.

'Ah, well, I have a good friend, Giles Robertson. He knows all about me, and he loves me all the same. He doesn't mind about the way I am or about Rebecca. He's still asked me to marry him.'

May stared at her. It sounded like a recipe for disaster. Giles was surely pinning his hopes on things developing between them despite what he knew about Florence. He was bound to end up heartbroken or, at the very least, disappointed and frustrated.

'Does he know what he's letting himself in for?' she asked.

'Of course. He's not stupid.'

'But have you actually talked about it?'

'Yes. We've gone through it all and he's still keen. Actually... I wasn't going to tell you this, but Giles has a "friend" too. So, you see, it will be mutually convenient.'

May's mouth dropped even further open.

'Have you told Ma and Pa?'

'Yes. They're absolutely delighted. They thought it would never happen. I think they are both secretly relieved. They'll never guess the truth. Not in a million years.'

May didn't reply immediately. She was wondering what they would think if they did know the truth. But still, being in London over the past few months had opened her eyes and broadened her mind and she wasn't shocked at Florence's proposal. What was more shocking in her eyes, was that Florence and Giles couldn't be open about who they were and who they loved.

After a while, she said, 'When's the service?'

'Next month. I was going to ask you to be my bridesmaid, but I'm not actually going to have bridesmaids. We're just going to have a quiet wedding at the register office in Midchester. I hope you'll come.'

'Of course. I wouldn't miss it for the world. But what does Ma say about not having a big church wedding?'

'Well, I think she's resigned to the fact that it's wartime and no one has much time or money. And she had the big wedding with Blanche. Do you remember?'

'How could I forget?' May couldn't help smiling at the memory.

Blanche had been married shortly before war broke out, and Wilhemena had insisted on an elaborate wedding with all the trimmings, even though Blanche's fiancé Conor and his father were anxious to get back to America as soon as they could. The whole thing had been arranged at breakneck speed and at great cost. All Blanche's sisters had been bridesmaids, decked out in pink satin, one hundred guests had been invited, and Blanche had been driven to the church in a coach and four.

'I couldn't go through that, especially not in the circumstances,' Florence said with a wry smile.

They were interrupted by Hadan and Wilhemena who had finished paying their respects to Mr and Mrs Winter and were ready to go home.

'Such a terrible, tragic day,' Wilhemena said, dabbing her eyes. 'It makes me cherish the ones I love all the more. And just to think, it could have been you, too, May.'

'Yes, I know, Ma, but please don't mention that here,' May whispered, tucking her arm into her mother's. 'Shall we go home now?'

The afternoon was drawing to a close and light was draining

from the sky as Barlow, Hadan's driver, drove them home to Rose Park. May stared out at the unspoilt countryside, the crops ripening in the fields, the hedgerows separating the meadows full of wildflowers, the verdant spinneys in the folds of the rolling hills. It was worlds apart from the shattered streets of the capital that she'd made her home, but still she yearned to be back there. Not just because she ached to see Gerald, but because she felt she belonged there now. She had a part to play, she had Ruby's legacy to live up to, and because she knew that what she was doing was making a difference.

17

RACHEL

ROSE PARK, 1980

THE MORNING after the night out in Midchester, Rachel awoke with a headache. She groaned and buried her face back in the pillow, remembering the evening, the exhilaration of seeing Daniel's band, followed by the strange, unsettling conversation with him in the snug of the Brave Old Oak pub. Why had he reacted so strangely when she'd probed gently for information about his father? She hadn't meant to irritate him, but his reaction had only served to pique her interest more. What had he to hide, she wondered. She sighed. There was so much that she didn't know about him and although he was always encouraging her to speak about her family, he gave precious little away about himself and his own background. He was such an enigma and she found it both tantalising and frustrating.

She forced herself out of bed and wandered along to the bathroom to wash. She had a plan for that morning: she was going to confront her grandfather and ask him for permission to go through some of the papers in his office. She would tell him, quite frankly, that she was looking into the history of the family and of Rose Park. Of course, she wouldn't tell him about the photographs she'd seen of him and his brother as very young children, or about the birth certificate of Henry Joseph Rose that she'd found in the records office in the Guildhall.

Just the thought of asking Hadan that innocent question filled her with trepidation, though. She remembered how, when she used to come to Rose Park for holidays when she was little, he would sit behind his desk in the office smoking a cigar and yelling at people down the phone. She realised that he still terrified her, even though he was ninety years old and bedridden. Still, she thought, examining her face in the bathroom mirror, she wouldn't be able to make progress in her search into the family's past unless she had access to all the papers, and Hadan's office seemed to be a likely source of useful information.

May was sitting at the table eating scrambled eggs when Rachel arrived in the kitchen. Just the sight of them made her stomach churn.

'Want some?' May asked between mouthfuls.

'No thanks. I'm feeling a bit dicky this morning.'

'Hangover?'

'Something like that,' Rachel said. 'I think I'll just have a piece of toast and a coffee.'

'Did you have a good time last night? You weren't very late back.'

'The band was really good,' she replied carefully, not wanting to get into a conversation about Daniel.

'It's nice that you're making friends and going out and about.'

Rachel put a piece of bread into the toaster and poured coffee from the pot that May had already made and topped it up with milk from the fridge.

'Is it OK if I go up and speak to Grandad this morning?' she asked.

'Of course. He'd love to see you. He gets quite lonely up there.'

Rachel had only been to see him a handful of times since arriving at Rose Park. She'd found those occasions both stressful and upsetting. It was hard for her to look at him, he was so diminished from the imposing, fighting-fit figure he'd once been, and it was hard too to be reminded of how old and weak he was. But still, she told herself, she should really make the effort to go more often. There was no excuse.

When she'd finished breakfast, she took a deep breath, set off up the stairs and made her way along the corridor to Hadan's room. She knocked on the door.

'Come in,' came the muffled voice.

She opened the door and went inside, closing it behind her.

'Ah, Rachel,' he said, looking up from his chair by the window. 'You haven't been for days. I'd given you up for lost.'

She walked towards him, trying not to register shock at the way he looked, the sunken eyes, the hollowed cheeks, the skin that was yellowing, like parchment. He was worse than when she'd last visited.

'I was wondering, Grandad, if you would mind if I tidied up your office.'

A frown instantly furrowed his brow. 'What the devil for?'

'I thought it might help, but I also ... well, I'm trying to do some research into the history of Rose Park and the family. I thought there might be something useful in there.'

Hadan's face changed colour from white to livid red. He spluttered and then began to cough. He carried on coughing and wheezing for what seemed like an age. Hastily Rachel rushed to fetch a glass of water from the basin and handed it to him. He took a sip and gradually the coughing subsided.

'Family history? What on earth for?' he choked. 'Has your mother put you up to this?'

'No, Grandad... It's my idea. I'm interested in the past, you know that.'

He fell silent then and from his expression Rachel guessed that he was thinking her request over. He was probably sifting through everything in his office in his mind, trying to remember if there was anything in there that he didn't want her to see. Then his eyes widened momentarily, and he started. He leaned forward and fixed her with his most terrifying look.

'I absolutely forbid it,' he roared at her, and she took a step back. 'You must not go in that room and you must not disturb any of my papers. I will know if you have, my girl, so don't you dare defy me. That room must stay exactly as it is until I'm in my box six feet under.'

THAT AFTERNOON AT FOUR-THIRTY, Rachel set off to the Quarryman's Arms, still reeling from her grandfather's outburst. It had made her even more convinced that there must be something in the office he didn't want her to see. Perhaps he already knew about his brother, but didn't want to share that knowledge with the rest of the family.

Her mother had been shocked when Rachel told her how he'd reacted.

'Please don't ask him again, Rachel,' she said, her face even whiter than usual, an anxious look in her pale blue eyes. 'It might send him over the edge.'

'I wouldn't dare!' Rachel said. 'And I wouldn't dare to go anywhere near his office after that either. The trouble is, I'll have to look somewhere else to find out any more about Henry Rose. I've just no idea where.'

Even now, walking to the pub hours later, a shiver went down her spine thinking about her grandfather's face, red with fury.

Jenny greeted her warmly as usual and she set to work cleaning the tables and polishing the glasses.

'I hear you had a good time last night,' Jenny said with a knowing smile.

'The band was great,' Rachel said. 'But how do you know?'

'Oh, Ray was in here at lunchtime. He told me all about it, and that he had to take you home.'

Rachel laughed. 'Yes, Daniel had to take Andy back. His van had broken down.'

'Ray's a good sort,' Jenny said. 'He said he'll be in again later on. It's his wife's bingo night and he likes to have a drink in here when she's out.'

It was around eight o'clock when Ray came into the pub. It was quite busy, a few customers were sitting at tables and others leaning on the bar and there was a gentle hubbub of voices. Most of them greeted Ray with a cheery wave or a pat on the back. He came to the bar and asked Rachel for a pint of Watney's. While she was drawing it, it occurred to her that Ray probably knew more about Daniel than most people and that he could be a useful source of information.

'Thank you again for the lifts last night,' she said, handing him the pint. 'Have this one on me.'

'Thanks, but it was no trouble. I'm always happy to help a friend out.'

'I hope Daniel got home OK last night,' she said. 'I haven't heard from him.'

'Maybe he'll be in later, but I doubt it. When I dropped by earlier on, he said he had a work deadline for tomorrow and he'd be working all evening.'

'Oh well... Ray, there's something I wanted to ask you.'

'Fire away,' he said, sipping his pint.

'Well, I happened to ask Daniel something about his father and he seemed quite annoyed. In fact, I think it might have been the reason he didn't take me home.'

Ray shook his head. 'No. He had to take Andy back. But he can be a moody bugger, I grant you that.'

'So, why would he get so annoyed about it? I just asked him if he knew who his father was, and he sort of clammed up. It obviously rattled him.'

'Yeah, well there's probably some history there,' Ray said, shaking his head. 'He might not want to admit to you who his father was.'

Rachel stared at him. 'Admit to me? Why ever not? Why would it matter to me? Do you know who his father is?'

'I do. And I'm going to tell you in confidence. Because he might not want you knowing, but I don't think it's fair to keep you in the dark.'

'So... tell me.'

'It was someone called Joe Harding,' he said.

'Joe Harding?' She frowned, she knew that name! Her mind cycled back over everything her mother had told her about the war. Then she remembered. Joe Harding, the boy who had shown her mother kindness on the farm, the one Hadan had forbidden her from seeing, the one who had cost May her job at the farm.

'I've heard of him,' she said at last. 'My mother knew him during the war.'

'Well, he's dead now. Died a few years back and it wasn't until after he died that Gill saw fit to tell poor Dan that Joe Harding was his father. He was gutted that he'd never had the chance to get to know him. But Joe was married to someone else. Gillian was just a fling. She didn't want to break up his marriage.'

'But why doesn't Daniel want me to know that Joe Harding was his father?'

Ray cleared his throat and took another sip of his drink.

'Because there's a longstanding feud between the two families I suppose. Goes way back to your great-grandfather's time. I don't know the details, but maybe Danny boy thought that it would put you off him if you knew.'

'But that's ridiculous. What does that matter to me? It's ancient history.'

'I know. It does seem a bit strange, but don't tell 'im I told you, whatever you do.'

Someone else came up to the bar to be served and Ray raised his glass to Rachel and shuffled away to talk to some of the locals.

For the rest of the evening, Rachel had half an eye on the door, but Daniel didn't come in. She wondered when she would see him again and wished she had the courage to find out where he lived and go and knock on his door. But she sensed that he wouldn't like that, and that his mother was a tough customer and might not be very welcoming to a member of the Rose clan.

She was glad when the evening was over, and she could leave the steamy pub and walk home in the cool night air. Her mother was still watching the scratchy black-and-white TV in the drawing room when Rachel got in.

'Would you like a hot chocolate?' May asked, getting up. 'I was going to make one for myself.'

'That would be lovely,' Rachel said, following her through into the kitchen and sitting down at the table.

'You look as though you have a lot on your mind,' May remarked. 'Is Pa's outburst still troubling you?'

'I'd forgotten about that,' Rachel said. 'No, it's something else.'

'You can tell me, you know,' May said, putting the saucepan of milk on the Aga.

So, Rachel told her about Daniel, about how he had taken her out, shown an interest in her, but how he had become rattled when she asked about his father.

'But I found out this evening who his father was. You're never going to believe this, Mum. His father was Joe Harding.'

'Joe Harding?' May's eyes widened in surprise.

'Yes. So perhaps Daniel thought that I might not want to see him because of the antipathy between the families. What do you know about the feud, Mum?'

'Not a lot really, only that it was the reason that my father stopped me working on the farm and forbade me having anything to do with Joe Harding. I know that Joe's grandfather was a union man and that he always made trouble in the quarry, getting the men to strike. Gabriel lost a lot of money through that. I think the animosity stems from that originally.'

'That doesn't sound very bad,' Rachel said. May put the cup of hot chocolate in front of her and she took a grateful sip.

'There was something else too,' May said slowly, as if long-buried memories were returning to her. 'Something that I'm not sure about. Something from around the end of the First World War. I don't know what happened, I just know that there was bad blood between the two families and that it stems from way back.'

'It must have been bad if people are still worried about it to this day,' Rachel said.

'Maybe you're right. But I'm not sure how we might find out more.'

When it was time for bed, it was with great trepidation that Rachel entered her room. She sat on the bed, the image of Hadan's fury still vivid in her mind, and hugged herself at the chill that ran through her. Were there ghosts from the past, living in the walls, here with secrets to reveal? She gave herself a shake before hurrying to the bathroom to brush her teeth.

But there was no feeling of foreboding this time, no apparent change in the light as she got into bed and pulled the covers up.

'Goodnight,' she said before turning off the bedside lamp.

The next morning, thankful for a good night's sleep, she woke early and went down to the kitchen. The questions from the day before were still burning in her mind.

Mrs Allen was at the sink washing up.

'I've already made you some toast and coffee, Rachel,' she said. 'Your mother has had hers and is up seeing to Mr Hadan's breakfast.'

'Thank you,' Rachel said, sitting down. 'I was wondering, Mrs Allen. Do you happen to know anything about the feuding between the Roses and the Hardings?'

Mrs Allen paused, wiping her hands, then said, 'Not a lot. I know that Mr Gabriel and old man Harding didn't get on. But Mr

Hadan and his son, Thomas I think it was, were the best of friends. Served in the First World War together, they did. Only Thomas Harding was killed. I'm not sure what happened after that. The last of the Hardings is dead now. Joe. And he and his wife didn't have any children...'

Just then the doorbell rang and Mrs Allen bustled away to answer it. Rachel could hear raised voices, so she went to investigate.

There in the doorway was Mrs Sutton's daughter. She was holding an old, black-painted wooden box.

'Ah, Miss Heywood,' she said seeing Rachel. 'I asked to come in, but for some reason was being told you were busy. Anyway.' she held up the box. 'I found this in Mum's belongings. It was my grandmother's. It was what she called her insurance policy. There are family papers in here. If you'd like to take a look, I could let you have it... at the right price.'

18

MAY

LONDON, 1941

MAY GRADUALLY SETTLED back into life in Dolphin Square after Ruby's funeral. She missed her friend minute by minute – she hadn't appreciated how much their little routines and constant light-hearted banter had kept her cheerful. Now she was all alone, and when she returned home from a night with the ambulance crew, dealing with death, devastation and horrific injuries, she had no one to talk to about it. Apart from Gerald, of course. But even though he'd told her she could come and see him or call him at any time of the day or night, she felt she couldn't wake him in the small hours when she got back from a shift. So, she had to bear those long nights alone and come to terms with the disturbing things she'd seen.

She and Gerald started to see more of each other from that point onwards. As he'd promised, at weekends, he would take her by public transport, if it was still functioning after the week's bombing raids, to hidden places in London that tourists and newcomers would never have heard of; to Abney Park Cemetery in Stoke Newington, a wooded sanctuary with an abandoned church. They walked between the neglected gravestones peering at the inscriptions, most notable of whom were William and Catherine Booth, the founders of the Salvation Army.

'That's uncanny,' Gerald said, looking at their elaborate gravestones. 'That's how we met – at the Salvation Army tea stall. Do you remember?'

'Of course,' she said, recalling that evening and how she'd immediately warmed to Gerald.

The cemetery was like a wilderness, and May found it hard to believe that it even existed there in the middle of that great city.

On other days, Gerald took her by bus to wander around the street markets in the East End, to eat pie and eels in a café beside Smithfield market, to Columbia Road to buy flowers, and to another cemetery, Kensal Rise, a much grander place than Abney Park, to see the graves of William Makepeace Thackery and Anthony Trollope.

She loved Gerald's company. She felt she could talk about anything with him and that he would never put her down or judge her. This was refreshing after a lifetime of being overlooked or even treated with contempt as the youngest sister. Gerald always took her seriously and respected her opinions. Gradually, as the weeks passed, the pain of losing Ruby was beginning to fade. She would never forget her friend, but her loss was no longer crippling. She realised one night, as she was walking back across the Dolphin Square gardens from a night on duty on the ambulance, that her heart was no longer so heavy with grief.

That weekend, Gerald took her to the Feldman Swing Club in Oxford Street. It was the first night she'd had off from the ambulance station since she'd returned to London from Ruby's funeral. Travelling there on the tube, she looked out at the platforms at people settling down for the night with their blankets and pillows, sheltering from the air raids, and a shiver went through her. The last time she'd set off from Dolphin Square to go to a nightclub was that fateful night of the bombing at the Café de Paris. What if this evening were to end in the same way? She glanced at Gerald sitting beside her. She couldn't bear to lose him as she'd lost Ruby. He'd become the most important person in her life.

The club was in a basement below street level, although May didn't feel reassured by that fact, given what had happened to the Café de Paris that was four floors underground. They went down a narrow staircase into a crowded, smoky cellar where people were dancing the jitterbug on the tiny dance floor to a jazz band playing on the podium.

'I thought that dance was banned,' May said and Gerald laughed.

'The jitterbug? Well, it is in most other places, but it's allowed here for some reason.'

There was something wild and free about the way people were throwing themselves into the dance, flinging themselves and their partners around the dance floor, twirling each other around in circles. It was so different from all the formal dances she'd ever seen before, she couldn't help smiling at the dancers. The sight of them lifted her heart.

'Let's try it ourselves later,' Gerald said.

'You're joking!'

'No, I'm not. But let's have a drink and something to eat first.'

They found a small table in an alcove with a good view of the band. Gerald asked what she would like to drink. She was about to ask for vermouth, but then the thought of it brought nausea flooding into her mouth. That's what she drank that fateful evening and she'd never be able to drink it again without thinking of poor Ruby, crushed under the falling masonry.

'I'll have a gin and tonic,' she said.

The waiter brought their drinks and some bar snacks – soused herrings, pickled onions and some slices of bread. They ate and drank and watched the dancing and basked in the pleasure of each other's company. Then, Gerald ordered more food –

borsch soup and chicken wings with mushroom puree, and sauteed potatoes.

The jitterbug ended soon after they'd arrived, and May was glad about that. She couldn't imagine jumping around after devouring herrings and pickled onions and all the other food she'd eaten. Thankfully, the music moved on to smoother jazz numbers.

'Shall we?' Gerald asked.

They'd never danced together before, and she was surprised at what a natural dancer Gerald was. They moved together as if they'd practiced for years and when she looked up into his eyes, she saw that he was looking down at her with an expression of pure love. He kissed her then, tenderly and lovingly, and held her tight as they swayed and moved together to the sound of the saxophone.

'Will you stay with me tonight?' he asked.

'I thought you couldn't have people in the flat?' she teased.

'No one will know,' he said, stroking her hair.

She didn't have the slightest hesitation about sleeping with Gerald. She knew that Ruby had been careless with her favours, and that it had sometimes made her unhappy. But, despite the age difference, May was quite sure that she loved Gerald and that she could trust him.

'I'd love to stay with you,' she said.

They carried on dancing until the club closed at two o'clock in the morning. May would have happily stayed all night if it had remained open. Down there in the smoke-filled room, with the languid jazz music filling her ears, it was possible to forget the war and the bombings and to enjoy the evening as if everything in the world was normal. The moment she emerged onto the street, and looked around, she knew that the reality of London as it was right then would hit her.

But when the club finally closed and the lights went on, they had to leave. They spilled out onto the pavement with all the other revellers and looked around them. Several of the shops that May remembered her mother bringing her to as a child had been gutted by bombs and their devastated carcases, grey and hollow in the moonlight, were a grim reminder of the war. Gerald took her hand.

'Don't think about it,' he said. 'Let's walk home, if you've got the energy? The tube shut down hours ago and it will take an age to get a taxi.'

So, hand in hand they crossed Oxford Street and made their way down Wardour Street towards Shaftesbury Avenue. A lot of the restaurants and theatres were either boarded up or had suffered bomb damage, but there were still many operating, although at that hour, everything seemed to be closed. There weren't many people around and it felt a little eerie walking through the bomb-damaged city virtually alone. It almost felt as if they'd survived the end of the world.

Piccadilly Circus was silent and dark and they made their way down to Trafalgar Square towards St James' Park. They walked along Horse Guards Road and past the rear entrance to Downing Street. It was shrouded in darkness and guarded by two soldiers with rifles. She wondered if Churchill was sound asleep in No. 10, or in an underground bunker somewhere, safe from the bombs.

At last, after almost an hour of walking, they found themselves striding along beside the River Thames. The bulky form of Dolphin Square eventually came into view. They walked, their hands still entwined, through the portico, and paused in the courtyard garden.

'Were you serious about staying tonight?' Gerald asked and she could hear the need in his voice.

'Of course,' she said, moving closer to him. He put his arm around her, pulled her in close and they walked together towards his block, then in through the entrance and into the lift. Going up in the lift they kissed, and almost didn't hear the bell when it reached the sixth floor.

Gerald's flat was chilly. He pulled the blackout curtains across the windows in the living room and put on a lamp. May blinked in the unexpected light.

'Brandy?' he asked, and she shivered again, reminded of the day Ruby had died when she'd come before. He must have seen her flinch because he said, 'I'm sorry. Something else then. Whisky perhaps, or Amaretti?'

'Whisky please.'

'I don't have ice I'm afraid,' he said, pouring a glass and handing it to her.

He sat down beside her on the settee and they both sipped their drinks. Suddenly May was nervous. She felt very young and very inexperienced, but still she knew that she wanted Gerald, that this felt right. He kissed her then and she put her drink down and responded to his kiss, their tongues meeting and exploring. Gradually, as the kiss became more passionate, she found herself leaning back and lying down. Then Gerald was moving on top of her, pushing the straps of her evening dress down, covering her neck and her breasts in kisses. She unbuttoned his shirt and slid her arms around his back and pulled him closer instinctively and soon, they were moving together as one.

When it was over and he was stroking her hair and looking into her eyes, the shrill of the air-raid warning sounded across the rooftops.

'Oh my God!' Gerald said jumping up and pulling his trousers on. May hastily pulled her dress back up and rearranged her underwear.

'We need to get down to the shelter,' he said.

How could they go down to that smelly shelter in the basement and sit with everyone else talking about the Blitz and the war and the price of butter after what had just happened between them? She wanted to lie with him, to savour the moment.

'No,' said May suddenly. 'I'm not going down there. I want to be here with you.'

He stopped buttoning his shirt and looked down at her and laughed incredulously. 'Are you serious?'

'Yes. I couldn't bear to go down there. Not after... well, I just want to be with you, Gerald. That's all.'

'We'll be taking a big risk,' he said. 'But if you really want to stay, we can.'

'I do,' she said, sitting up and looking into his eyes.

'Alright,' he said. 'Shall we go to bed, then?'

They went into Gerald's bedroom, slipped out of their clothes and got between cold linen sheets and held each other tight. But in that second, through the window came the drone of bombers and the whine of incendiary bombs. The sky was lit up with fire.

'That sounds really close,' said Gerald, getting out of bed and going to the window. 'It's definitely somewhere in Pimlico, or Westminster maybe.'

Within seconds the drone of the engines became a deafening roar and there was an explosion so close and so loud that it rocked the building.

'My God! That's here. They've hit the next door block,' Gerald said.

May got out of bed, pulled a blanket around her and went to the window. Sure enough, the next block along from them, Frobisher Block had a huge, gaping hole in its façade and flames pouring out of what had been the roof a few seconds before.

'We should go and see if we can help,' May said. 'Do you have a jumper or something I could put on over my dress?'

Gerald was already pulling on his clothes. He rummaged in a drawer and took out a grey sweater and handed it to her. May put on her dress and pulled the sweater on over it. Then, they went out onto the landing and ran down the stairs, not wanting to risk the lift in case this block was hit too.

When they went out into the courtyard, May stopped and looked at the building, aghast.

'That's the block above the shelter, isn't it? Frobisher?'

'I think so,' Gerald said grimly.

They rushed towards the burning block and saw that others were running across the courtyard towards it too. She spotted Jane and Tommy from her ambulance crew amongst those rushing to help. Already the tall flames licking roof of the building were being doused by giant jets of water from the other side. The fire crews must have been out on the street that ran along the outside of Dolphin Square within minutes of the blast.

Everyone crowded around the entrance to the shelter. The steps were unobstructed at the top, but a few steps down the front wall of the building had fallen in, blocking the passage below.

An ARP warden who had arrived with the others took charge.

'There are about sixty people in there,' he said. 'We need to dig through that wall and get through to the stairs below to get them out.'

Some of the men scrambled down and started pulling loose bricks away from the entrance to the passage. People quickly formed a line to pass them back up to the top.

'I know where the gardeners keep their shovels,' May said. She remembered Ruby chatting to one of the gardeners one day while he put his tools away.

'Show me,' said Gerald.

They ran to the hut which was tucked away in a far corner of the complex but when they tried the handle it was locked. Without pausing, Gerald kicked the door. It only took a few kicks before it caved in. Although it was dark inside, in the light from the fires, May could see several spades and shovels hanging on the wall. She and Gerald gathered them up and hurried back to the rescue point. The men working to remove the bricks and rubble took them gratefully. They worked more quickly after that and had soon cleared a man-sized hole in the entrance to the passage. Two of them went down and returned a few minutes later helping an injured woman to the surface. Blood was pouring from a wound on her forehead and she looked very shocked.

The men helped her out and sat her down on the lawn. Jane had brought the dressings box from the ambulance and instantly got to work cleaning her wound.

'Do you think the ambulance could come inside the courtyard?' May asked.

'Yes. Go and tell Ernie we need all the ambulances we can get here. As he said, there are sixty people down there. They might all be injured.'

Already there were four or five dazed people sitting around on the grass. Someone had fetched a floodlight and set it up pointing towards the passage so the rescuers were no longer working in darkness. They were working frantically, as quickly as they could. Already there was an ominous smell of escaping gas in the air and everyone was terrified of an explosion.

May ran as quickly as her legs would carry her to the ambulance garage. Ernie had already worked out what was happening, and the crews were assembling in the ambulances.

'There are a lot of injuries in the main courtyard,' May told him. 'The shelter was hit.'

She got inside her own ambulance beside John and they drove in convoy up the garage ramp, round to the front of the building, through the archway and across the courtyard to where all the injured people were sitting in a group dazed and confused.

As May got out of the ambulance and went to fetch a stretcher, she realised that the raid was still going on in the skies above. The drone of German aircraft filled the air, the howl and screech of bombs and the boom of explosions. She hoped against hope they wouldn't hit Dolphin Square again.

For the rest of the night, she worked tirelessly alongside the rest of the crew and the other rescuers, checking the injured, loading them onto stretchers, carrying them to the ambulances and delivering them to St Thomas' hospital across the river. Gerald stayed all night too, helping the ARP wardens bring the injured up the narrow passage to safety.

Finally, when dawn came and the bombing raid was over, over sixty people had been rescued from the basement shelter and taken to hospital. The ARP warden who had been there from the start came to thank everyone.

'Thank you, miss. Your dress looks a bit the worse for wear,' he said and May looked down at her cream-coloured evening dress that was covered in mud and bloodstains, as was Gerald's grey sweater.

'It doesn't matter,' she said. She was just relieved that everyone had survived. What did a dress matter in the face of that?

Gerald came over and put his arm around her. 'If it wasn't for your insistence, we would have been trapped down there, and possibly injured.'

May fell into his embrace. They had been lucky. Very lucky.

'So much for spending the night together,' he said, kissing her hair.

'It's alright, Gerald,' she said. 'There will be other times, I hope.'

'I'll make sure of it, don't you worry,' he said, hugging her tightly.

19

RACHEL

ROSE PARK, 1980

RACHEL STOOD in the hallway of Rose Park staring at Alice Johnson, who stood there holding a battered wooden box, a defiant expression on her face. She was a stout woman, with an unflattering “pudding basin” haircut and an abrasive manner.

‘As I said, it belonged to my grandmother,’ she was saying. ‘It contains some papers that I think your family might be very interested in.’

‘What’s this?’ Rachel heard her mother’s voice behind her.

‘Mrs Johnson thinks we might want to buy the contents of that box,’ Rachel said as May came to stand beside her.

‘I’ve never heard the like,’ Hilda Allen chipped in. ‘You should be ashamed of yourself, Alice Johnson. If your mother knew what you were up to, she would have your guts for garters.’

‘It sounds like blackmail to me,’ May said.

Alice Johnson blinked, her face growing red with outrage.

‘It’s nothing of the sort,’ she said. ‘When you came round to Mum’s house the other day, asking my mother for information, I got to thinking. I remembered this box and I dug it out and had a look through it. What I found in there in all likelihood answers the questions you were asking my mother. But times are hard, so I couldn't possibly let you have this information for nothing.'

'I don't understand,' May said. 'What exactly is in there?'

'Well, I can't tell you that, can I? Not before we've agreed a price.'

May sighed. 'I suppose you'd better come through to the kitchen and we can talk properly.'

They trooped along the passage to the echoing kitchen and sat down around the big, scrubbed table. Alice Johnson looked around her in awe.

'I've never been inside Rose Park before,' she said in reverential tones, 'Now I know what they were talking about. I've never seen anywhere like it.'

'Let's get to the point, shall we?' May said.

Rachel watched her mother admiringly. Often seeming shy and afraid of conflict, there were times when May came into her own and showed that under that mild exterior lurked a strong backbone and nerves of steel.

'The point is,' Mrs Johnson replied, meeting May's gaze, 'that you want to know about a child that was born to your grandparents before your father was born. The answer is inside this box. My grandmother kept some important papers. As I told you before, she was worried about her position after Miss Emily died and she thought she might need a bargaining chip.'

Rachel's heartbeat sped up. Was this true? Was all that was separating them from the truth of little Henry Joseph Rose the lid of that battered box? She wanted to intervene, to say that they would pay whatever Alice Johnson wanted, but she held back, knowing that was impulsive and foolish. It would be better to leave it to May.

'So how much are you looking for?' May got straight to the point.

'I want at least two hundred pounds for it.' Alice Johnson lifted her chin defensively.

May laughed. 'You've got to be joking! I don't have that sort of money.'

'But your father does.'

'I'm not going to trouble him with this,' May said in a steely tone. 'I will give you fifty pounds and that is an end to it. It's all I have.'

The abrasive woman laughed. 'I'll settle for a hundred, no less.'

May sighed. 'I could always have it for free... If I call the police. Once they've arrested you for attempted blackmail, I'm sure they'll be happy to share the contents of the box with me. Take my offer, or I'm picking up the phone.'

Wow, thought Rachel, wanting to applaud her mother.

Alice Johnson's face went red with fury as she considered the offer, blinking quickly. In the end she said, grudgingly, 'Alright. I suppose it's better than nothing.'

'Wait one moment. I will fetch the money. But if I find that there is no useful information in that box, I won't hesitate to call the police.'

Alice Johnson narrowed her eyes and said, 'Oh, I think you'll find that it answers your questions.'

May left the kitchen and Rachel and the two older women sat in silence, listening to her footsteps echoing down the passage, then running up the stairs. The silence around the table was beyond awkward, it was excruciating.

Fortunately, May was back in double-quick time holding a few ten-pound notes. She stood beside Alice Johnson and counted them out onto the table. Mrs Johnson drew in a deep breath, picked them up and put them into her handbag.

'You've got it at a knock-down price,' she said. 'And that proves exactly what the contents of that box proves about your family. That you're all mean-spirited and self-serving.'

'I think you should leave right now,' May said, tight-lipped. 'Mrs Allen, would you please show Mrs Johnson out?'

Alice Johnson swept out of the room, her nose in the air, with Hilda hurrying behind her. May sank down in a chair and put her head in her hands.

'That woman,' she said. 'The cheek of her!'

'You were awesome, Mum,' Rachel said, 'so brave.'

May huffed. 'I don't know about that. I just couldn't back down. Such an awful woman.'

'I know, Mum. She's horrible. But let's not think about her. Shall we open the box?'

'Why don't we take it into the drawing room? I don't necessarily want Mrs Allen to know about it,' May whispered. 'It will be all round the village in a flash.'

May picked up the box and the two of them walked together along the passage, across the hall and into the huge, old-fashioned drawing room, with its hunting prints on the walls. It was still furnished with chintzy cushions and elaborate floral curtains that Wilhemena had chosen in the 1960s. May sat down on one of the wide settees and Rachel sat beside her.

'You open it,' May said putting the box down on the coffee table in front of them. 'I don't think I can.'

Rachel could hardly keep her hands from shaking as she pulled open the lid of the wooden box and peered into it. Inside were three brown envelopes. She took the top one out and studied the post mark. It was stamped from somewhere indistinct in Derbyshire. She looked more closely. Somewhere called Stanley Common. It was addressed in formal handwriting to Mr Gabriel Rose, Rose Park, Perry Cross, Northamptonshire and dated sometime in June 1895.

She pulled a letter out of the envelope and opened it up.

'Shall I read it to you, Mum?'

May nodded.

'*Dear Mr Rose,*

Thank you for visiting Stanley Manor Asylum this week with your son Henry. I have examined the doctors' reports and discussed his case with our resident physician, Dr Ramsay. He is of the opinion that Henry is suffering from grand mal, as your own doctor suggested, and would benefit from long-term residential care here.

I suggest that you bring him and his belongings as soon as you are able. Please send a telegram to let us know when you will be arriving. If you come by train our driver will be able to collect you from Belper station.

I look forward to hearing from you,

Your faithful servant,

Charles Jacobs

Chief superintendent, Stanley Manor.'

RACHEL LOOKED up from the letter into her mother's eyes.

'How terrible!' May said. 'He was ill, so they sent him away. I wonder what in the world happened to him?'

'No wonder Emily died of a broken heart,' Rachel murmured.

'Yes. No wonder. It's incredible. I wonder if Pa knows anything about it?'

'He would have been five when this letter was written, so it's doubtful,' Rachel said. 'Shall I read the next one?'

The next letter was written two years later. Again, it was from Charles Jacobs to Gabriel Rose.

'*DEAR MR ROSE,*

As I mentioned at your last visit, I'm afraid Henry's health is not good at present. And his behaviour when he is well is causing us serious concern. He is often disruptive towards other patients, causing arguments and fights. He was particularly difficult after your last visit when you brought your wife and younger son. He took a long time to settle down and threw numerous tantrums after your departure, obliging us to use restraints upon him.

In view of that, and for the safety of the staff and the other patients, could I please ask that you refrain from bringing other members of your family when you visit in future. I understand that you need to see your son from time to time, but it would be good to keep those visits to a minimum. Say, once every six months?

I look forward to hearing from you,

Your obedient servant,

Charles Jacobs.'

RACHEL FOUND herself stumbling over the words while reading that letter. The tragedy of the whole situation was hard to bear. Looking up at May she saw she had tears in her eyes.

'How terrible…' May said. 'How truly terrible.'

'What is grand mal, I wonder?' Rachel asked.

'It's a serious form of epilepsy, I believe. That was what they called it in those days.'

'So, this letter proves that Grandad must have gone to visit his brother in the home. He would have been seven then.'

'So, he might remember,' May said. 'But if he does, he's certainly never mentioned it. He's kept it a secret for ninety years.'

'I wonder what happened to poor Henry?' Rachel mused, dipping into the box and taking out the third envelope.

There was no letter inside this one. Instead, there was a wad of folded papers and when Rachel opened them out, she saw that they were invoices, brittle and yellowing with age. They were all headed. "For the care of Henry Joseph Rose", and must have been submitted monthly. Various items were listed and itemised on each, including food, laundry, nursing care, doctors' care, medications. The bills all came to around £10 each.

Rachel handed them to May, who studied each one carefully.

'Ten pounds would have been a lot of money in those days,' May said. 'Although Gabriel was a rich man, it would have eaten into his earnings.'

'I wonder what happened to Henry,' Rachel said. 'Do you think he got better and was discharged? If so, he would surely have contacted his only brother.'

She couldn't get over this revelation about her grandfather's family. To have discovered a relative who had been sent away to an asylum simply because they had epilepsy was stunning. How would poor Emily have felt about that? It was interesting that the letters and invoices were all addressed to Gabriel. Although, Rachel reflected, that was probably how things worked in those days. But poor Emily, banned from even visiting her child because her presence unsettled him to such an extent. She must have been devastated. The reasons for her depression and withdrawal from the world were becoming more apparent. No wonder there was a sinister atmosphere in her old room.

'I have no idea what happened to him. I wonder if Stanley Manor is still exists? They might have some records,' May said.

'We could go there, couldn't we?' Rachel said on an impulse.

'I suppose we could. It's probably only an hour or two's drive from here. We could go and see if the place is still open. It would be good to have a day out. And I could tell you more about what I did during the war on the journey.'

'What about Grandad, though?' Rachel asked.

'Well, we need only be gone a few hours. Mrs Allen can manage. If we set off in the morning after I've seen to his bath and breakfast, she can give him his lunch and we could be back for teatime.'

'Alright. As long as we're back by four thirty. I need to work in the pub tomorrow evening.'

'Of course. We'll make sure we are.'

Rachel didn't want to miss her next shift. Tonight was her night off, but there was a chance that Daniel might come into the pub the following evening. She hadn't seen him since the evening she'd gone to see the band at the Brave Old Oak, and she was missing him and beginning to worry that she might not see him again. Added to that, if he did happen to turn up, she wanted to find a way of asking him about the Harding family and letting him know that she knew who his father was, and that it didn't change anything for her.

THE NEXT MORNING, when May came down from giving Hadan his breakfast, she looked pale and careworn.

'He made a terrible fuss about me going out,' she said. 'Honestly, it's like being a prisoner. He wanted to know all about where we were going. I'm afraid I had to make up a little white lie. I couldn't tell him we were going anywhere near Derbyshire or he might have suspected something. I said we were popping into Northampton to buy you some things for when you go to college. I hope that sounds alright?'

'Of course.'

Mrs Allen was keen on finding out where they were heading, too. She asked all sorts of subtle and not-so-subtle questions, but May managed to evade them all.

'We'll be back by four o'clock, I promise,' May said, getting into the car. They drew away and Rachel waved out of the back window to Mrs Allen who stood by the front door, wringing her hands, watching them go. She had clearly realised they were duping her and looked disgruntled.

May drove while Rachel read the map for her. It wasn't far to the M1, the roads weren't busy and they covered the miles quickly. It felt good to be away from Rose Park and Rachel couldn't wait to get to Stanley Manor and see if there were any clues about Henry from almost a hundred years before.

On the way, May told Rachel more about her role on the

Dolphin Square ambulance crew during the war. Rachel was amazed that May had never spoken about it before, but now that she had opened up, she seemed to have remembered everything from every one of those terrible nights – every victim she'd helped, every devastated building she'd visited. Rachel wondered how she would have coped in similar circumstances. She'd never had to face anything remotely like it in her life, and she was a similar age now to the age May had been then. How easy her life had been in comparison. She had been hoping that May would tell her more about Gerald and why their romance had ended, but May said she was saving that until they were back at Rose Park.

They turned off the motorway and headed north, it was only another few miles on the local roads, then they drove into Stanley Common. It was a pretty village with Victorian cottages grouped around a huge village green. There was a little shop on one side of the green. Rachel got out of the car and headed towards it.

The woman behind the counter was very friendly. Rachel bought apples, crisps and some bottles of Coke.

'Do you know where Stanley Manor might be?' she asked.

The woman frowned. 'Stanley Manor? I don't think there's anywhere around here by that name. I'm sorry, love.'

'It used to be a mental asylum, I think. Around a hundred years ago,' Rachel said.

'Well, there is a big place a couple of miles away called the Manor House Hotel. That might be it,' the woman said handing Rachel her change. 'You need to head out of the village that way,' she added, pointing past the green, 'carry on, turn left and it's about a mile along that lane. You can't miss the signs.'

The shopkeeper's directions were accurate. There was a sign to the hotel at the turning, and soon they were heading along a narrow lane towards it. They came to an entrance flanked by red-brick gatehouses with a large sign saying, "Manor House Hotel", and May swung the car through the tall gates. The long, winding drive led through a spinney and over the hill and when they emerged from the wood, they had a view of the grand house at the bottom of the hill. It was a huge, red-brick, gothic pile, with arched windows, and little fairytale towers at either end. It was surrounded by manicured lawns and on one side was a golf course.

The car park in front of the building was full of rather expensive-looking cars.

'Oh dear. Do you think we can park here in a Mini Metro?' May joked, reversing into a space between a Porsche and a BMW.

They walked up the front steps and into the reception hall, where a uniformed receptionist greeted them.

'We have a rather unusual request,' May told her. 'We believe a relative of ours stayed here as a child almost a hundred years ago. Do you happen to know anything about the history of the building?'

'I'm not sure, madam. If you'd like to take a seat, I'll ask the manager to assist you. Can I ask your names please?'

They gave their names, then sat and waited in armchairs around a coffee table, admiring the panelled interior, the stained-glass windows and the well-heeled guests going to and fro. Soon, a grey-haired man in a smart suit came to speak to them.

'Mrs Heywood?' he came up to May and shook her hand, then did the same to Rachel, 'Miss Heywood? I'm David Morrison, the manager here.'

He sat down between them in another armchair.

'I understand you've been inquiring about the history of the building?'

'Yes, we have records from the 1890s that suggest it might have been a mental asylum. Provided we have the right building, that is.'

May handed him one of the invoices and he read it, frowning slightly.

'Henry Joseph Rose...' he said. 'Do you know, that name rings a bell, but I'm not sure why.'

'We believe he was brought here when he was a young child. But we don't know how long he stayed,' Rachel said.

'Yes,' the man said, handing the invoice back to May. 'It was indeed an asylum. Right up until the 1950s. I'm afraid no records remain from that time. The building had been abandoned for ten years by the time the hotel chain bought it. They then gutted it completely,' he said and paused for a moment. Then he went on, 'Ah! I think I know now why that name might be familiar to me. If you follow me, I will show you.'

They followed Mr Morrison through the passageways, tiled with patterned colourful tiles, to a back door and out into a cobbled courtyard. They crossed the courtyard and on the other side was a red-brick chapel.

'This was built in 1840 at the same time as the house,' he said. 'The family who built it were very devout. It is no longer used as a chapel. We use it to house the visitors' creche. I won't take you inside. It can be rather noisy!' he said smiling.

Instead, he opened an iron gate at the side of the building and led them behind it into a small graveyard, shaded by spreading chestnut trees. Unlike the graveyard at Rose Park, this one was well kept, the gravestones were free of moss and the lawn was mown.

David Morrison took them to the far corner of the graveyard and pointed to a simple limestone grave. 'This must be a sad moment for you. I'll leave you alone. I'll be in reception when you've finished,' he said.

Rachel stared at the words engraved on the limestone slab. "*Here lies Henry Joseph Rose, born June 5th 1888, died July 7th 1899. Beloved son of Gabriel and Emily Rose and brother to Hadan. Taken far too young. This stone was hewn from the quarry at his birthplace.*"

'Oh Mum, how sad!' Rachel said, feeling numb with shock.

'He was only eleven. Emily died less than a year after that. She must have just faded away.'

May put her arms around Rachel and they hugged for a long moment.

'What a tragedy. For Emily, for Henry, for all of them,' May said. 'And for poor old Father too.'

20

MAY

LONDON, 1941

BEING with Gerald made it possible for May to bear the horrors of the Blitz. His strength and his calm nature gave her strength too. Without him, she knew that she would have crumbled months before. She never asked him about his work, but sometimes she would catch him frowning, his eyes faraway, or deep in thought. She would ask him what he was thinking but he would never tell her.

'There are things I need to keep to myself,' he would say. 'Things I can't speak about. Some of them keep me awake at night.'

'I wish I could help you, Gerald,' she would say, but she was aware that, however much she got to know him, part of him would always remain an enigma to her. She had to accept that, but for someone so young, it was difficult to come to terms with the fact that the one she loved had to have secrets from her.

After the bombing of Dolphin Square, the air raids intensified in frequency and severity throughout April and May 1941. The night of Wednesday, April 16th was particularly savage. There were so many casualties in London, over 1000 dead and 2000 more seriously injured, May read in the newspapers afterwards, that it became known as "the Wednesday". The newspapers reported that 685 aircraft dropped 890 tons of high explosives and 4200 incendiary bombs. Almost every borough in London was hit.

That night, the air-raid siren sounded around ten o'clock and that was immediately followed by the drone of German bombers and the rattle of anti-aircraft fire. May and her crew were called to several incidents during that night, the first of which was a huge fire in a street in Westminster, a short drive from Dolphin Square. When they arrived, the fire crews were already there, dousing the buildings with their hoses. The hoses were powerful – because of the pressure of the water it took two men to hold one of the large hoses, but it seemed that the whole street was on fire and the desperate attempts of the firemen to douse the flames made little impression on the wall of fire that was consuming the Victorian apartment blocks.

When the crew arrived, the road was awash with water and strewn with burning debris from the building. Firemen were bringing out exhausted, terrified people, mainly women and children, and May and the crew did their best to ease their pain before taking them off to St Thomas' hospital across the river. One woman, a mother of four children, two of whom had choked to death in the smoke before they could be brought out, looked so exhausted and beaten that May feared for her life. She performed mouth to mouth resuscitation on her and when she'd finished, the woman looked up into her eyes and said, 'Hold me.'

May put her arms around the woman, but within a few seconds she felt her body going limp. The life had drained from her. May gasped and slapped the woman's face, felt her pulse frantically, but there was nothing. May had seen a great deal of death and destruction over the past few months, but this young mother dying in her arms shocked her to the core.

She had to carry on, helping to pull trapped people from the burning building, loading them onto stretchers and taking them to hospital in the ambulance. In the small hours, the façade of the building, that had been so weakened by the bomb and the fire, collapsed into the street, with a great rumbling noise that sounded like another explosion. By then, all the casualties had been taken to hospital and only the dead remained under the rubble of the collapsed building.

May and her crew finally arrived back at the Dolphin Square garage at around three o'clock in the morning, but from the drone of aircraft and the constant boom of explosions, and the colour of the sky, it was clear that the air raid was continuing unabated. They cleaned and restocked the ambulance, got cleaned up as best they could in the washroom and drank a welcome cup of tea, but then Ernie came to them from the switchboard, his face white.

'Paddington station's been hit by a parachute mine,' he said. 'It's not on our usual patch, but the crews there need backup. I wouldn't ask, but they're desperate. It sounds serious.'

'It's alright, Ernie. We'll go,' Tommy said, gulping his tea down and standing up. The crew followed Tommy back to the ambulance. They set off through the stricken city, headlights dimmed, bell ringing. Progress was slow. Buildings were collapsing across roads everywhere and they had to reverse up and make many diversions en route.

When they reached Paddington station, the damage the bomb had wreaked was clear to see by the light of the full moon. It had landed partly on the station forecourt and partly on the buildings. There was a huge crater in front of the station and the whole of the front wall of the station building was blown out. Piles of rubble shrouded in clouds of dust were all that was left.

The crew left the ambulance alongside several others parked up in front of the bombed-out building. They took two stretchers and went inside the station.

May looked round at the devastated station building with a sinking heart. Surely many people must have died here. The station was kept open at night and it was often busy into the small hours. One of the platforms had been reduced to rubble by the blast, but others were still open, and she was astonished to see passengers seated on benches on the platforms, still waiting for trains.

An ARP warden approached them. 'It's the waiting room on platform 1. It collapsed when the front of the building was bombed. There are several people trapped inside. We've got rescue workers pulling them out right now.'

They followed him to the front of the building where an entire wall had collapsed in on itself. Rescue workers had already dug a hole in the rubble and were bringing out survivors. May was shocked at the state of them, most were bleeding profusely, some were unconscious, but then Jane touched her arm and said, 'Those ones weren't so lucky,' and May followed her gaze to a dark corner of the station where rows of bodies, their faces covered by coats lay.

There were several other ambulance crews there, waiting to take survivors to hospital. May and her crew worked tirelessly all night, helping the rescuers bring out those trapped in the collapsed waiting room. It must have been very crowded when the bomb had hit, May thought. Most of the survivors had severe cuts and bruises, many had head wounds, and some had broken limbs. One man's leg was severed at the knee, and another had such a deep wound to his stomach that he was bleeding to death, fading away before their eyes. Jane quickly stemmed the flow of blood with bandages and they loaded him into the ambulance.

Once the survivors were clear of the rubble, the crew cleaned and patched up their wounds, and ferried them to the nearby Hammersmith hospital. May sat in the back of the ambulance with the patients, holding their hands and talking to them, trying to stop them losing consciousness. Several didn't make it, dying in the back of the ambulance during the journey and on more than one occasion, May found herself arriving at hospital, holding the hand of a dead person. After the experience of watching the young mother die earlier that night, this left her dazed and confused and feeling lower than ever.

When they finally arrived back at Dolphin Square it was daylight. May felt exhausted and drained, her body was weak and she ached all over, almost as if she'd been in a fight. That night had taken it out of her like no night before it.

She couldn't bear to go back to an empty flat, so she made her way to the 6th floor of the opposite block and knocked on Gerald's door. When he opened the door and saw her standing there, bloodied and filthy and white-faced, he gathered her in his arms, took her inside and plied her with brandy as he'd done once before. Then, they went to bed and held each other tight until Gerald's alarm went off at seven thirty.

She didn't want to let him go, but she knew she had to. He slid out of bed and went to the bathroom.

When he came back, she lay there and watched him dress, pull on his pants, then his white shirt and button it up, then his suit trousers, securing them with navy braces. She loved watching him. She was getting to know his little mannerisms and habits and they endeared him to her even more. And he looked even more handsome than ever, in his smart suit and tie.

'Are you going out today?' she asked.

'Yes. I have to go into work for a meeting. But you can stay here. Just remember to pull the door firmly shut when you leave. It will lock itself. Oh, and don't tell a soul you've been here.'

'Alright,' she said. After he'd closed the front door, she turned over and went back to sleep.

She was woken mid-morning by hammers and drills in the block opposite. They were already repairing it after the bomb damage last month. She went to the window and stood behind the curtain to take a look. The building was covered in scaffolding and a hive of activity. Watching the builders out there working hard to repair the damage wrought by the bombers, it struck her how resilient this city was. Everywhere there had been damage, the very next day a clean-up operation was started and where possible, buildings were shored up and repaired. If they were beyond repair they were quickly demolished. Londoners were determined not to let the bombing beat them. It made May feel a little better, watching the activity. It gave her hope. She hadn't been able to save everyone, but there had been many survivors last night, and without May's crew more would have died.

She moved away from the window and as she did so, she knocked a book off the sill. It was *1984* by George Orwell that she knew Gerald had been reading recently. She picked it up to put it back and a letter fell out. There was no envelope, and it was a handwritten note. It was only a page long. She knew it was wrong to read it, but her eyes were drawn inexorably to the flowing handwriting. It was dated April 10th 1941, and what she read blew her world apart.

Dearest,

I know things weren't good between us before you left but I miss you and I wish you would come home. I am doing my best to face my demons as you call them, but it is even harder without you here. I wish you would just come down and we could talk it over sensibly,

Your ever loving,

Helena

May read and re-read the note several times over, until the implications of it sank in. She went over to the bed, sat down and let the tears come. She sobbed her heart out. What had she done to deserve this? Gerald had seemed the most trustworthy, truthful of men and she'd thought she could let herself love him without fear of getting hurt. How wrong she had been. This letter was proof that he was either married, or heavily involved with another woman. How could he have done this to her?

When she stopped crying, she let out an angry roar which made her feel a little better. Then she dressed in her filthy uniform as quickly as she could, found a paper and pen on Gerald's desk in the living room and wrote him a note, which she left on the kitchen table. Then she left the flat, banging the door shut behind her.

Dear Gerald,

I know about Helena. You have broken my heart. Don't try to contact me. I don't want to see you again.

May.

21

RACHEL

ROSE PARK, 1980

ALL THE WAY back to Rose Park from Derbyshire in the car, Rachel and her mother talked about their extraordinary discovery at the Manor House Hotel. They were deeply saddened by what they'd learned, both trying to come to terms with the secret that Hadan had kept from the family for his entire life.

'What a terrible decision Gabriel made, to send his own son away, to banish him, simply because of his condition,' May said. 'And poor, poor Emily. Perhaps she tried to resist, but was overruled.'

'Do you think we should tell Grandad that we know about what happened to Henry?' Rachel asked. 'I mean, he might feel better about it if he knows that it's all out in the open.'

'I'm really not sure,' May said, shaking her head. 'He could have told us about it at any time, and he chose not to. But I wonder why? Why was it such a secret?'

Rachel thought for a moment. 'In those days an illness like that might have been regarded as a source of shame,' she suggested. 'Gabriel might have thought that it was some sort of judgment on him, a stain on his family. We know he had a temper and that he was a proud man. It was probably him who wanted to keep it a secret.'

'Yes, and perhaps Pa just carried on keeping the secret because he was so ashamed of what his father had done. Or perhaps it was simply too painful for him to talk about.'

'Maybe,' Rachel agreed.

'It would be good to understand more about it,' May said. 'I will try to think of a subtle way of introducing the subject to Pa.'

By the time they arrived back at Rose Park, it was mid-afternoon and Rachel had to rush to get ready for her shift at the pub. She put on some tight jeans, an embroidered white cotton top, then sat down at the dressing-table mirror in the Pink room, put gel in her hair and brushed it to give it more volume, before paying particular attention to her make-up. If Daniel did happen to come in to the pub that evening, she wanted to be looking her best.

She was walking along the village street towards the pub, as usual enjoying the beauty of the late afternoon and the birdsong in the trees and hedgerows, when she heard the sound of an engine behind her and the toot of a horn. She turned to see Daniel driving towards her in his van. He drew up beside her, stopped the van and wound the window down.

'Hey, Rachel. How are you?'

As usual, she was struck by his good looks. He was smiling at her, and his smile seemed so genuine she couldn't help smiling back.

'I'm fine thank you.'

'Look, I'm sorry I haven't been around much lately. I've been busy at work. But we've got another gig tonight. Do you fancy coming along?'

'Alright. Where is it?'

'It's actually at the Barley Mow, where we went to play pool the other week.'

'OK. That would be great,' she said.

'I'll be able to take you there in the van this time. Our set's not on until eleven. What time do you finish at the pub?'

'Ten thirty.'

'OK. I'll be in the Quarryman's then. See you later,' he said with another broad smile then drove away, leaving Rachel with her thoughts scattered and her emotions in a turmoil.

Much as she was attracted to Daniel and was flattered by the attention he was paying her, she was still slightly wary of him. He hadn't been in touch since that evening at the Brave Old Oak and if he was genuinely interested in her, surely he would have been? Perhaps tonight was the night to tell him that she knew who his father was? Although she would have to work out a way of doing that without betraying Ray's confidence.

The pub was quiet that evening and the time dragged. Rachel found herself clockwatching until the hands of the clock finally crawled round to ten twenty-five and then her eyes were glued to the door. Daniel came in just after ten thirty, came up to the bar and kissed her on the lips. Again, she felt herself blushing. She was sure that a hush had descended on the room and that everyone had turned to look at them. Jenny came over and said, 'Hey, lover boy, leave my barmaid alone, won't you?'

'Come on, Jenny!' he laughed. 'It's the end of Rachel's shift. I'm taking her off to another gig.'

'Well, you be careful, won't you,' she said.

'Always,' he replied with a wink.

Rachel collected her bag and jacket and joined Daniel, then they walked out to the van together.

He drove quickly and skilfully through the lanes, and they didn't speak for a few minutes. Then he said, 'Look, I'm sorry I was a bit offish the other night. I didn't mean to be. It's just that I'm a bit sensitive about my dad. I didn't know who he was until recently. I'm just getting used to it.'

'It's fine,' she said, wondering how she was going to get him to admit that his father was Joe Harding.

'So, are you going to tell me who he was?' she asked.

'It won't mean anything to you,' he said. 'You aren't from the village.'

'It might. Try me.'

'OK. If you insist. His name was Joe Harding. Now does that mean anything to you?'

Rachel was taken by surprise. She hadn't expected him to come straight out with it like that. Perhaps it wasn't such a big secret after all.

'I have heard that my great-grandfather had some sort of feud going on with the Hardings. But I don't know what it involved. That's all. Do you know anything about it?'

'Not really, no. It was a long time ago. But I do know that your grandfather and mine served together in the First World War. So perhaps the rift had healed by then.'

'Maybe,' Rachel said uncertainly, remembering how her mother had told her that Hadan had forbidden her from working on the farm where Joe Harding was working in 1940. There must have still been animosity then, but she didn't want to mention that to Daniel for some reason.

They had reached the next village now and Daniel had slowed down and was looking for a parking place near the pub. He finally found one and manoeuvred into it.

'Come on,' he said, smiling at her. 'Let's go and enjoy ourselves instead of raking over ancient history.'

He got out of the van, opened the rear doors and started unloading the equipment for the gig.

'Do you want to meet me inside the pub? The rest of the band should be there already.'

'OK. Do you want a drink?' she asked, and he shook his head.

'I'll wait until after our set for that.'

She went inside the pub alone, feeling a little self-conscious, but as soon as she stepped through the door, Andy came over to her. 'Hi, Rachel, nice to see you again. Do you want a drink? Is his lordship here yet?'

She laughed. 'Yes please. A gin and tonic if that's OK? And yes, he's just getting his stuff out of the van.'

Daniel appeared after a few minutes and the band set up in a corner of the bar. There were fewer people here than had been at the Brave Old Oak. Rachel found herself a seat and sipped her drink.

They played their set, starting with a medley of songs from the seventies and moving on to that year's hits. Once again, she was impressed by their versatility and skill. She hadn't seen many live bands, but they made a good job of sounding equally convincing when playing "Mr Blue Sky" by the Electric Light Orchestra as they did when playing a hit by The Jam or David Bowie. The audience were as enthusiastic as the previous time, and Rachel found herself clapping and cheering at the end of each number.

When they'd finished, they came to join her at the table and the landlord brought them pints on the house. Everyone was in jovial mood. Two other girls came over and were introduced as Caroline and Sally; they were Tim and Andy's girlfriends. They sat either side of Rachel and she was pleased not to be the only female in the group. Everyone chatted amiably for half an hour or so, then Daniel said, 'I think we'd better hit the road. I've got work in the morning. Rachel, shall we go? I'll take you home.'

She waited until he'd collected his equipment from the corner of the pub, then said her goodbyes and went out to the van with him.

'Do you mind if we take a slight diversion?' he asked. 'I need some petrol for the morning.'

'Of course not,' Rachel said. She didn't feel tired. The gig had stimulated her. She felt alive and full of energy. He started up the van and they moved off.

'Do you mind if I smoke?' he asked. 'I always feel like one after a gig.'

'Of course not.'

'Do you want one? Come to think about it, I've never seen you smoke.'

'I do have the odd one at parties sometimes,' she admitted. 'I wouldn't mind one now.'

He stopped the van and got a packet of No 7s and a lighter from his pocket. He lit a cigarette and handed it to her. Then he lit one for himself and set off again. Rachel wound the window down and took a long drag on the cigarette. She hadn't smoked for a while. It felt good, the relaxation spread through her body straight away, but she was glad she'd managed to resist the urge to take up the habit full time.

They didn't speak as Daniel drove towards the main road. Then he turned towards Midchester and drove the couple of miles to the petrol station. He pulled in under the glare of the neon lights. He got out to fill the van up with petrol and stubbed his cigarette out. Rachel realised that hers had gone out. She'd have to wait until Daniel came back with his lighter. As Daniel filled up, she thought there may be a spare lighter in the glove-box. As he walked across the forecourt to the kiosk to pay, she opened it up and a wad of papers fell out onto her lap. She picked them up and was about to put them back when she happened to glance down at one of them.

A bolt of shock went through her. It was a copy of her grandfather's birth certificate, then she looked at the next one, that was a copy of his marriage certificate to Wilhemena. Her heart beating fast, incredulous, she carried on leafing through the papers. There were copies of birth certificates and marriage certificates for the entire family, then there were newspaper clippings about the quarry, about how Hadan had sold it to a big mining company after decades of family ownership. There were also newspaper articles about Rose family weddings and births and other family events. She was staring down at the last of these in disbelief when she heard Daniel's hand on the door handle.

She turned to look at him, white-faced.

'What on earth is all this?' she asked.

His face changed from smiling to ugly anger in a flash.

'What the hell were you doing nosing around in my glovebox? Those are private papers.'

She stared at him, anger boiling up inside her now. 'These are all about my family,' she shouted. 'What are you playing at, Daniel? Is this why you've been taking me out? So you can get information about my family? Why would you need that?'

'No... no. It's not like that at all,' he said. 'I was doing a piece for the newspaper. Local history. Your family is the most prominent family in the village. I wanted to write an article about them.'

'Bullshit!' she said. 'If you were doing that, why didn't you just ask me? I would have happily told you everything I knew. Why be so secretive about it? You've really blown it now.'

'Look, you don't have to believe me, but it's the truth.'

She looked him in the eyes, tears clouding her own vision, but she held them back. He was looking at her with his most appealing look, as if he really cared about her, but something told her it was all a sham.

She steeled herself. She shouldn't have trusted him, and she mustn't fall into his trap again.

'I don't believe you. You're up to something and it involves my family. I'm not going to fall for your bullshit anymore. Take me straight home,' she said as coldly as she could.

Daniel drove her home in strained silence and when he pulled up outside the gates of Rose Park, she jumped out of the van.

'I'm sorry, Rachel,' he said. 'Don't let's part like this. Can't you forgive me?'

She looked at him again, thinking about the kisses they'd

exchanged in this very spot on that first evening, how thrilled she'd been at his touch, but how all that pleasure had dissipated in a few lightbulb moments.

'Just leave me alone,' she said. 'I don't want to see you again.'

She slammed the van door and ran down the drive without a backward glance. She heard the van skid as it turned round then roar away up the lane and as she ran, she thought about her mother and Gerald and the parallels between their two situations.

22

MAY

APRIL,1941

Two days after "the Wednesday" when May had fled from Gerald's flat having read the letter from Helena, she took the train to Wolverton en route to Rose Park for Florence and Giles' wedding. She was glad now that she hadn't asked Gerald to accompany her to the wedding. If he'd received an invitation, questions would inevitably have been asked as to why he didn't arrive with her. She'd been in two minds whether or not to invite him before her earth-shattering discovery. But just as she had at Ruby's funeral, her instinct had been to keep their relationship a secret, not to subject him to Hadan's scrutiny and to the inquisitive gaze of the rest of the family. She knew they would judge him, that they felt they could because she was the youngest child and they thought she couldn't be trusted to make her own decisions.

She felt lonely and distraught on the train journey from Euston, going over and over the traumatic conversation she'd had with Gerald the previous evening. He'd come up the stairs to the flat at around six o' clock and knocked loudly on the door. She'd tried to stand firm and ignore him, but he'd carried on knocking and calling through the letter box until she'd given in and opened the door to him. She did it partly because she didn't want the neighbours to complain to Ruby's father.

'We have to talk, May,' Gerald said when she opened the door. 'Can I come in?'

She held the door aside, her heart pounding. She was so drained and low from the terrible night with the ambulance and the discovery of Helena's note that she felt she had no resources left to deal with him.

'I don't know what there is to say,' she said, and they both sat down on opposite sides of the living room, staring at each other.

'I owe you an apology,' he said. He looked as drained as she felt, white-faced and distraught.

'I should have told you, May, but I simply didn't know how. I was trying to find a way, but the longer we were together the harder it seemed to be, and the deeper I fell in love with you the more difficult it became.'

'So, what is there to tell? You're married. That's all there is to it. I trusted you, Gerald, and you deceived me. I won't ever be able to trust you again.'

'But you can trust me, May. I love you and I'm so, so sorry. Let me explain about Helena.'

'Go on.' She wanted to hear what he had to say, but she couldn't imagine that anything he said would make her any less angry or humiliated than she felt at that moment.

'I met her at Oxford. She was attractive in a flamboyant sort of way – a party girl, always the centre of attention, always with a host of admirers, but she chose me, and I was flattered. We courted for a few months towards the end of the third year. She was studying languages. After the exams, she told me she was pregnant. I was flabbergasted. I thought we'd been careful, but of course, I did the honourable thing and asked her to marry me. As soon as we were married, she told me the baby wasn't mine, it was one of the fast set, one of the rich, titled, braying idiots she used to hang around with.

'She said there was no chance of her marrying him. I was devastated, May. She'd used me. But a few weeks after that, she lost the baby. She was so cut up about it that she started to drink heavily. She'd always been a social drinker but after that she started to drink on her own. She would drink all day when I was out at work, and when I came home, she'd often be out cold surrounded by empty bottles. I lost track of the number of times I called an ambulance to take her to hospital. That went on for a couple of years, then I couldn't stand it anymore. I told her that if she didn't stop drinking, I would leave her. She tried half-heartedly for a while, but it didn't last, so in the end I did leave. An opportunity came up at work to stay in the flat in Dolphin Square on a surveillance exercise, so I jumped at it.'

May looked at him, at his open, honest face, and a chink of pity opened up in the wall of resentment she'd built around herself that day.

'You still should have told me, Gerald. At the beginning. I might have understood then. But not now. It's too late now.'

'Don't say that. Please don't say that. I love you, May, you know that. More than anything. I would have asked you to marry me already but for... but for...'

'But for the fact you already have a wife,' she couldn't resist saying.

'I'm going to divorce her. She will never change. She's never really acknowledged she has a problem. It's been over between us for a long time.'

May stared at him, self-pity welling up inside her. How could she have been so trusting? Perhaps her family were right. Perhaps she wasn't capable of making her own decisions. This was the only real one she'd ever made and what a monumental mess she'd made of it.

'If you need time, take as long as you like. Just tell me that you won't cut me off before you've thought about it properly. I have some assignments to go on for work over the next few weeks. Why don't you think about it while I'm away?'

'Assignments?' she asked, but she knew he couldn't and wouldn't tell her more. 'Lying comes easily to you Gerald, doesn't it?' she burst out. 'You lie all the time for your work, so lying in your private life must have been just as easy.'

He shook his head. 'No! No. I hated lying to you. It was agony for me. But as I said, I just couldn't find a way of telling you. I'm so sorry, May. Please forgive me.'

She looked at his earnest face, his eyes full of love for her and she felt her wall of reserve crumbling.

'I will think about it. But I can't promise anything. I might just find it too hard to forgive you.'

'Thank you. You won't regret it, I promise you.'

She was silent, wondering if she'd made the right decision.

'I will come and see you when I get back,' he said. 'It will be in mid-July. In the interim, the War Office will probably give up the lease on the flat, so why don't we agree to meet somewhere else? How about on the steps of the Tate Gallery? It's close to where we first met. I will write to you with the exact date I'll be back. If you need me, you can write to me at this address.'

He took a card out of his pocket and handed it to her. She glanced down at it and saw that it was a PO Box number.

'Alright,' she agreed reluctantly, already berating herself for being weak. It would have been far better, she told herself, to have ended it there and then, rather than to have this ongoing, tenuous arrangement dragging her down. But still, looking at him, she knew she still loved him and it would take a lot for her to stop.

Looking out of the train window at the rolling countryside, she saw the familiar sights of the outskirts of the little railway town of Wolverton, the train sheds, now munitions factories, and the streets of red-brick houses. The train crossed the water meadows where cattle grazed and waterbirds waded, rattled across the bridge over the River Ouse and then puffed into the station with a blast of its horn.

May gathered her bags and got out of the carriage and looked around. At first, she thought no one had come to meet her, but when the steam cleared from the platform and passengers began to move away from the train, she was surprised to see Wilhemena standing there at the bottom of the station steps. May's heart surged with joy to see her mother. She hadn't realised how much she'd missed her, and she ran forward and flung her arms around her. Wilhemena looked mildly surprised at such a display of affection.

'I didn't want to trouble Barlow,' she said. 'So, I came myself. Honestly, May, I'm quite glad to get away. My nerves are worn to a frazzle by this wedding already. Florence is being very bossy about arrangements.'

'Really? You do surprise me,' May said with laughter in her eyes.

She walked beside her mother to the car and got into the passenger seat.

'So, how are things in London, May?' Wilhemena asked as she started the engine. 'The papers yesterday were full of terrible news.'

'I know. Yes, I was on duty. It was... it was very shocking.'

'You don't have to do it, you know, my darling.'

'Yes, I do, Ma. We've been through all this before.'

'Alright. I won't go on.'

Wilhemena drove on, quickly and erratically as she always did, overtaking a builder's truck before swinging quickly back onto her own side of the road just as another lorry came around a bend.

'I'm so pleased Florence is settling down at last,' Wilhemena said brightly, changing the subject. 'Giles seems such a steady chap. And so good-looking! But what about you, May darling? Have you met anyone down in London?'

May looked at her mother's profile. At her perfectly coiffed hair, her silk blouse and matching pearl earrings and necklace. She was almost other-worldly, May decided, in that she'd never had to work or live anywhere other than in rambling country houses, served by a multitude of staff. She took it all for granted and anything remotely out of place in that perfect, peaceful existence worried her terribly. May knew that Wilhemena would never understand about Gerald. She would blame May herself for getting involved with a married man, rather than offering her sympathy. So, just as Florence had decided to hide her true preferences from her parents, May decided that she would never be able to tell them the truth about Gerald.

'No one special, I'm afraid, Ma,' she sighed.

'Oh, May darling. What an awful bore for you. I was hoping that the horrors of the Blitz might at least have been compensated for by some thrilling wartime romance.'

'Sadly not,' May said and looked out of the window at the familiar, rolling fields.

They were almost at Rose Park now and all these fields belonged to her father, as did the cattle in them and the honey-coloured farm buildings nestling in the valley. She was happy to be home, in that old, familiar world, unchanged for centuries, untouched by the war.

FLORENCE AND GILES' wedding at Midchester Register office went off without a hitch. It was just as Florence had wanted it. There were a few friends she'd made from Bletchley Park, others from her university days in Cambridge and a couple of old school-friends. Equally, Giles had invited a similar number of family members and close friends. Florence wore a simple grey suit and hat and Giles a morning suit with a chrysanthemum in his buttonhole. He was indeed very good-looking – tall, with intelligent dark eyes and wavy dark-brown hair.

Everyone went back to Rose Park where Wilhemena had laid on a buffet in the drawing room. It was a beautiful spring day and the French doors were flung open to the terrace. Everyone got mildly drunk on local beer. May looked around for Rebecca, but she clearly wasn't there. When she and Florence found themselves alone in the kitchen at one point, May asked about her.

'You don't expect her to come to this charade, surely?' Florence snapped.

'What does she think about it all?' May found herself asking. She didn't want to hurt Florence with her questions, but she was genuinely interested.

'She thinks it's a convenient smokescreen. Which is exactly what it is.'

'I'm sorry, Flo, I didn't mean to upset you. I'm just curious.'

'Don't worry. I shouldn't have snapped at you. The truth is, I feel a bit on edge. Things are very tense at work and... well, neither Ivy nor Blanche is here and that's a bit sad. This wretched war, May!'

'I know. It sometimes feels as if the world has turned upside down,' May replied.

There must have been something in her tone that caused Florence to frown and look at her closely.

'Is everything alright with you, May? You're looking a bit peaky.'

May dropped her gaze to the floor. She desperately wanted to confide in someone about Gerald, but now wasn't the time to tell Florence. Whatever the circumstances, it was Florence's wedding day after all. It wouldn't be fair.

'I've seen some terrible things with the Ambulance Service,' she said. 'It takes a bit of getting over.'

'I'm sure it does.' Florence stroked her cheek. 'Poor you. You're very brave. You know you can always come to me if you ever need to talk about anything. Anything at all. I know Mother isn't much good like that and with Ivy and Blanche abroad we only have each other now.'

'Thank you, Florence,' May said and they hugged briefly.

'Now, I need to be getting along. Giles and I need to be heading off very soon. The story is we'll be going off to some hotel somewhere, but in actual fact we're going home to Bletchley Park and we'll have a quiet celebration in the pub there with Rebecca and Robert. Take care, won't you, my darling.'

'Yes. You, too. Thank you, Flo.'

Florence rushed off to find Giles and soon everyone was gathering outside the front door to wave them off in Giles' Triumph Roadster. May stood and waved along with everyone else.

Florence knelt up on the front seat and waved to much clapping and cheering. As Giles accelerated away down the drive, her hat flew off and landed on the gravel, much to the hilarity of the guests. They didn't bother to turn round and go back for it, so May wandered down the drive to pick it up. It was bottle green with blue feathers and looked like an exotic bird resting there. She picked it up, stroked the feathers and thought about her sister. How brave she was, and how resourceful, taking this opportunity to make the best of her situation. From what she'd seen of Giles, she was sure that their friendship was a happy and supportive one and she was glad for Florence that she had such a good friend. She hoped that they would be able to make their unconventional arrangement work.

She walked back towards the house, watching the wedding party standing on the steps. Wilhemena and Hadan stood beside the door, chatting to Giles' parents, while the guests milled back into the house for more drinks. From where she stood, it could have been a scene from any country wedding. She wondered how many of the guests knew the surprising truth.

23

MAY

LONDON, 1941

THE DAY AFTER THE WEDDING, May went back to London and the chilly, empty flat in Dolphin Square. She felt lonelier than she'd ever felt before. She missed Ruby more than ever now. She missed her cheerful companionship, her quick sense of humour and her positive attitude to even the bleakest of situations.

She tried to imagine what Ruby would have advised her about Gerald, but she just couldn't. Her situation was so outside the realms of either of their experiences that she simply couldn't think of what Ruby might say. Ruby's own dalliances had all been with eligible officer-types, some of them caddish and arrogant, but none of them married. Thinking it over, she realised that Ruby had never got to know Gerald, although May had told her all about their meetings. Ruby had been sceptical.

'He sounds quite interesting, May, a bit of an enigma, perhaps. But are you quite sure he's your type?' she'd said once.

'What is my type though?' May answered. 'I'm not quite sure myself. But I *am* sure that my type is probably not your type,' and Ruby had laughed heartily and agreed with her.

If Ruby had known he had a wife drinking herself to death somewhere in the suburbs, she would have probably advised

May firmly against having anything to do with him. But even though May now had the benefit of hindsight, she didn't think she would have done anything differently since she'd first met Gerald. She was relieved in a way that he had gone away, it made things easier, but she did miss him. She missed his comforting embrace when she came home after a rough night and she missed his passionate kisses, but she also missed his friendship and his company. She'd grown to rely on it since Ruby's death, far more than she'd realised.

On the Monday evening, she put on her uniform and went back to work, taking her place at the table in the common room with the rest of her crew. For the next few hours, they chatted and played cards as usual to pass the time. Looking round at their faces though, May could see that, like her, they were all on tenterhooks, waiting, listening out for the tell-tale wail of the air-raid siren followed by the drone of enemy aircraft and the ack-ack of anti-aircraft fire.

She realised, looking at the familiar faces of the crew, that she knew them all very well now. Tommy, a former soldier, discharged from the army on health grounds, thin and nervy, with his anxious smile and dark hair slicked back with Brylcreem. John, portly, balding and friendly, a former butcher by trade. And diminutive Jane, with her short, dark curls, a no-nonsense nurse. They'd been through so much together, and they were bound by those shared experiences, almost like family, even though they all came from such different backgrounds.

May wondered if she could confide in any of them. They all knew about Gerald, from the odd comment she'd dropped, although they didn't know his name. They joshed her gently about him, always referring to him as 'May's fancy man' or 'Mr Rose'. She decided she couldn't bring herself to tell them about the rift. She would rather keep the information to herself. She didn't want to look weak; confidence and strength were important qualities for the ambulance crew. So, she battled on, forcing a smile when they joked about her lack of prowess at cards and joining in with the general banter just as she normally did. But inside, her heart was bleeding and she would have loved to be able to let her guard down for just a moment and allow the tears to fall.

That night was the first time for weeks that they hadn't been called out to a raid. As the evening wore on, the others told her about Saturday when the bombing had been almost as heavy as on "the Wednesday". Again, May had read about it in the paper on the way back to London on the train. Over 1000 tons of high explosive were dropped on London, including 250 parachute mines and over 150,000 incendiary bombs from 783 sorties by the Luftwaffe.

'We were called to a street in Kennington where some houses and a church had taken a direct hit,' Tommy told May. 'There were people trapped down in the cellar. ARP wardens did their best to get to them, but when they finally dug deep enough, there was no one alive, they just found bodies,' he said, shaking his head. 'There was a gas leak, so that must have been what killed them.'

'Then we had to go to Waterloo Bridge. That had been hit too,' Jane said. 'There were people trapped on the bridge in buses and cars. Fortunately, only with superficial wounds. We managed to get them all to hospital.'

'It was scary, though,' John put in. 'The raid was raging on all the time we were out there. Jerry planes flying low all around. We could have been hit at any time.'

'And the flares!' Jane said. 'There was no moon that night, so the bombers used flares to light their way. The sky was all lit up like it was broad daylight.'

'I'm sorry I wasn't with you,' May said.

'Everyone has to have some time off,' Jane said patting her hand. 'How was your sister's wedding?'

'Oh, it was very nice, thank you,' she said.

'Did your fancy man go with you?' Jane asked and the others sniggered.

'No. I went on my own,' May replied stiffly and the others exchanged looks. She could tell they wanted her to go on and explain why, but she couldn't face telling them the truth. She remained silent.

In the morning, she went back up to the flat, ate some toast and slept soundly until early afternoon. When she got up and looked out of the window, there was a removals van pulled up outside Gerald's block and furniture was being brought out by men in brown overalls. So that was it. He'd gone away and the flat was being emptied. It felt like the end of an era, and as if every trace of their love was being erased.

The days wore on in the same vein. As April moved into May and the roses came out in the Dolphin Square gardens, May would catch their scent on the evening air on her way to work and would feel a pang of homesickness. She would pluck one and breathe in its heavenly smell and be transported back to her home. Rose Park was always smothered in roses from spring to late summer. Hadan prided himself on the beautiful displays in the gardens and on the white and pink ramblers that climbed up the front of the house, filling the rooms with their delicate scent.

Now she was alone, May began to miss home in a way that she hadn't in the previous months. She would sometimes call Wilhemena who would always say, 'There's no real news to speak of. Your father's working hard as usual. Oh, I had a letter from Blanche the other day. Everything is fine with her...' and then she would take the opportunity to try to persuade May to go home. It was only now, that she was all alone, that May began to be tempted, but she resisted that temptation. She needed to be strong and to see out the Blitz.

For a few weeks after the devastating April raids, there were no air raids at all and May got used to going down to the garage to play card games and to wait. Although waiting was tedious and stressful in its own way, it was nowhere near as bad as the reality of seeing innocent people crushed by falling buildings and injured by flying masonry and glass.

'Do you think it's over?' May ventured to ask the crew one day in early May.

'I doubt it,' Tommy said, shuffling his cards. 'Jerry won't give up that easily.'

After a few weeks though, May had a new worry to add to her problems. Her period was late, and she began to obsess that she could be pregnant. Whatever would she do if she was? She battled on, hoping she was late just because she was unhappy and not eating properly, but knowing that she really should see a doctor. The family doctor at Perry Cross always reported everything about the family's health to Hadan as a matter of routine, so that was an impossibility. She didn't know any doctors in London, although she'd spent enough time hanging around in hospitals. She wished Ruby was there to advise her, or even Gerald. There had been no word from him, although she wasn't surprised, she didn't expect to hear from him until July.

On 10th May there was another fierce air raid. People had got used to evenings without the danger, so were out and about enjoying the spring weather. May's crew was called to an incident in Southwark where a street of shops with flats above them had been hit by incendiary bombs. When they arrived, the whole street was engulfed in fire. Firemen with high-pressure hoses were dousing the flames, but like earlier fires that May had witnessed, the hoses were doing little to dampen the ferocity of the blaze. The road surface was lethal too. It was covered in broken glass and debris and two inches deep in water. May and the crew waded over to where ARP wardens were dragging people out through the smashed plate-glass front of a shop. It was instantly clear that the first two were dead, so they were laid out on the pavement and covered in coats. The third was a woman with multiple cuts and wounds, in particular an ugly gash to her stomach.

'Come on. Bring the stretcher.' Jane beckoned May close and knelt down to stem the bleeding with bandages.

May stared at the blood oozing from the woman's stomach, the glistening of her exposed intestines. She felt nausea rise in her stomach and within seconds, had to drop the stretcher and run behind a pile of rubble to vomit.

She took deep gulps of air and when she felt well enough, she went back to the stretcher. Jane had finished bandaging the woman by then. She didn't say anything, but she gave May a look and they both lifted the woman onto the stretcher, then hurried with her over the debris and rubble and along the slippery road to the ambulance. John and Tommy were bringing another casualty to the vehicle at the same time.

'Let's get off to St Thomas',' John said. Another ambulance had just drawn up beside theirs, but it didn't look as if anyone was alive in the building.

They all slid onto the front seat and set off down the wrecked street, lights dimmed, avoiding debris and collapsing buildings. They reached the hospital, and after they'd unloaded the patients, and were stowing the stretchers back into the ambulance, Jane took May aside.

'You're expecting a baby, aren't you? I saw you being sick behind the rubble. You've never done that before.'

May instantly felt herself blushing. 'I'm not sure, but I think I might be,' she admitted.

'Well, I *know* you are. Your face has filled out over the past few weeks. The way you carry yourself too. It looks different. Take it from me, I can tell.'

'I don't know what to do,' May said weakly as they walked back to the ambulance.

'What does your fancy man say about it?'

'He doesn't know. He's away... and in any case. We've... well, we're not seeing each other anymore.' It felt good to be able to tell someone the truth at last.

'Oh, poor you, May dear. But you do need to see a doctor. When we get back to the garage, I'll give you an address.'

THE DOCTOR'S surgery was in a run-down street in Lambeth behind St Thomas' Hospital, and May sat in a waiting room with some very sick-looking people, who coughed and spat and groaned in pain. They wore ragged clothes and looked dirty as well as down at heel. At last, her name was called, and she entered a small, dimly lit surgery that at least looked clean. Doctor Peters was much older than she expected. He must have been in his seventies at least.

'My colleague, Jane Jeffries, recommended you,' May said and the old man smiled.

'Ah, Jane. Heart of gold, that one. She used to help out here sometimes before the war. Now, what can I do for you, my dear?'

'I think I might be pregnant,' she said, and his face fell.

'I don't offer that sort of service, I'm afraid,' he said stiffly, and May frowned. 'I am semi-retired now, and certainly not a wealthy man, but I haven't yet resorted to that sort of practice.'

May understood, and hastened to reassure him. 'No, no. I'm not looking for any sort of service, Doctor,' she said. 'I just want to know if I am or not.'

'Pop up on the bench,' he said, drawing back a curtain. She did as he asked and he examined her quickly with deft, but cold hands.

'I'm afraid so,' he said. 'Not sure if that's good news or bad news, but it's incontrovertible. Two to three months I would say. Now, if you live nearby, there's a clinic in St Thomas' that cares for local women. You might want to pop in there to get checked over as things progress.'

Outside on the street, May wandered up to the Lambeth Palace Road to get a bus. She couldn't get over his words, 'as things progress'. It sounded so certain, so inexorable, so set in stone. Things were going to progress and there was nothing she could do so stop them. If she'd felt alone before, she felt it even more now. Who could she turn to? Her mother wouldn't understand, and her father would probably be so furious with her that he could well turn her out on the streets. She needed to keep it a secret for as long as she could.

The bus arrived and she got on and climbed up to the top deck with other passengers. There were a couple of women with babies and small children sitting at the front gossiping. One baby was crying loudly, but the women ignored him and carried on chatting. A week ago, May would have found them unremarkable, but now she couldn't stop looking at them. That was what her life would be like in a few months. It was terrifying.

The bus lumbered past wrecked buildings and bombsites in various stages of repair in amongst the houses and shops. Children played on piles of rubble and dogs rooted around in the dust. How she longed for the beauty of Rose Park at moments like this, but she knew she couldn't go there until she'd worked out what to do.

For the rest of the journey, over Westminster Bridge, around Parliament Square and down Millbank to Pimlico, she thought hard and by the time she got off the bus outside Dolphin Square she'd made some decisions. She would write to Gerald straight away and tell him the news. She would need his help in the future, whatever she felt about him at that moment. She would confide in Jane too and she would tell Florence. Florence would be able to help her somehow, of that she was sure.

24

RACHEL

ROSE PARK, 1980

MAY FELL SILENT, and Rachel stared at her mother, taking in the implications of what she'd just said.

'You really had a baby during the war? I can't believe it, Mum.'

May nodded but said nothing.

'So, what happened to him or her? Where are they now?'

'I'll tell you tomorrow, Rachel. Don't you need to get off to the pub now?'

Rachel sighed and checked her watch. 'Yes, I suppose so. But I'm dreading it this evening. And I don't know how I'll be able to wait until tomorrow to hear about what happened. Why haven't you told me about this before?'

She felt bruised by this news, hurt that her mother hadn't trusted her with the truth.

'Because I promised I would keep it a secret. But the time seems right for you to know now. You are grown-up, just about to go off to university. When you said that you wanted me to tell you what I did during the war, I made the decision to tell you everything.'

'Who did you make that promise to?'

May sighed. 'Like I said, I'll tell you tomorrow. That's the deal.

I've been telling you what I can about the war during the afternoons while Pa is asleep. I need to go and wake him up now.'

'I can't wait, Mum.' Rachel said and she meant it. Never in her entire life had she suspected that she might have an older brother or sister. By the time May had met her father and given birth to Rachel, she was thirty-nine years old, and she'd told her that although they'd tried for another child, they hadn't been able to conceive. But Rachel had never even thought that there was a sibling in the world somewhere, around twenty years older than herself.

May got up from her deck chair and dusted her skirt down.

'I hope it goes alright this evening. Perhaps Daniel won't come into the pub after all,' she said, squeezing Rachel's arm.

Rachel had told May about the extraordinary discovery of the papers in Daniel's glovebox. May wasn't as taken aback as she had been.

'He's a journalist, Rachel,' May said. 'Perhaps what he said was true, it was research for a story about local families. But I have to admit, it's quite odd that he didn't mention it to you.'

'Extremely odd. He's been pumping me for information all along,' she said. 'Only I didn't notice at first. I thought he was just genuinely interested in me. What an idiot I've been!'

'Not at all. You mustn't blame yourself. Perhaps it's got something to do with the feuding between the two families,' May suggested. 'Have you thought of that?'

'Maybe,' Rachel said, but she didn't think it could be that.

Now, May picked up the tea tray and they walked together across the sweeping lawn towards the house.

'Have you thought of a way of asking Grandad about his brother yet?' Rachel asked and May shook her head.

'I'm not sure it would be kind. He clearly wanted to keep it a secret, otherwise he would have told us. Is it fair to bring up something like that on his deathbed?'

'Maybe not. Anyway, we know about Henry now, we know

that he died when he was very young, a year before his mother. We'll never prove that it was that that led to Emily's death, but it seems very likely.'

Rachel went up to her room to get ready for the evening shift. Looking in the mirror, she recalled the day before, when she'd taken so much care getting ready in case Daniel had happened to come into the pub. Now, she brushed her hair and applied her makeup to please herself. It gave her confidence to be looking her best, and she might need all the confidence she could get if Daniel were to come in this evening. She wondered, as she put on her lipstick, if her brother or sister looked like her. Where did they live now? Did they have children? The shock she'd initially felt at May's revelation had quickly turned to curiosity and she couldn't wait until the next afternoon to hear more.

Later, when she arrived at the Quarryman's Arms, Jenny greeted her warmly as usual.

'How did it go last night, my love? Was the band good?' Jenny called from the far end of the pub where she was cleaning the tables.

'Yes. The band was good, it's just that... well, I had a bit of a difference of opinion with Daniel afterwards.'

Jenny stopped what she was doing and came closer. She looked concerned.

'I'm sorry to hear that. I'm not surprised, mind. Has he been messing you around? He's done that plenty of times before, I can tell you.'

Rachel shook her head. 'Not exactly. It was really odd. I was looking for a lighter in his glove compartment, and all these papers dropped out. They were copies of *my* family's birth and death certificates, press clippings about family events. It was weird. It felt... well, like a massive invasion of privacy.'

'My God. How odd!'

'He said he was doing a newspaper article about local landowners, but I didn't believe him. He's been trying to get information about the family out of me ever since we met. I've no idea what he's up to, but I don't trust him an inch now.'

'I'm not surprised, my love. He's always up to something. I would steer clear of him from now on if I were you.'

'I intend to,' Rachel said. 'Do you want me to clean behind the bar?' she asked, putting on an apron.

She got on with sweeping the floor and setting out the glasses. Soon it was opening time and she began serving the usual smattering of locals – men from the quarry dropping in for a pint after work, farmers and labourers and the odd couple, popping in for a drink as part of an evening stroll. She kept an eye on the door in case Daniel came in. She'd agreed with Jenny that if he did, Jenny would serve him, but much to her relief, he stayed away that evening.

As they were clearing up after closing time, Rachel brought the subject of Daniel up again with Jenny.

'Can you think why he might be so interested in my family?' she asked, and Jenny paused with four glasses in her hand.

'Well, since you mentioned it, I've been wondering about something,' she said. 'This is a small village and there are often rumours swirling about the place. I tend to let them wash over me, but my granny, the one I told you about, she remembers everything. She probably knows things about Daniel Walters that the rest of us never knew or have forgotten. Why don't I take you round to meet her tomorrow?'

'That would be great, but could it be in the morning?' Rachel asked, anxious not to miss her afternoon under the oak tree with May and the revelations she hoped that it would bring.

'I'll check with her. She's very old, but as bright as a button. She remembers everything. Why don't you give me a call around ten, by which time I'll have had time to speak to her.'

Jenny's grandmother lived in a thatched cottage smothered with yellow roses along a narrow lane on the edge of the village. When Rachel knocked on her door at eleven o'clock the next morning, it was Jenny who opened it. She was smiling conspiratorially.

'I've told Granny what happened with Daniel, and she thinks she might know what it's about.'

'Really?' Rachel asked, suddenly excited. 'Did she tell you about it?'

'No. She wanted to talk to you first. Come on in. The kettle's just boiled.'

The front door opened straight into a colourful sitting room, bathed in sunlight. One wall was lined with books, there was a multi-coloured rag rug on the floor and several vases of roses dotted around the room. Jenny's grandmother was sitting in an armchair, but she got straight up when Rachel entered. Rachel immediately saw that she was a sprightly lady, far more so than Mrs Sutton, but she guessed she must be quite a bit younger too.

'My name is Nellie,' she said, holding out a bony hand. Rachel took it and was surprised at the strength of her grip. She had beautiful blue eyes and her skin was heavily wrinkled and nut brown from the sun. Her hair was startlingly white, contrasting with her skin. She was dressed in an orange patterned skirt and a white T-shirt and flip-flops.

'Here's the tea,' Jenny said, bringing a loaded tray through and putting it on a coffee table in the middle of the room. 'Oh, and Granny made scones. They're a real treat, I can tell you. Oh, do sit down, Rachel.'

Rachel sat down opposite Nellie, and Jenny handed her a mug of tea and a buttered fruit scone on a plate. She took a bite of the scone and understood instantly what Jenny had meant. It was melt-in-the-mouth delicious, and she had to restrain herself from devouring it all in one mouthful.

'Jenny tells me you're interested in Gillian Walters' boy,' Nellie said, taking a bite of her own scone.

'I'm curious about him. He's been investigating my family records, and taking me out, pretending he's interested in me, and I'd like to know why.'

Nellie laughed. 'Well, you are a pretty girl. All the Roses were great beauties. And he does have an eye for the ladies, that one.'

Nellie sipped her tea then put it down and leaned forward, fixing Rachel with her disconcerting blue gaze. 'I think I might know why he's interested in you and your family. But it's a long, long story. I'll try to tell you as quickly as I can.'

'Take your time, Granny,' Jenny said. 'I love a good story and I'm sure Rachel does too.'

'Alright. Well, here goes. When I worked at Rose Park, I was only in my teens. Wilhemena and Hadan had already been married a couple of years, but there were rumours circulating even then. Wilhemena didn't like the rumours and she got rid of a lot of staff because she thought they were gossips. I was one of those, but that wasn't until I'd been there a couple of years, so I gleaned a lot of the gossip in that time.'

'So, what were the rumours?' Jenny asked.

'Well, they were all about the two families – the Hardings and the Roses. A lot of this happened before my time, so some of these details might be a bit vague. But as far as I know, it all started when old Mr Gabriel and William Harding had a falling out over conditions for the men at the quarry. William Harding was a union man. At first, Mr Gabriel was refusing to pay them for breaks during the day, so they went on strike over it. It escalated from there. They were always at loggerheads over something – pay and conditions or working hours, holidays, things like that.

'The two men developed a real hatred for each other. Mr Gabriel had forbidden young Hadan from playing with William Harding's son, Thomas, although they were exactly the same age. Only, when Miss Emily sank into a deep depression and took to her bed, when the boys were still young, maybe five or six, young

Hadan was left to his own devices. Some of the kitchen maids were meant to look after him, but he was always running away. The girls had other duties and weren't trained nannies, so had no idea what to do with him. He ran wild and he always wanted to do what was forbidden. So naturally, he started to play with young Thomas Harding.

'They were best friends for years. Thomas was a good-looking boy, a real charmer and clever too. People thought that Hadan felt a bit inadequate beside Thomas and although they were friends, they were always competing over something. They were inseparable as youngsters, but they started to play with a young girl in the village, Beth Carey. Beth was very pretty and both boys fell in love with her, so the rumour goes.

'Of course, your grandfather was sent away to school, and that meant Thomas had a chance to get closer to Beth without any competition, and when Hadan came back, he didn't have a chance. Beth and Thomas got married a couple of years before the Great War broke out. That was when Hadan and Thomas fell out.

'Your grandfather and Thomas Harding met up again when both joined up for the Northamptonshire Regiment at the outbreak of war. Your grandfather was an officer and Thomas a foot soldier. I don't know how true this is, but again, the rumour mill has it that due to your grandfather's bungling orders, Thomas was killed during an offensive in the Battle of the Somme. During that same battle, mustard gas was deployed by the Germans and your grandfather sadly breathed it in. Some say that affected his temperament. He came back from the war a changed man.'

'That makes sense,' Rachel said, nodding. 'He's renowned for his bad temper. He's also really volatile. It's like being on eggshells, being with Grandad.'

'So, when he came back from the war in 1917 – and these are rumours again, I have to say – he made a beeline for Beth Harding. He told her he'd always loved her, and he hadn't stopped even though she was married to his best friend. People say that they had some sort of liaison. It didn't last long, but a few months after that, Beth gave birth to a baby boy.

'Mr Gabriel quickly married your grandfather off to your grandmother, Wilhemena, but all the servants knew what had happened. Some of them, caught gossiping before the wedding, were let go. But the village was full of it. William Harding and Beth passed the baby off as Thomas', saying that the baby was late, but everyone suspected they were being paid by your grandfather to do that. Gradually, over the years, the rumours died down. Beth died about twenty years ago now, and her son, Joe Harding, lived in the village until he died a few years ago.'

'Joe Harding?'

The old lady nodded. 'That's the one, my dear. Now, I don't know how much of this is speculation and how much of it is fact, but that is what people thought. Your grandfather will know the truth.'

Rachel's mind was racing with all this new information to digest. Everything was falling into place now. That explained why Hadan had forbidden May from having anything to do with Joe Harding. He was her half-brother, so Hadan must have been terrified of them getting close.

'So, Daniel had recently found out that he was Joe Harding's son,' Rachel said, 'and he'd heard the rumour about Joe Harding being my grandfather's son, and he was looking into the family tree. If it's all true, it must mean that Daniel is my cousin.'

'And there's your answer,' Jenny said. 'That's why he was trying to find out about your family. You can bet your bottom dollar that he thought he might get a slice of your grandfather's inheritance when the time comes.'

Shock washed through Rachel at this thought. It was so obvious, when you thought about it. And then she remembered something else.

'I saw him in Northampton when I went up to the Guildhall, talking to a woman. Someone told me later that he'd been there to see a family solicitor. Maybe he went to ask her about that.'

It felt like completing a complicated jigsaw puzzle, all the random pieces were now falling into place. In the maelstrom of feelings that were swirling around in her head and heart she couldn't work out whether to be glad that she had another cousin, or annoyed that Daniel had tried to manipulate her. One thing she was sure about though; she couldn't wait to tell her mother about it.

25

MAY

LONDON, 1941

THE FIRST THING May did when she got back to the flat after Doctor Peters had confirmed her pregnancy, was to force herself to sit down and write to Gerald. It was difficult, and she had to screw up many attempts and throw them in the bin before she came up with something she felt happy about posting.

DEAR GERALD,

I know we parted on bad terms, and I'm only writing to you now because I have something important to tell you. I am expecting your baby. I saw a doctor today and he confirmed the news. This is a shock for me, and I don't know how I feel about it. I do know though, that I won't be able to tell my parents, who wouldn't understand, and would probably disown me and cut me off without a penny.

I intend to stay in Ruby's flat as long as I can. At least it is private here. Please write to me as soon as you get this. We need to speak as soon as possible.

Yours, May

. . .

SHE COULDN'T BRING herself to sign off with "Love, May", not because she didn't love Gerald; in spite of everything that had happened, she knew in her heart that she was still deeply in love with him, but because she was still angry with him for having deceived her.

She sealed the envelope, put a stamp on it, addressed it to the mysterious PO address he'd given her, then walked down to the post office in Sussex Street to post it. Men were still working on the bomb-damaged block opposite, but it was almost finished. There was definitely the feel of summer in the air now. There was blossom in the trees that lined the street and if she closed her eyes and listened to the birdsong, she could almost believe there was no war on. But her heart and head told her otherwise. Ruby was never far from her thoughts, and she only had to close her eyes for a few seconds before the image of one of the badly injured people she'd helped during an air raid would come into her mind. She knew the experience had changed her for ever and that she would never forget any of them.

JANE REFUSED to allow May to continue working on the ambulance crew once her pregnancy had been confirmed. May was reluctant to tell the others on the crew about her condition, but Jane told her to leave it to her. May trusted her completely. She was sure that Jane would find some ingenious way of letting the others know that she couldn't continue working, without giving away her secret.

Every morning when she awoke, she would run down the stairs to the postbox, unlock it and peep inside, but every morning she was disappointed. Perhaps Gerald hadn't received her letter, perhaps he had but didn't want to write back, perhaps he'd been sent abroad? She had no way of knowing the answer to any of these questions. All she did know was that he hadn't written to her.

In desperation, she would walk down Millbank to the Tate Gallery and walk up the steps to the front door. There was a sign on the door saying that the gallery was closed, and all the paintings had been taken to safety in the countryside, or to be stored in underground stations. Standing back from the front door she could see that the building itself had sustained damage like so many others. Part of the roof was covered in a tarpaulin and some of the windows were boarded up. She would stand there feeling foolish for a few minutes, then walk home slowly, staring at the pavement. What a fool she was to think that Gerald might simply turn up on the steps of the Tate unannounced. She was grasping at straws, she knew that.

The days became long and lonely for May. Once a week she went along to the mother and baby clinic at St Thomas' Hospital to be weighed and measured and generally prodded around. She got to know some of the other young mothers at the clinic, most of whose husbands were away serving in the army, so she didn't feel so out of place being alone.

Jane came to see her every couple of days, and often brought something from her rations – a couple of potatoes, some butter, or a few slices of bacon.

'Won't you go short?' May would ask, reluctant to accept the gifts.

'You have to keep your strength up,' Jane would say.

She would often stay for a couple of hours and chat, or they would take a walk beside the river together. May was surprised by what a good friend Jane had become and how solicitous she was of May's welfare. But Jane knew that May was completely alone, that she couldn't tell her parents and that Gerald was nowhere to be seen. She was clearly concerned about how May might cope in that situation.

There were sometimes air raids in the evenings, and when

she heard the air-raid siren, May would lean out of the window, watching the bombers fly over and the sky glow with orange light from the fires, listen to the sound of ack-ack gunfire. At those times she felt a little guilty that she wasn't out there with her crew, but she knew that Jane was right and that it wasn't fair to risk the life of her baby. Sometimes she would go down to the shelter in the basement, but she always loathed doing that. It made her feel claustrophobic and confined, and reminded her sharply of how much she was missing Gerald.

One day, she happened to look out of her window when she noticed that the windows of Gerald's old flat were open. A thrill of excitement went through her. Perhaps someone was cleaning it, perhaps Gerald was back? Either way, whoever was there might know something about his whereabouts. She went out of the flat and quickly hurried over the courtyard and into the block, then took the lift to the sixth floor. Her heart was pounding when she knocked on the door. There were footsteps inside, were those Gerald's? The door was opened by a tall, thin man wearing pebble glasses.

'Yes?'

'I'm looking for Gerald Clifford,' she said.

The man blinked. 'I don't know anyone by that name,' he said.

'He used to live here. It was rented for him by the government. Are you... are you a civil servant too?'

'I couldn't possibly say, but I'm afraid you won't find anyone of that name at this address,' he said. 'Now, if that's all, I'm very busy.'

Behind him, through the door, she caught a glimpse of radio equipment on the desk in the spare room. It was the same equipment Gerald used to use. The man started to close the door, but May pushed it open.

'Please! I know you're in the same line of work as him. He had a radio like that. I really need to get in touch with him.'

The man sighed impatiently. 'There is no one by that name at this address and there never has been, so if I were you, I would go away and forget all about him.'

He pushed the door shut and May stood there on the landing opening and shutting her mouth in astonishment. What did he mean, 'no one by that name'? Was Gerald Clifford a false name? Did he use another name for his work? Perhaps he had several identities. She wandered back, puzzling over the strange exchange with the tall man. What did it all mean? Whoever Gerald was or had been seemed to be slipping from her grasp, part of a complicated web of deceit that she'd become embroiled in. She even wondered if she'd dreamed it all, but then she put her hand on her belly and remembered. The living proof was growing inside her.

AFTER ABOUT A MONTH, the air raids on London lessened and then stopped altogether. The newspapers said that it was because of Hitler's decision to focus all his forces on the invasion of Russia. Now the repair and clean-up of London began in earnest. Everywhere May walked was a hive of activity with the sound of hammers and saws ringing in the air as buildings were being repaired, or demolished if they were too badly damaged, and rubble was being loaded into lorries to be taken away.

May took the train to Bletchley Park to pay Florence a visit. She had sent Florence a note beforehand to let her know she was coming, and Florence had written back to say she was looking forward to seeing her. May kept recalling the conversation they'd had at Florence's wedding. 'You can always come to me if you ever need to talk about anything,' Florence had said. Well now, she *was* coming to her, and she really needed her help and support.

To her surprise, Florence was waiting on the station platform when her train pulled in. They hugged when May got off the train.

'I had a day off so I thought I would come and meet you,' Florence said.

'Thank you. I wasn't sure quite how to get to Bletchley Park from here,' May replied, relieved.

'It's not far, but I brought the car anyway. Are you quite alright, darling?' Florence asked, holding May at arm's length and peering at her. 'You look a bit odd, if I may say so.'

May had wanted to be strong, to tell Florence everything calmly and in good time, but at her sister's words, her resolve melted and she burst into tears. Florence held her tight until her sobs subsided while other passengers pushed past them towards the station exit.

'Let's go for a cup of tea,' Florence said, 'and you can tell me all about it.'

There was a small, old-fashioned café inside the Victorian station building and they found a table in the corner. May dabbed her nose while Florence ordered tea and biscuits. The waitress, her hair wrapped up in a scarf, watched them with curiosity in her eyes.

'So, tell me all about it,' Florence said, leaning forward and looking at May intently.

'I'm pregnant,' May answered immediately and Florence sat up straight and blinked in surprise.

'Good God. I didn't even know you had a boyfriend.'

'I haven't. Well, not now anyway. I found out he was married, so... well, he's gone away for his work and we're not seeing each other at the moment.'

'He sounds a complete cad!'

'Oh no! He's not like that at all. He's had a difficult time, his wife's an alcoholic. It's a long story.'

'So, it's been going on a while with him?'

'A few months, yes. I had no idea, until I was sick one time on one of my shifts on the ambulance. I don't know what to do, Florence. I haven't anybody I can turn to.'

'Well, you've got me,' Florence said. 'So, don't despair. I realise that you can't tell Ma and Pa. They would never accept it, and they would never get over it either. I take it you're going to go ahead and have the baby?'

'Yes,' May muttered.

'I would say I feel sorry for you,' Florence said, sipping her tea, 'but I don't feel sorry at all. Frankly, I'm jealous.'

'Jealous?' May was stunned. How could anyone be jealous of her and the mess she'd got herself into?

'Well, put it this way, I'm never going to be in your position, am I?'

May looked at her sister's face and realised what she was saying, and her heart instantly filled with sympathy.

'I'm so sorry, Flo, I didn't think. How tactless of me,' she said, reaching out for her sister's hand.

'Not tactless at all,' Florence said briskly, giving May's hand a brief squeeze. 'It's just the way things are.'

When they'd finished their tea, they went out to the car park where Florence's car, an old Austin A40, was parked up. Florence drove them the two miles or so to the little terraced house she and Giles rented in a street on the edge of Bletchley Park.

'This is home!' she said, parking outside. 'It's pretty small, but it's cosy and we like it here.'

'We?' she asked.

'All four of us. Rebecca lives here too. Robert, Giles' friend, lives next door and everyone comes and goes more or less as they please. We're like a happy family.'

'I'm so pleased for you,' May said. 'And I can't wait to meet Rebecca.'

'And she's looking forward to meeting you too. Come on, let's go inside.'

The house was a lot bigger than it appeared from the street, with a long hallway, with rooms off on either side, leading to a small kitchen at the back. Florence beckoned May through the house.

'I expect Rebecca's out in the garden,' she said. 'She usually is.'

May followed Florence through the small kitchen and out into a sunny courtyard garden, where a tall woman with a mop of curly blonde hair was kneeling, weeding a raised bed full of flowering herbs.

'Rebecca. Meet my sister, May,' Florence said, and May could tell from the way she raised her voice that Florence was a little nervous about the meeting.

Rebecca stood up, dusted down her skirt and took off her gardening gloves. She held out her hand and May shook it.

'Lovely to meet you, May. I've heard a lot about you,' Rebecca said smiling. She had twinkly blue eyes and a delicate featured face with high cheek bones. She was beautiful, and May could instantly see how Florence could have fallen in love with her.

'I've made some cakes. Shall we sit out here and have a drink? There's some lemon barley water in the fridge.'

They all sat down at a little wrought iron table and chairs and ate Victoria sponge and drank barley water, enjoying the afternoon sunshine.

After a while, Florence said, 'Do you mind if I tell Rebecca about your problem, May?'

May was a little reluctant, but Rebecca seemed such a loving, open person that she couldn't really object. 'Of course, it's fine,' she said.

'May is pregnant, Rebecca, and she doesn't know what to do.'

'Oh, May,' Rebecca said, smiling broadly, 'Congratulations. Whatever the circumstances, bringing a new life into the world is always a source of joy,' then she leaned over spontaneously and hugged May.

'I hadn't really thought about it like that, but I suppose you're right,' May said.

'Do you want to keep the baby?' Rebecca asked.

'Well, I don't want to have an abortion, and I don't want to give it up for adoption either. But bringing up a child on my own would be difficult.'

'May, you are far too young to be tied to a child,' Florence said. 'Especially with no man around to help you.'

'Did Pa help Ma with us?' May asked, laughing.

'No, of course not. But Ma had nannies and housemaids. She didn't really need his help, did she?'

'No, I suppose not,' May said.

She felt at a loss as to what to do. Florence was right, she wasn't ready to bring up a child alone. If Hadan found out he would cut off the small allowance which was keeping her going at present, and she had no qualifications for any type of employment. And in any case, if she was working, who would look after her baby? She'd come here for answers, but so far, Florence wasn't helping much.

Suddenly she felt weary. The sun beating down in the suntrap garden was giving her a headache. She felt sweaty too. She wiped her hand across her brow.

'Are you alright?' Florence asked. 'You look a bit peaky.'

'It's the sun, I think,' May said.

'Why don't you go up and have a lie down. You must be tired after the journey. I'll show you the guest bedroom.'

May followed Florence into the house and up the narrow staircase. The guest room was at the front of the house looking over the street. It was only a box room but furnished beautifully with floral curtains and a matching bedspread and pretty watercolours on the walls. The bed had an old-fashioned brass bedstead and beside it was a washstand complete with a china jug and bowl.

'What a lovely room,' she exclaimed.

'Oh, that's Rebecca's doing. She's got a talent for that sort of thing,' Florence said proudly. 'Now, you lie down and I'll bring you a glass of water.'

May kicked off her shoes and took her dress off, then she slid between the cool sheets. Florence tiptoed in with her water and put it beside the bed.

'Sleep for as long as you like. We'll be downstairs preparing supper. Giles will be back soon, and Robert. We can all have supper together. You'll like them both.'

May sank back on the pillows and drifted off. She slept for a long time. She was dimly aware of people moving about downstairs, the front door slamming as Giles came in, and him calling 'Hello!' and the others hushing him. When she finally awoke properly and checked her watch it was six o'clock. She yawned and stretched and got out of bed.

When she went downstairs, she could hear voices from the dining room, which was at the front of the house. She opened the door and went inside. They were all sitting at the table, having a drink. They all turned to look at her, smiling. Florence got to her feet.

'Come in, May. You met Giles at the wedding, but this is Robert.'

Robert had blond hair, swept back from his face, and wore horn-rimmed glasses which gave him an intense, intelligent look. He held up his glass. 'Good to meet you, May,' he said, smiling with his perfect white teeth.

'Come and sit down,' Florence said. 'You probably won't want a G&T. Would you like some more lemon barley? Rebecca's cooked stew and dumplings. We were just waiting for you to start.'

May sat down at the end of the table between Rebecca and Giles and Florence brought her drink. Everyone was talking about their colleagues, exchanging anecdotes about them and laughing gently.

Rebecca brought the food and dished it out onto the plates, and everyone tucked in. It felt good to have company for once and May realised how much she missed the ambulance crew and her regular evenings chatting and playing games with them. She looked around the table at four happy faces and was glad that Florence had found three such genial companions and that their arrangement seemed to be working out so well.

When the meal was over, they all went through to the sitting room where there was an upright piano and Robert played some ragtime and some popular music. The others sang along and May joined in too. When it was bedtime, Florence went up with May and sat on the bed while she got into her nightdress.

'What do you think of our little household?' she asked.

'Oh, I think it's wonderful, Flo. It's great that you all get on so well. I'm so happy for you.'

Florence picked at the bedspread and May could tell that she had something to say.

'What is it, Florence?'

'Do you think you and your man will get back together?' she asked.

May's spirits fell. She didn't want to think about Gerald when she was feeling so positive, but she sat down on the bed beside Florence and told her about the strange meeting she'd had with the man in Gerald's flat.

'Is Gerald an intelligence officer then?' Florence asked.

'Yes.'

'He probably operates under a few different names. They often do,' Florence replied.

'I don't know if he's ever going to come back,' May said. 'He seems to have disappeared completely. He told me I could write to him, and I did, but he hasn't replied. He said he would come back in July, but I've no idea whether he will. And even if he does, I don't know if I can ever trust him again.'

'Look,' Florence said, 'why don't you wait and see if he comes back? Perhaps you'll be able to patch things up and settle down and have your baby together.'

May hung her head. She couldn't imagine that would ever happen. In her bones she had a strange feeling that Gerald was never coming back.

'And if he doesn't come back,' Florence said, 'I have another idea.'

'Oh?'

'We talked it over downstairs while you were asleep. If you agree, we thought that Giles and I could adopt your baby. You could still see him or her whenever you wanted to, so you wouldn't have to give them up to strangers, and one day, you'd be able to tell them the truth. I've always wanted children, but thought it would never be possible. Perhaps this way would help us all out?'

May stared at her, recalling her sadness in the station café when she'd said she was jealous of May's pregnancy. Her life and that of her friends was warm and supportive and complete in every way but this. Perhaps this was the answer to May's prayers after all. The more she thought about it, the more it appealed to her. After a few minutes' thought, she looked into her sister's eager eyes and said, 'Yes. I think that might work, Florence. What a brilliant idea. I'm so glad I came to see you.'

26

RACHEL

ROSE PARK, 1980

ONCE AGAIN RACHEL found herself staring at her mother. This was the second revelation about the family that day and she was finding it hard to take it all in.

'So, is that what you did?' she asked, still trying to process the information.

May nodded. 'Your cousin Lawrence is Florence and Giles' adopted son. But I'm his birth mother.'

'That's incredible, Mum. I can hardly believe it.'

She thought about her cousin, a rather bumbling, disorganised character who ran an antique shop in a little town outside Oxford and she recalled the unkind words that her grandfather had said about him on the first day of her visit. He'd said he didn't set much store by Lawrence's common sense, and she knew what he meant. But despite his lack of business acumen, Rachel knew Lawrence to be a decent human being, kind and generous and always amiable and friendly when they met. Thinking about it, she realised that she didn't know him very well. They'd only met a dozen times or so in the whole of her life. She wondered then if May had deliberately kept them apart.

'Does he know about it, Mum?'

'Yes. Florence told him as soon as he was old enough to understand. I suppose he was about ten then. Since then, I've always been to see him a few times a year. I usually spend a couple of days with him when I stay with Florence.'

So, that was why May was such a frequent visitor to Oxford. The draw wasn't her sister, it was in fact, her secret son.

'But why didn't you tell me about it?'

May sighed. 'I wanted to. Believe me, I longed to at times, but... well, I never actually told your father. For some reason, I never had the courage to explain about Gerald and what happened during the war. I decided not to tell him. And that meant I couldn't tell you.'

'But it's years since Dad died,' Rachel said, still not understanding. 'Why didn't you tell me after that?'

'Oh, I don't know my darling. I think secrecy had probably become a habit by then. It was a bit like Gerald not telling me about his wife, there just didn't seem a right time. But I decided, when you said you wanted to hear what I did during the war, that now was the right time to tell you. I realised that I couldn't put it off any longer.'

'I wish you'd told me sooner,' Rachel said, biting her nail, once again feeling the pain of her mother's secrecy. 'You know, I always longed for a brother or sister. It felt so lonely sometimes, growing up an only child. Especially after Dad died. It would have made a difference.'

'I'm so sorry, Rachel. You didn't seem lonely... you know, we don't always make the right decisions about things like that. If I'd realised you were desperate for a brother or sister, I might have told you before.'

'So, you still haven't told me everything, did you have the baby in London?'

May shook her head. 'No, I stayed in Ruby's flat for several months. It was quite difficult at times, because Ma and Pa used to try to get me to go home. The Blitz was over by then, so I didn't have the excuse of the ambulance service. I went back a couple of times for weekends until the baby started showing, but after I was about five months pregnant, I had to stay away.

'When I had about month left to go, I went to stay with Florence. Giles had a friend who was a doctor. He took care of me. I actually gave birth in that little box room I'd stayed in that first night. Then, the doctor helped us go through the formalities of the adoption process. Florence was right about it. I never felt as though I was giving my child away, because I could see him whenever I wanted.

'And I know that he made Florence and Giles, and also Rebecca and Robert, very happy indeed. He grew up with two mothers and two fathers. He might seem a little odd to you, Rachel, but he is the most settled, grounded individual I've ever encountered, and I put that down to his enlightened upbringing.'

'I'm still finding it hard to take in. Especially after what I found out about Daniel this morning.'

'I know. That's extraordinary too. I was astonished when you told me about that. It's amazing. I wonder if it's true?'

'I think it must be. There can't be any other explanation. I'm going to ask Daniel about it when I can find the courage. But tell me what happened to Gerald, Mum? Did you ever see him again?'

May shook her head and an expression of sadness crept into her eyes. 'I wrote a few times to the PO Box number he'd given me, but there was never a reply. And I used to go down and wait on the steps of the Tate Gallery sometimes too. Foolish, I know because I had no idea if or when he might go there, but for some reason the hope kept me going.'

'What do you think happened to him?'

May shrugged. 'Perhaps he read my first letter and was scared off. Perhaps he wasn't ready to be a father. I have no idea. It's strange though, I didn't think he would be the type to just up and leave like that. He seemed dependable and decent, despite everything that happened.'

'Did you try to find him?'

May nodded. 'I even went to MI5 while I was in London. I went into the front entrance on Millbank. It wasn't very far from Dolphin Square in fact. There was a security man on the desk, and I asked to see Gerald Clifford. I said I knew he was one of their agents. He told me outright that there was no one with that name employed there and I went away crying. I realised that Gerald Clifford must have been a false name that he used to disguise his real identity, or perhaps it was his real identity... I was so confused by it all.'

'You know that records are released every so often about Military Intelligence, don't you? I read about it in the paper once. I'm not sure how many years they keep them for. Twenty or thirty maybe, but maybe we could go and do some research?'

'Yes, maybe. It all seems such a long time ago, Rachel. It's all in the past. I'm not sure I want to go dredging all that up now.' May looked at her watch. 'I need to go in and see to Pa now. He wasn't at all well this morning. I don't think it will be long now, Rachel.'

'Perhaps we should tell him about Daniel?' Rachel said. 'It might give him some sort of... well, closure about the past. And he might want to meet Daniel. He is his grandson after all.'

'Perhaps. But we decided not to upset him by telling him what we knew about his brother. This might upset him more.'

'I doubt it. What would be upsetting about finding out you have another grandson?'

'Hmm, let me think about it. I'll try to sound him out.

Two days later, Rachel stood outside the offices of the Public Records Office in central London. She'd made some preliminary phone calls and discovered that records of the Intelligence Service were released after thirty years. She couldn't wait to go there and find out what she could about Gerald, so she'd made an appointment to view the archives from 1941. The previous day, she'd been to the public library in Northampton and looked at national newspaper archives for the war years. She'd made some interesting discoveries by scanning newspapers from April-July 1941. In amongst the reports of air raids, she discovered a tiny report buried in the bottom of the news columns, about a stabbing in Pimlico on June 10th of a man known as John Jackson. That was in the London *Times*, but she carried on looking through all the newspaper archives available and discovered a grainy photograph of John Jackson. She took a photocopy of it, but she didn't show it to her mother straight away. She wanted to find out more about John Jackson before she did.

Now, she entered the chilly, forbidding building and was directed to a room on the first floor where the archives of Military Intelligence records from thirty years before were stored. An unsmiling woman on the desk gave her a box of microfiches and she took them to a machine and started scrolling through them. She was particularly interested in the date of the John Jackson stabbing. Something told her that the newspapers hadn't revealed the true story and that there was more to discover.

With bated breath she found an entry dated June 10th 1941 and scrolled through various reports. Then she came to one that made her pause. "Agent 54, killed in the line of duty on the evening of June 10th." Agent 54 had infiltrated a right-wing group and gathered a list of its members. These were identified in the files as being a fifth column of Nazi sympathisers who were making preparations for a German invasion.

"John Jackson was stabbed leaving a meeting of the group on the evening of June 10th. Agent 54 was known variously as Thomas Stafford, John Jackson, and Gerald Clifford. He was a brave agent who gave his life in the line of duty."

When she got home, she showed it to May.

'I went to the public records office in London to see what I could find about Gerald. I think this is him,' she said, handing the photograph to her, together with a copy of the news report. May stared at it for a long time. After a while, Rachel saw that her hands were shaking.

'It's him. It's Gerald. So, he didn't abandon me after all. Thank you, Rachel. Thank you so much for finding out about this. It makes such a difference.'

Rachel was glad that she'd been able to help her mother come to terms with the past. She could see that it made a huge difference to May to know that Gerald hadn't abandoned her. He had died serving his country before he could have even read her letter.

LATER ON THAT MORNING, May came downstairs from Hadan's room smiling.

'I think you were right, Rachel. I think it might be a good idea to introduce him to Daniel. He was getting very morose earlier, saying that he'd made a lot of mistakes in his life and he'd let people down. I think it might cheer him up to see the living proof of his so-called mistake. It might show him that things didn't turn out so badly, despite all his misgivings.'

So, the following day, Rachel walked through the village to Lime Kiln Lane where Daniel lived with his mother. She'd got Daniel's address from Jenny. As he hadn't been into The Quarryman's Arms since their altercation about the papers she'd found in his glovebox, she'd decided to take matters into her own hands. She felt emboldened by the information she'd gleaned about her family over the past days and weeks. She'd had time to process everything and although the past had sometimes seemed like a complex web of overlapping lies and betrayals, everything was gradually falling into place and was now becoming clearer to her. What she'd gleaned lately both through the photographs and records she'd found, the people she'd spoken to and through her mother's honesty, were some positive things as well as some betrayals. Having thought about it long and hard, she decided to focus on those positives. She'd gained a brother, or at least half-brother she hadn't known about, and a cousin too, and she'd enriched her understanding of many people she'd been quick to make assumptions about before.

Number 11 Lime Kiln Lane was a neat, Victorian cottage with a small front garden. Daniel's white Escort van was parked by the gate. She had timed it just right; she knew he would be back from work by now and probably wouldn't have gone out again. She opened the gate with trepidation but took a deep breath and pushed away her nerves. She needed to be strong and calm for this conversation. She knocked on the front door and waited, trying to keep her breath even, but her heart was pounding against her ribs which was unnerving. The door opened and Daniel stood there. He was dressed in smart trousers and a shirt and tie, which looked a bit incongruous with his stubbly chin and wavy dark hair. She'd never seen him like that before, but she guessed that that was how he must dress for work.

He stared at her, looking momentarily disconcerted.

'Rachel! What a surprise,' he said, recovering himself quickly. 'Would you like to come in?'

'Yes. We need to talk,' she said, stepping into a small hallway.

'Come through to the kitchen. Mum's out at the moment. At her evening class. Would you like something to drink? Tea? Or I've got some beer in the fridge.'

'Oh, beer would be nice,' she said.

He asked her to sit down at the small, square table and she looked round at the cosy kitchen. Gillian was clearly an arty person. The walls were painted navy blue and the cabinets and the floor scrubbed pine. The window blinds looked as though they had been hand-painted with a colourful floral design.

Daniel got two bottles of Watney's pale ale out of the fridge, uncapped them and put them on the table.

'Do you want a glass?' he asked.

'No thanks, I'll drink it from the bottle.'

He sat down opposite her. 'So, what did you want to say?'

Rachel took a sip of beer.

'I know why you were trying to find out about my family,' she said. 'I mean I know the real reason. Not the reason you told me the other night when I found those papers.'

He swallowed and looked at her for a moment, then asked, 'Why don't you think what I said was true?'

'I had an instinct about it that's why. And now I know the truth. You are my cousin. You are Joe Harding's son and Joe Harding was my grandfather's son by Beth Carey, or Harding as she was later.'

Daniel's eyes widened in shock. 'Who told you that?' He was blushing now, as if caught red-handed.

'What does it matter? It's true, isn't it?' She didn't take her eyes off his face even though she knew it was making him squirm.

He dropped his gaze and focused on his beer bottle.

'Alright, it's true. Or at least I think it's true. I went to a solicitor to see if there were any tests that could be done to find out the truth, but she said there weren't. That there were only witness statements and documentary evidence.'

'Ah,' Rachel said, triumphant. She'd known that was why he went to the solicitor. 'So you wanted to prove it in case you might be able to lay claim to some of my grandfather's estate, didn't you?'

'No! No! It was nothing like that. I swear, Rachel. I'm not interested in his money. I just wanted to be absolutely sure that it wasn't all speculation before I came forward. You know, I grew up an only child with a single mum. To find out that I had a huge family out there was mind-blowing.'

This time it was Rachel who had no words. This struck such a chord with her that she knew it must be true. So, it wasn't about the money at all. It was about belonging, being part of something. And he didn't want to hope it was true until he could be sure.

'And was taking me out about that too?' she asked and he laughed and shook his head.

'I was curious about you, yes. But the more I got to know you, the more I got to like you. You might not believe it, but it's true.'

She looked into his eyes, trying to see whether he was speaking the truth, but she couldn't tell. She guessed she would never know for sure.

'Mum and I think it would be a good idea for you to come and meet my grandfather. It would be good for him to see you before he dies.'

'But he doesn't even know about me. He must think that my dad never had any children.'

'Do you want to meet him?'

Daniel shrugged. 'Of course, but I never thought it might be an option. It feels a bit daunting, if I'm honest.'

'Would you come with me now? I don't think there's much time.'

'I suppose now is as good a time as any.'

May was in the kitchen, waiting for them. Rachel introduced them and they shook hands. 'I'm glad to meet you, Daniel,' May said. 'I think we ought to go up straight away, he gets very tired in the evenings.'

They all went up to Hadan's room. Rachel felt sick with apprehension as they stood outside his door. She'd wanted Daniel and Hadan to meet, but was this really the right thing to be doing? But it was too late for qualms now. Her mother was turning the handle and opening the door. They all walked inside and stood a little awkwardly in a row just inside the door. Hadan was seated in his chair with his back to them, looking out of the window at the afternoon sun on the golden meadows beyond the park.

'Pa, we've brought someone to meet you,' May said and Hadan visibly stiffened.

'Who the hell wants to see me?'

'His name is Daniel, Pa. And he's your grandson.'

'Don't talk nonsense. I only have two grandchildren. Don't try to trick me, May. I'm an old man, but I've still got my marbles.'

'It's not a trick, Pa. Daniel is Joe Harding's son. And Joe Harding was your son, wasn't he, Pa?'

There was a long silence from the chair by the window. Hadan was motionless. He didn't even turn his head. The tension in the room was palpable.

'Let me see him,' he finally growled.

Daniel walked forward and stood in front of Hadan's chair. He held his hand out, but Hadan didn't take it. He sat forward, rigid. Then he cried out, in a quavering voice. The voice of a child.

'Henry? Henry? Is that you?'

Chills went through Rachel. May stepped forward, 'This is Daniel, Pa. Your grandson. Henry was your brother, wasn't he?'

Hadan reached out and held Daniel's hand.

'Henry was sent away,' Hadan said, 'a long way away from home to a hospital. My father wanted to pretend he didn't exist. From that moment on I was an only child. But my mother never forgot him. We went to see him there sometimes, in the hospital, but he was changed. Maybe it was the medication. He was deeply unhappy there. He never wanted to play with me. Poor mother, she was broken by it. So broken that she stopped living. She stopped being a mother to me and took to her bed.

'I was left to run wild. That's when I met Thomas Harding,

and we became friends. That lasted for years, until we became rivals, over Beth Carey. She was the most beautiful girl I'd ever seen in my life. We both fell in love with her. I was sent away to school and didn't have a chance. But I had my chance later on, when the war came and Thomas was killed, that's when Beth and I became close. But it all went wrong when she got pregnant. That's when the rot set in. Her and old man Harding, Thomas' dad, they made me pay for it then. And I paid heavily, believe me.'

'Paid?' Daniel asked. 'Did they blackmail you?'

Slowly, Hadan nodded. 'I paid for that boy, or they said they would tell the world. I was married by then and had a reputation to protect. I paid for my mistakes alright. Many times over.'

There was silence, while Hadan's eyes rested on Daniel's face. 'I don't blame you for any of this, boy. I'm glad you came. I'd like you to stay and talk to me. May, Rachel, could you give us a few moments, please?'

'Of course, Pa.'

Rachel took her mother's hand and left the room quietly, as Daniel drew a chair up to sit beside his grandfather and talk, to try to make up for a lifetime of missed opportunities.

EPILOGUE

ROSE PARK, SUMMER 1980

THE COFFIN that bore Hadan Rose from St Matthew's church in the village of Perry Cross to its final resting place in the little graveyard at Rose Park, was pulled by four black horses with plumes of red feathers on their bridles. Hadan's will had made several stipulations about his funeral, including that he should be buried beside Wilhemena in the family graveyard at Rose Park. The family followed the coffin carriage on foot and Rachel walked beside May, who was struggling with the emotion of the occasion.

On the other side of May, walked Lawrence. He'd arrived the previous evening and May had explained to him that Rachel was now aware of their relationship. Rachel had chatted to him long into the night, wanting to know all about his childhood, about how he felt about May when he discovered the truth, whether he'd ever been tempted to tell Rachel and others the family secret of his birth. May had also told him what they'd discovered about Gerald's death and he'd studied the photocopy of the newspaper cutting carefully, trying to glean some insight into his father from that grainy photograph. His face had crumpled with emotion as he looked at it. He'd been truly moved by the knowledge that Gerald had died before he'd discovered about May's pregnancy. Prior to that he'd been under the impression that his father just hadn't wanted to know.

She'd asked him how he'd felt about keeping such an explosive secret. 'Guilty at times,' he admitted, 'but it was Mum's wish. I couldn't really go against that. I'm glad that it's all out in the open now though, Rachel,' he said, giving her a hug.

Looking around her, Rachel saw many sad faces in the procession. May was clearly devastated, tears running down her cheeks unchecked, despite the fact that her father had been difficult and demanding, right to the end. On the other side of May, walked her two aunts, Blanche who had flown in from her home in the Philippines two days before Hadan's death, and Florence, who walked slowly with her head bowed, her arm tucked into Rebecca's who walked beside her.

Rachel had hardly met Blanche before and was keen to get to know her eldest aunt. Blanche had been pleased to talk and had promised to tell Rachel all about what happened to her during the war before she returned home. 'I'm staying for ten days, so there should be plenty of time for that,' she'd said.

When they were about halfway to Rose Park, Rachel noticed someone walking on the other side of her and turning she saw Daniel fall into step with her. Over the past few days they had talked a lot and had managed to bury their differences. He'd been introduced to Blanche and Florence, both of whom had been amazed and delighted to welcome a new nephew into the family.

Rachel still felt hurt that Daniel had been so secretive about what he was doing, but she was sure she would get over that in time. He smiled at her tentatively and she smiled back. She was thinking about what he'd said the day after Hadan had died.

'You know, after our argument the other evening, I realised how much you'd started to mean to me, Rachel. I wasn't honest with you, and I realise now that that was a mistake. Do you think, once the funeral is over and everything starts to settle down, that we might... well, that we might start again?'

She still wasn't sure how she felt about that. Everything had been so up in the air lately that she didn't know what to think. But she did know that she didn't bear grudges for long and she understood why he'd been so keen to find out what he could about his father's family. After all, that was exactly what she herself had been doing, and she was glad that she'd discovered so much about her family that summer.

Looking around her, it seemed that the whole village had turned out to say goodbye to Hadan. The streets were lined with people who bowed their heads as the coffin rumbled past. In paying their respects to Hadan Rose, they were also saying goodbye to the last one hundred years and a little bit of their own past at the same time. There would never be a landowner like Hadan at Rose Park again, lording it over the quarry and all the farms too. The day of his passing was a landmark. His kind belonged firmly in the past.

It was with great trepidation that Rachel took herself to bed that night. She sat on the bed in the Pink room, half expecting to hear her grandfather's booming voice, or to feel the oppressive atmosphere she'd felt before. But there was nothing but silence, no chill in the air, no diffused light. It seemed that Daniel had been a great comfort to Hadan in his final hours and that her grandfather's soul was at rest.

'Goodnight, Grandad,' she said, slipping under the covers. 'Sleep well.'

AFTERWORD

Thank you for reading *Kiss From A Rose*. I hope you enjoyed reading it as much as I loved writing it! Please sign up to my newsletter at the following link—

https://www.annbennettauthor.com/signup for information about my upcoming releases. If you do, you will receive a free download of one of my books. You can also follow my Facebook page for updates about my writing.

If you've enjoyed the book I would really appreciate it if you could leave a review on Amazon. It will help inform potential readers about the book and raise its profile. It will also help me to reach more readers.

You might like to read *The Lake Pavilion,* which is also set partly in a small village in middle England, inspired by Pury End, the village where I was born. It is also set partly in British India in the 1930s. Please turn over to read an excerpt.

EXCERPT FROM THE LAKE PAVILION

Prologue

Darjeeling, India, April 1935

THE LITTLE TRAIN up to Darjeeling took all afternoon, weaving its way through the mountains, stopping at tiny village stations along the route to take on passengers. It was dark when it finally puffed into the station on the edge of the town. As Amelia got out of the carriage and took a breath of the crisp mountain air, she noticed that it was so much cooler and fresher up here than it had been lower down in the valley.

From the station platform, Amelia could see the lights of the little town spilling down the steep surrounding hills. She had visited Darjeeling with her parents for short breaks during the hot weather, but they hadn't had time to go there for at least three years. She asked a rickshaw-wallah to take her to the Planter's Club. It was where she'd stayed with her parents and where her father used to lodge when he came up on Mission business. It was the only place she knew in the town.

The Planter's Club wasn't too far from the station, a sprawling white-painted building with balconies overlooking the mountains. Amelia felt a prickle of nerves as she stepped into the entrance hall alone, with its stuffed leopard and tiger heads displayed on panelled walls. There was a musty, damp smell about the place, that mingled with the odours of smoke and alcohol. She could hear the hum of voices and the chink of glasses from the nearby bar.

The old man on the desk peered at her from behind thick glasses and confirmed that there were rooms available. She was shown along the gloomy passages by a bearer who carried her trunk on his head and a holdall in each hand. On the way, they passed the open door of the billiard room, where a group of men were standing around the table in a haze of cigar smoke. The room she was given on the first floor was sparse but comfortable with an old-fashioned bathroom next door. It felt like pure luxury compared to the family bungalow down in the village that she'd left behind. And not too expensive either.

She sank down onto the strange, saggy bed, suddenly overwhelmed by her loss, and the fact that she was now completely alone in the world. As well as this all-consuming grief, a new panic set in. She needed to do something quickly to provide a living and a home for herself. Her parents had never earned much, and what money they did have they'd contributed to the poor or to the church. They'd left her next to nothing. She had a few scant savings, but she knew they wouldn't last long. She resolved that the next day she would go to the local hospitals and see if there were any vacancies for carers. She lay down on the bed, exhausted. She'd barely eaten that day, but she couldn't face going down to the dining room alone. Eventually, she closed her eyes and fell into a fitful sleep.

Chapter 1

Kate

Warren End, Buckinghamshire

April, 1970

It was starting to rain as Kate turned the car off the main road and headed down the hill between the lines of towering chestnut trees. Mist descended on the gently sloping fields and she switched on the wipers, her spirits sagging. It had been raining the day she left, twenty-five years ago, but over the decades she'd envisaged her homecoming so differently. Each time she'd imagined going back there, she thought of the place bathed in sunlight; the sun sparkling on the village pond, the honey-coloured, thatched cottages basking in the warmth of a summer afternoon.

She crossed the brook in the dip and accelerated up the last hill, passing the sign for "Warren End". Her heart beat a little faster in anticipation and she gripped the steering wheel. The car crested the hill and there it was, laid out before her; the village, just as she remembered it. She drove slowly down the hill, past the modern houses and rows of Victorian workers' cottages on the outskirts and turned right at the crossroads.

The whole place seemed eerily empty. There were no children playing hopscotch in the middle of the road, no dogs lounging in the sun or women sitting on front walls gossiping. The buildings on the High Street were the same as the ones in her memory, though. Stone cottages, some of them thatched, some with slate roofs, but looking closely, she saw that there were subtle differences. Both the Methodist Chapel and the blacksmith's forge had been converted into houses, with bottle glass windows and colourful window boxes. In fact, each and every house looked as though it had undergone a facelift since Kate's childhood. Nothing was shabby and workaday now. There was no peeling paint anymore, no rickety outhouses or corrugated tin roofs. Neat porches had been built, houses tastefully extended, thatch renewed. Hanging baskets now hung from eaves, front gardens had been turned to gravel and outside each house, instead of the workers' vans of her memory, smart cars were parked up.

Kate had never considered it before, but Warren End must now be a commuter village, within easy reach of Bletchley and the fast trains to London. It was strange. She'd expected to see the same familiar faces she'd grown up with. In her mind's eye they wouldn't have aged and they'd still be dressed exactly the same. How hadn't she realised that, like her, they would all have moved on?

She crossed the top of the narrow lane where the smallest cottages were and glanced tentatively down it. It had been where the poorest estate workers had lived in her day. A shudder went through her as an unbidden memory surfaced. Did Joan still live there? What was she like now? Had she married and had a family? All these thoughts crowded Kate's mind and she tried to banish them as she turned back to focus on the road.

She drove on past another row of gentrified cottages and rounded a sharp bend. There it was, the imposing gateway to Oakwood Grange. Stone pillars topped with concrete balls, large white gates that stood open. She pulled the car off the road and in through the entrance, tyres scrunching on gravel. She bit her lip. It was hard to believe that this was all hers now. She drove on through the oak trees on the perimeter and the house came into view. It was still beautiful, if, unlike the rest of the village, a little shabby now. The house was what an estate agent would describe as a "Victorian gentleman's residence". Large and square with beautiful nineteenth century lines. Built of pale stone with a pillared porch at the entrance and an octagonal tower on one corner, looking out over the fields and woodland that dipped away to the west.

Kate got out of the car and stared across at the house, the rain beginning to soak through her sweater. She was half afraid to approach the building, such was the power of the past. As she stood watching, the front door opened, and a short woman with grey hair, dressed in a blue overall came out onto the step.

'Is that you, Miss Hamilton?' the woman called, and from somewhere in the depths of her memory, Kate recognised the voice.

'Yes! One moment. I'll get my things.' She grabbed her bag from the back seat and hurried through the rain to the shelter of the front porch.

The woman opened the door wider for her to pass. Kate stood in the front hall, taking in the sweeping staircase, the oak panelling, the tall grandfather clock. The memories came flooding back.

'The solicitor asked me to come and open up for you today, make sure the place is clean.' The woman closed the front door. Her eyes flitted to Kate's and away again and Kate realised that she was nervous.

'Thank you,' said Kate. 'That was very thoughtful.'

'I don't suppose you remember me,' the woman smiled. 'But I remember you from when you were young. I'm Janet Andrews. I live in one of the cottages down Clerks' Lane.'

'Oh yes! Of course. I do remember you,' and the image of a young, careworn housewife surfaced, hanging out washing in her back garden with a baby balanced on one hip, a cigarette drooping from the side of her mouth, curlers in her hair. Janet would only be ten years or so older than Kate herself.

'You used to be as thick as thieves with that young Joan Bartram, didn't you?

Kate ventured an uncertain smile, wondering fleetingly just how much Janet knew of the truth of what happened that last summer.

'Poor Joan still lives down that lane,' Janet went on, and a wave of surprise went through Kate at the confirmation of something that she'd half expected. She wondered why Janet had referred to her as "Poor Joan".

'She lives in one of the estate cottages, a few doors along from me.'

'Oh,' Kate said, not knowing how to respond. 'Joan and I lost touch, I'm afraid.'

Janet paused for a moment, then said, 'Well, look at me! Standing here gossiping, when you're wet through and catching your death. Come on through to the kitchen. The Aga's on and it's warm as toast in there.'

Kate followed Janet along the flagstone passage and into the cavernous kitchen, with its high ceilings and big sash windows that looked out over the wet lawn. She automatically went over to the Aga and stood with her back to it. As the heat began to warm her through, she remembered how her great-aunt Amelia used to do exactly the same. A pang of guilt shot through Kate. She shouldn't be here.

It had been a shock to get the solicitor's letter the previous week, telling her that Oakwood Grange had been bequeathed to her in Amelia's will. Her immediate feeling was that Amelia shouldn't have left her the house. After all, she hadn't exactly been a dutiful great-niece. The last time they'd seen each other was at Kate's mother's funeral three years or so before. They'd exchanged Christmas cards of course, but Kate was acutely aware that she should have done more. She should have visited Amelia, offered her help and company. She'd suspected that Amelia had become eccentric and reclusive as she got older, and probably far too fond of the whisky. Nobody had actually told Kate, but she was sure that was what had shortened Amelia's life.

'She died peacefully, your auntie,' said Janet, filling the kettle at the Butler sink. 'You mustn't worry about her last years. She had plenty of help, here in the village. I was here every day to clean, the district nurse used to drop in, the vicar. She had lots of friends and neighbours.'

Kate stared down at a dip in the worn flagstones, where generations of housemaids must have stood in front of the scrubbed table to chop vegetables and roll pastry. Was Janet referring to the fact that Kate and Amelia had become strangers, or was she just trying to set her mind at rest? Did she know that it wasn't through neglect that Kate hadn't come back? It was simply that she couldn't face up to the past.

'The solicitor said that you're an architect now. Is that right?'

'Yes,' said Kate, brightening at the change of subject. 'I work in London. Big projects mainly now.'

Janet crossed to the Aga and put the kettle on the hot plate.

'Do you have a family?'

'No... no, sadly not.'

'It was dreadful about your brother,' Janet went on with a sympathetic look.

'Roy? Yes. He died in France a few months after the D-Day landings. Poor Mum and Dad never got over it. It's why we moved away from the village, in fact.'

Janet shook her head. 'Terrible business. I expect they wanted a new start.'

'That's right. They did.'

But the new start hadn't really helped them. They'd grieved for their only son for the rest of their lives. Her father had suffered a breakdown and never fully recovered. He'd died, a broken man, in 1950. Her mother had battled on but had never got over her loss. They'd moved to East Anglia shortly after Roy's death, where Kate's mother had relatives, but even in their new home, they couldn't move on. They'd set up a bedroom for Roy there, a replica of his room in their house in Warren End. It had become a sort of shrine, where his framed photographs stood on the table, his school prizes were displayed on the walls, his football boots, still muddy from his last match, were lined up with the rest of his shoes in the bottom of the wardrobe. Kate had tried to hide it from her parents, but she began to resent Roy after a time. He'd always been her parents' golden boy as the pair grew up. He was always put first, Kate's needs and wants came secondary to his as a matter of course. And even in death he came first in their affections. His achievements overshadowed her own, even when she won a place at university to study architecture and later won prizes and awards for her designs.

Janet filled the teapot and put it with a mug and a jug of milk on the table. 'I'd best be getting on,' she said. 'I've made up the guestroom at the top of the stairs for you. I'll see you at the funeral tomorrow.'

'Thank you. And of course, I'll see you there.'

'The Women's Institute has organised a get together in the village hall afterwards. We thought you wouldn't want the bother of having people in the house.'

'Oh, I wouldn't have minded at all, but that's very generous of them.'

Janet crossed the room and lingered in the doorway.

'I was wondering... would you like me to carry on here? Cleaning, that is? As I said, I used to come in for your auntie every day, but I could carry on once a week if you like?'

Kate didn't intend to be in the house any longer than strictly necessary. Just long enough to clear the place and get it on the market, but she didn't want to offend Janet, and in any case, it would be good to have it clean for potential purchasers to view.

'That would be great. How about Wednesday mornings?'

Janet smiled. 'All right. I'll be here at nine sharp. But I'll see you tomorrow anyway.'

Her footsteps echoed across the hall, the front door slammed, and Kate was alone in the house.

SHE SAT at the kitchen table for a long time, sipping her tea and letting the atmosphere of the old place seep through her; the wind in the eaves, the rainwater in the drainpipes, the creaks of the old timbers. She'd never been alone in this house before. It had always been somewhere she'd been in awe of when she was young. And all these years later, she still felt nervous about exploring it by herself. But, she'd finished her tea and there were no excuses. Gathering her courage, she got up from the table, left the kitchen and crossed the hall to the large living room with the octagonal bay window. It was just as she remembered, with a pale blue Chinese carpet on the floor and prints of landscapes and hunting scenes on the walls. It was still furnished with the same chintzy sofas and chairs that Kate recalled from the 1940s.

On the mantlepiece above the marble fireplace stood several photographs of Amelia and James. One of them in lace and morning suit on their wedding day in 1940, a couple more of them both on horseback with the local hunt, and various other portraits of them together as they grew older. In all the pictures Amelia was smiling, and it hit Kate afresh how beautiful she had been with her slightly exotic looks. No wonder Great-Uncle James had fallen for her when he met her working as a chambermaid in a London hotel, and had given up his status as a confirmed bachelor to marry her in his late middle-age. Peering at these fading portraits of Amelia and Great-Uncle James now, they appeared to be the very image of a devoted couple. Kate sighed heavily. How deceptive appearances could be.

There was one picture that surprised Kate though, and she picked it up and stared at it closely. She could have sworn that it hadn't been here when she used to come to Oakwood Grange as a child. It was of a young Amelia, possibly fifteen or sixteen, between an earnest looking man and a rather dowdy woman. They were standing under some lush greenery, in front of a backdrop of snow-capped mountains. These must be Amelia's parents, the missionaries. Suddenly Kate remembered. They had taken Amelia out to India to live in a remote village in the foothills of the Himalayas when she was in her early teens. She'd not returned to England until her mid-twenties. It was odd that Amelia had virtually never referred to her time in India; she had no Indian memorabilia in the house and it simply never came up in conversation. Kate frowned, wondering. It had never struck her before how strange that was. And it felt a little odd too, that this photograph hadn't been here before. She set it back down and continued on her tour of the downstairs, lingering at the door of the large dining room, with its polished oak floor and gracious furniture. James would always invite Kate's family round for Christmas dinner and she would feel out of place in these intimidating surroundings, like the poor relation that she was. She used to wish that they could spend Christmas alone as a family, at home in the comfortable schoolhouse that went with her father's job as headmaster of the village school.

She closed the door on the memories, and moved on to the next room, which used to be Uncle James' study and which Amelia must have taken over after his death. The oak desk with its tooled leather top was covered in papers and there were files and notebooks piled up on it. There was a cut glass decanter, almost empty, on the desk too. Kate sat down in the leather chair, remembering how James used to sit in here puffing on a pipe as he scanned the Financial Times for the latest share prices. She could almost smell the tobacco he used to favour; spices, fruit and vanilla combined. The room couldn't have been decorated since his death shortly after Kate's father's and the ceiling was yellowed with age and years of smoke.

Kate glanced at the papers on the desk. The solicitor had told her she needed to sort through Amelia's bills and find out what needed to be paid. The chaotic look of the paperwork made her heart sink. She thought wistfully of her office in Lincoln's Inn Fields, a picture of calm and order, white walls with pale oak furniture and thick white carpet, everything in its place. The rain was still pouring down outside and there was nothing else to do, so she sat down and started to sort the bills and letters into piles.

Gas bills, electricity bills, water, rates, letters from the bank. Before long she was making some sort of order out of the chaos.

The sky was darkening outside by the time she'd finished. She found a pile of cardboard folders on top of a bookshelf and filed the letters according to subject matter, promising herself that she would return to the task after the funeral. She wondered about putting them away rather than leaving them out on the desk. She pulled open the desk drawers one by one. In the top one, a jumble of old pens, paperclips, drawing pins, and bottles of dried up ink. In the second, a pile of unused writing paper, and in the bottom one nothing at all, but the drawer wouldn't pull out. Curious, Kate knelt down and peered inside. A card-backed envelope was sticking in the mechanism, stopping the drawer from opening properly. With a little effort she pulled the envelope out and stared at it. She recognised Amelia's writing on the front; "Amelia Hamilton – Personal".

Feeling a little like a snooper, Kate fished inside the envelope. There was only one sheet of thick cream coloured paper inside. She pulled it out and scanned it quickly. She read it three times before the meaning of the words sunk in.

"*I, Amelia Alice Holden, of the Russell Hotel, Bloomsbury, London WC1, hereby renounce and relinquish the name of Holden and will henceforth adopt for all purposes and be known by my maiden name of Collins. Signed as a deed this 1st day of February 1938, before William Smith, Solicitor and Commissioner for Oaths, Bedford Square, Bloomsbury.*"

Kate stared at the words, frowning. She'd never known Amelia going by the name of Holden. She'd always been Amelia Collins, and after she'd married Uncle James, Amelia Hamilton. Kate went through the possibilities, but there was only one that seemed remotely plausible to her; Amelia had been married before and had renounced her former married name. But it didn't seem possible. Why would Amelia have hidden that fact? Had she been involved in some sort of scandal and wanted to put it behind her? Amelia had always had an air of mystery about her. It had hardly been credible to Kate that she had been the child of missionaries. But there was the picture on the mantlepiece to prove it. And after all, Amelia was no stranger to scandals. Kate's hands began to tremble as she remembered back to that last summer in Warren End. She'd tried so hard to forget the terrible events of those days and her part in what had happened. After all, it was why she'd stayed away ever since. She'd known it would be difficult to come back, but she'd not realised quite how quickly the old memories would resurface, and alongside them that deep feeling of guilt that burned through her soul.

ACKNOWLEDGMENTS

AND AUTHOR'S NOTE

The village of Perry Cross was inspired by Pury End in Northamptonshire, the village where I was born. I lived there until I was eighteen, in a converted pub, The Bricklayers Arms (the inspiration for The Quarryman's Arms in *Kiss From A Rose*, of course). The surrounding countryside and villages also inspired many of the descriptions in this book. There is no Rose Park at Pury End, but there are several large estates in the vicinity and there is also a quarry on the edge of the village, known as "the Lime Kiln".

I read a lot about the Blitz in London and remember my mother, who grew up in Harrow, talking about it. My chief source of information on the Blitz was the excellent *The Bombing of London 1940-41* by John Conen.

I know Dolphin Square in Pimlico quite well from having worked in nearby Westminster for twenty years, and having had friends who lived in the complex. It has a fascinating history, which is why I chose it as a home for Ruby.

I'd like to thank my sister Mary Clunes, and my brilliant ARC readers for their feedback, Trenda London for her editorial insights and Lauren Finger for her painstaking proofreading. Finally, a big thank you to everyone who's read my books and supported my writing down the years.

ABOUT THE AUTHOR

Ann Bennett has written several historical novels, many set in India or South East Asia. This is her sixteenth book. Her first novel, *Bamboo Heart: A Daughter's Quest*, was inspired by her father's experience as a prisoner of war on the Thai-Burma Railway. *Bamboo Island: The Planter's Wife*, *A Daughter's Promise*, *Bamboo Road: The Homecoming*, *The Tea Planter's Club* and *The Amulet* are also about WWII in South East Asia. With *The Fortune Teller of Kathmandu*, they form the Echoes of Empire collection.

Ann is also author of *The Lake Pavilion* and *The Lake Palace*, set in British India during the Burma Campaign in WWII, *The Lake Pagoda* and *The Lake Villa*, both set in French Indochina during WWII. Ann's other books, *The Runaway Sisters, The Forgotten Children, The Child Without a Home* and bestselling *The Orphan House*, are published by Bookouture.

For more details please visit www.annbennettauthor.com

ALSO BY ANN BENNETT

Bamboo Heart: Daughter's Quest

Bamboo Island: The Planter's Wife

Bamboo Road: The Homecoming

A Daughter's Promise

The Tea Planter's Club

The Amulet

The Fortune Teller of Kathmandu

The Lake Pavilion

The Lake Palace

The Lake Pagoda

The Lake Villa

The Orphan House

The Runaway Sisters

The Child Without a Home

The Forgotten Children

Made in United States
North Haven, CT
04 April 2024

50889078R00168